ZORRO

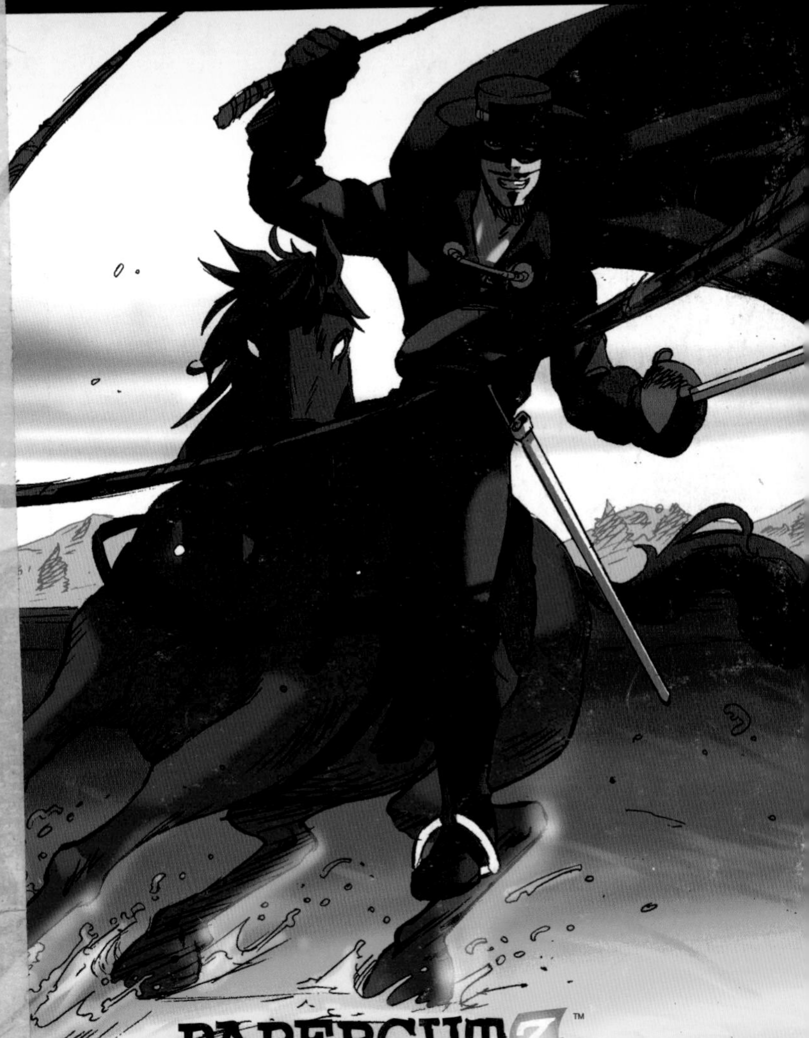

PAPERCUTZ™

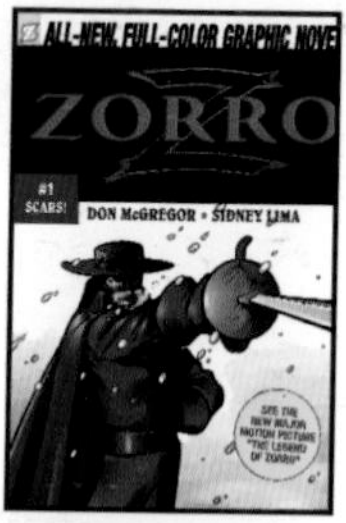
ALL-NEW FULL-COLOR GRAPHIC NOVEL
ZORRO
#1
SCARS!
DON McGREGOR • SIDNEY LIMA

Graphic Novels
Available from Papercutz

1 Scars!
2 Drownings!
3 Vultures!

$7.95 each in paperback
$12.95 each in hardcover

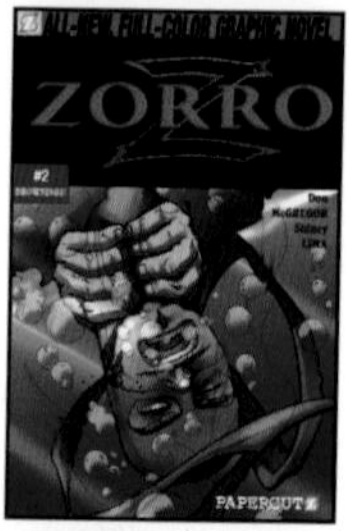
ZORRO
#2
PAPERCUTZ

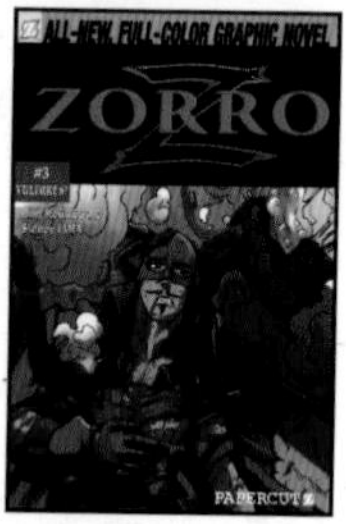
ALL-NEW FULL-COLOR GRAPHIC NOVEL
ZORRO
#3
PAPERCUTZ

Please add $3.00 for postage and handling for the first book, add $1.00 for each additional book.
Send for our catalog:
Papercutz
555 Eighth Avenue, Suite 1202
New York, NY 10018
www.papercutz.com

ZORRO ®

#3 "VULTURES!"

DON McGREGOR • Writer
SIDNEY LIMA • Artist
Based on the character created by
JOHNSTON McCULLEY

New York

This is for my Grandson, KRISTOFFER MOURITZEN, who at 2 years old already knows what he likes and doesn't like — is already a force of independent nature in his own right —and is an expressive story-teller, who uses his voice and face and hands to bring the story home, stories that would make some people's jaws drop if we did them in comics. –D.M.

Vultures!
DON McGREGOR — Writer
SIDNEY LIMA — Artist
MARK LERER — Letterer
MARCOS De MIRANDA — Colorist
JIM SALICRUP — Editor-In-Chief

ISBN 10: 1-59707-020-3 paperback edition
ISBN 13: 978-1-59707-020-1 paperback edition
ISBN 10: 1-59707-021-1 hardcover edition
ISBN 13: 978-1-59707-021-8 hardcover edition

10 9 8 7 6 5 4 3 2 1

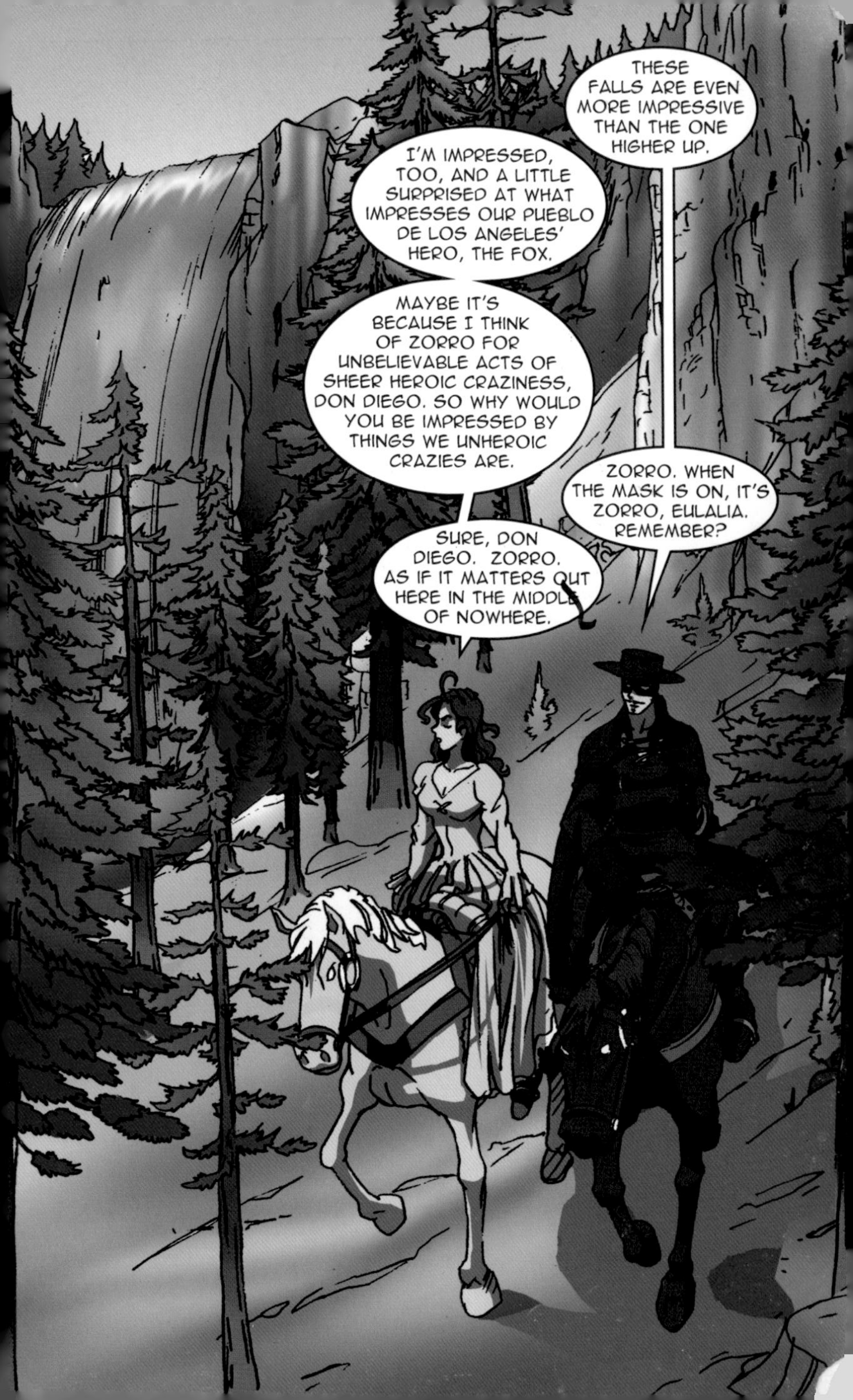
THESE FALLS ARE EVEN MORE IMPRESSIVE THAN THE ONE HIGHER UP.
I'M IMPRESSED, TOO, AND A LITTLE SURPRISED AT WHAT IMPRESSES OUR PUEBLO DE LOS ANGELES' HERO, THE FOX.
MAYBE IT'S BECAUSE I THINK OF ZORRO FOR UNBELIEVABLE ACTS OF SHEER HEROIC CRAZINESS, DON DIEGO. SO WHY WOULD YOU BE IMPRESSED BY THINGS WE UNHEROIC CRAZIES ARE.
ZORRO. WHEN THE MASK IS ON, IT'S ZORRO, EULALIA. REMEMBER?
SURE, DON DIEGO. ZORRO. AS IF IT MATTERS OUT HERE IN THE MIDDLE OF NOWHERE.

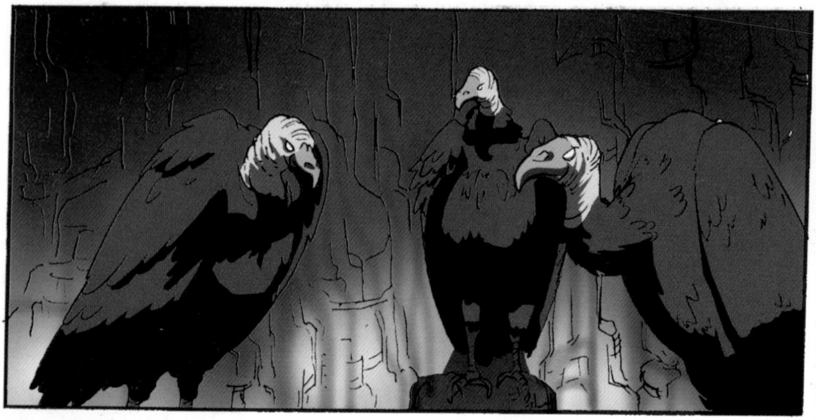

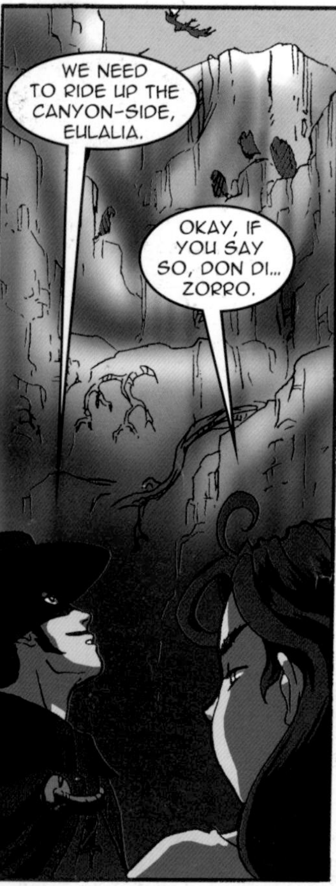

WE NEED TO RIDE UP THE CANYON-SIDE, EULALIA.
OKAY, IF YOU SAY SO, DON DI... ZORRO.

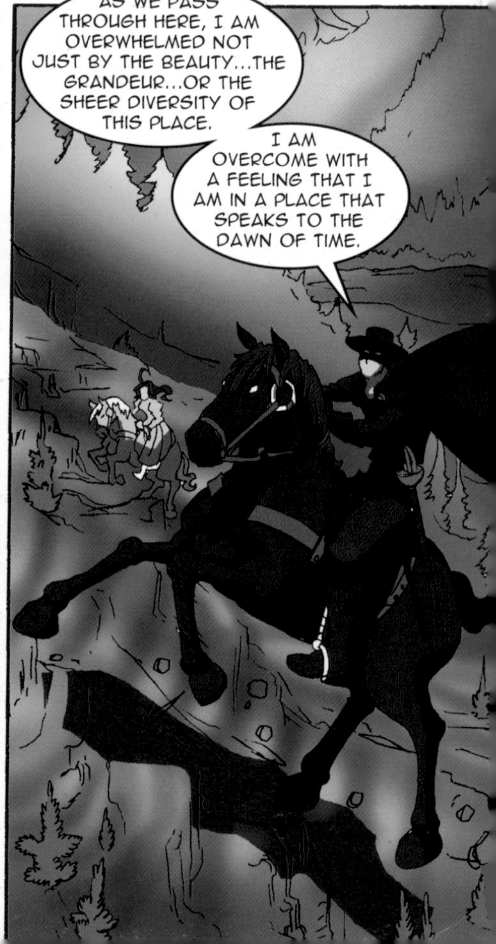

AS WE PASS THROUGH HERE, I AM OVERWHELMED NOT JUST BY THE BEAUTY...THE GRANDEUR...OR THE SHEER DIVERSITY OF THIS PLACE.
I AM OVERCOME WITH A FEELING THAT I AM IN A PLACE THAT SPEAKS TO THE DAWN OF TIME.

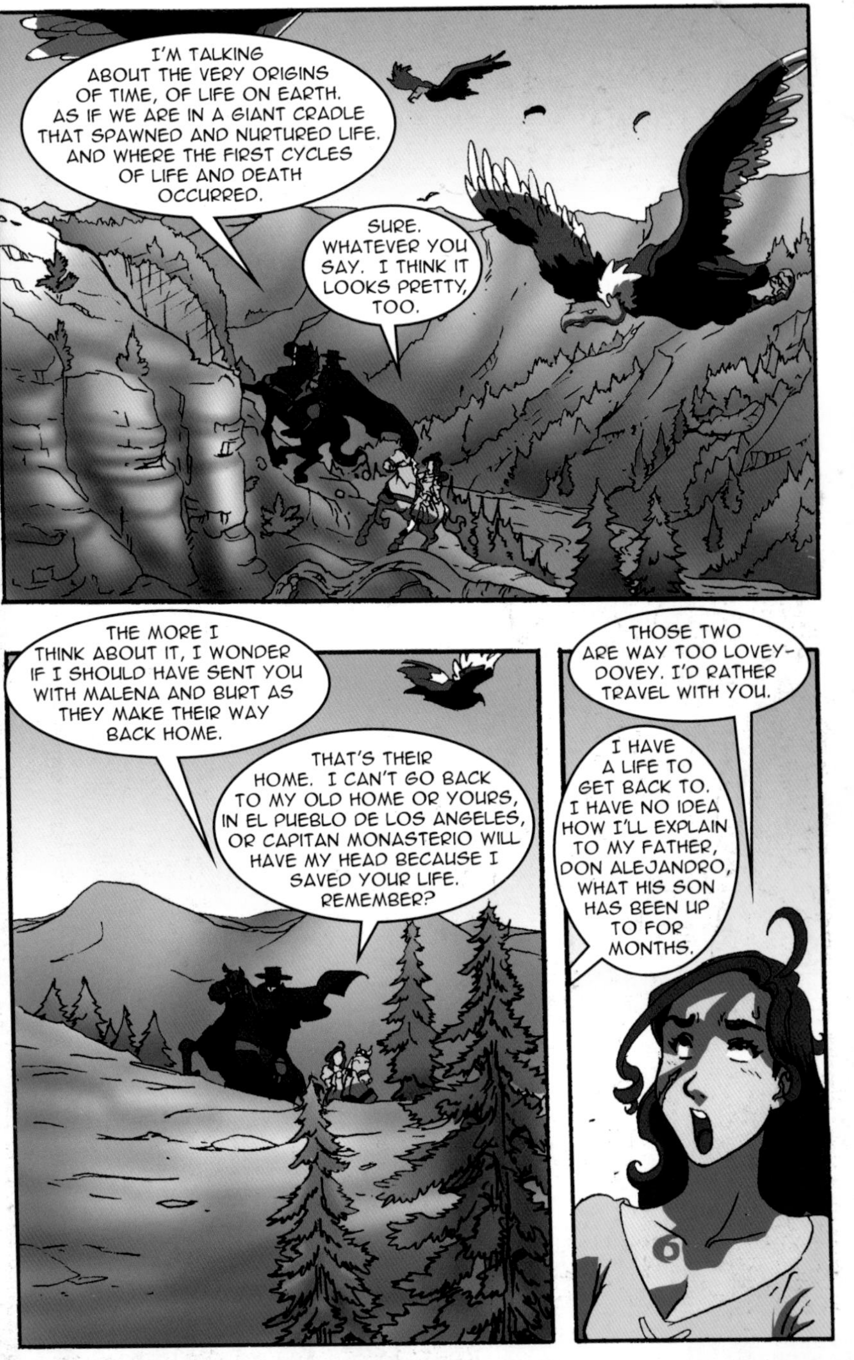
I'M TALKING ABOUT THE VERY ORIGINS OF TIME, OF LIFE ON EARTH. AS IF WE ARE IN A GIANT CRADLE THAT SPAWNED AND NURTURED LIFE. AND WHERE THE FIRST CYCLES OF LIFE AND DEATH OCCURRED.
SURE. WHATEVER YOU SAY. I THINK IT LOOKS PRETTY, TOO.
THE MORE I THINK ABOUT IT, I WONDER IF I SHOULD HAVE SENT YOU WITH MALENA AND BURT AS THEY MAKE THEIR WAY BACK HOME.
THAT'S THEIR HOME. I CAN'T GO BACK TO MY OLD HOME OR YOURS, IN EL PUEBLO DE LOS ANGELES, OR CAPITAN MONASTERIO WILL HAVE MY HEAD BECAUSE I SAVED YOUR LIFE. REMEMBER?
THOSE TWO ARE WAY TOO LOVEY-DOVEY. I'D RATHER TRAVEL WITH YOU.
I HAVE A LIFE TO GET BACK TO. I HAVE NO IDEA HOW I'LL EXPLAIN TO MY FATHER, DON ALEJANDRO, WHAT HIS SON HAS BEEN UP TO FOR MONTHS.

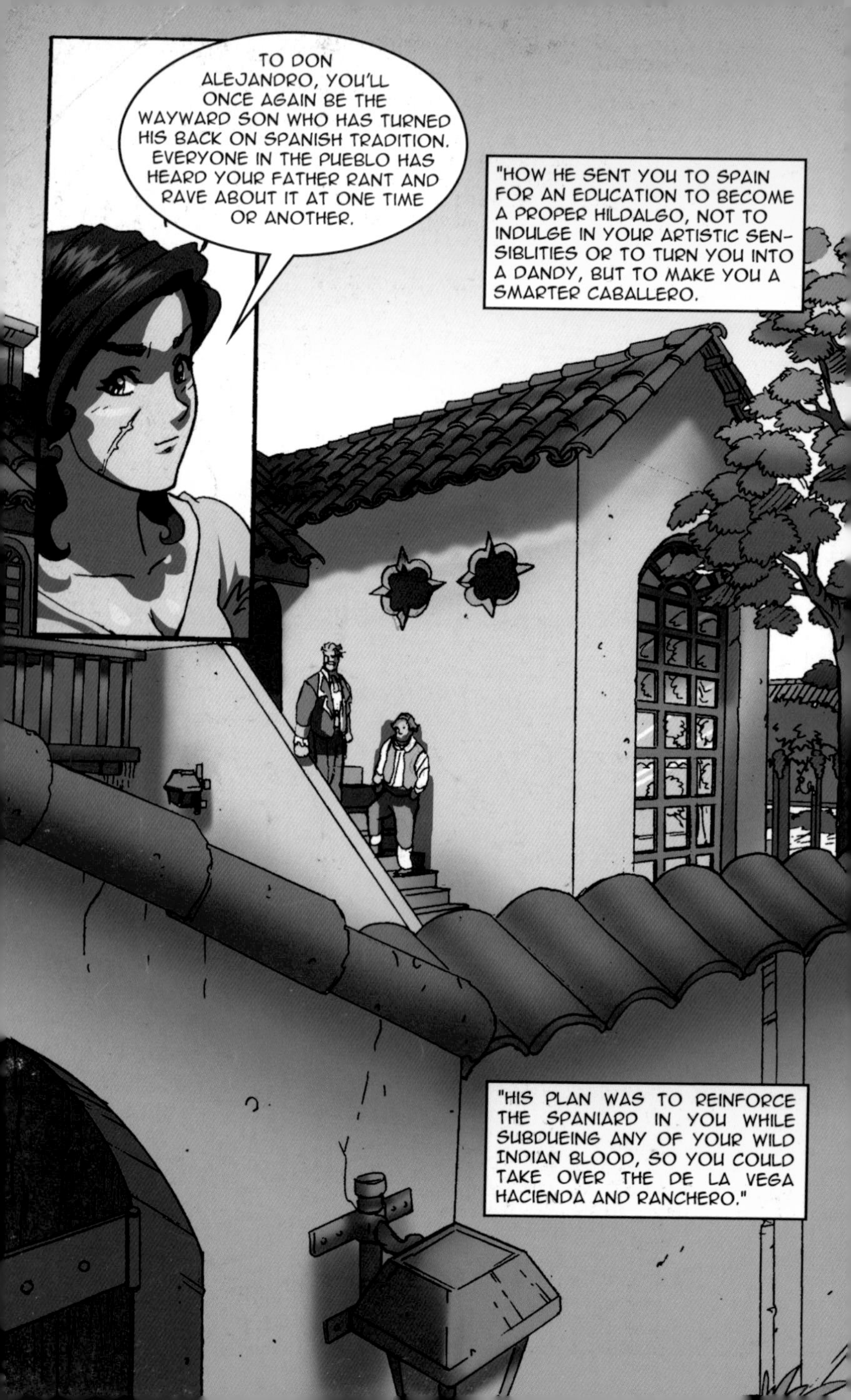
TO DON ALEJANDRO, YOU'LL ONCE AGAIN BE THE WAYWARD SON WHO HAS TURNED HIS BACK ON SPANISH TRADITION. EVERYONE IN THE PUEBLO HAS HEARD YOUR FATHER RANT AND RAVE ABOUT IT AT ONE TIME OR ANOTHER.
"HOW HE SENT YOU TO SPAIN FOR AN EDUCATION TO BECOME A PROPER HILDALGO, NOT TO INDULGE IN YOUR ARTISTIC SEN-SIBLITIES OR TO TURN YOU INTO A DANDY, BUT TO MAKE YOU A SMARTER CABALLERO.
"HIS PLAN WAS TO REINFORCE THE SPANIARD IN YOU WHILE SUBDUEING ANY OF YOUR WILD INDIAN BLOOD, SO YOU COULD TAKE OVER THE DE LA VEGA HACIENDA AND RANCHERO."

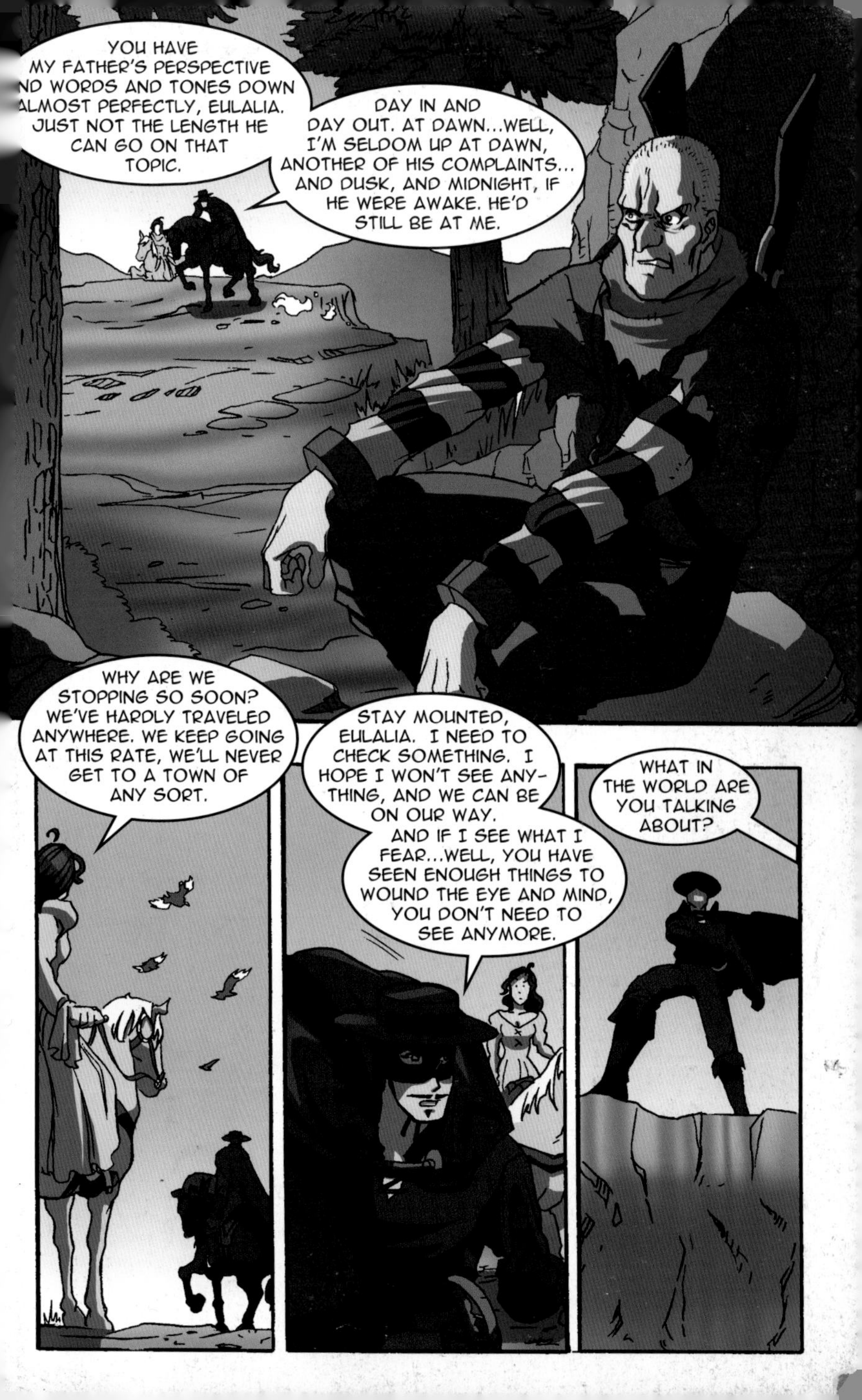
YOU HAVE MY FATHER'S PERSPECTIVE AND WORDS AND TONES DOWN ALMOST PERFECTLY, EULALIA. JUST NOT THE LENGTH HE CAN GO ON THAT TOPIC.
DAY IN AND DAY OUT. AT DAWN...WELL, I'M SELDOM UP AT DAWN, ANOTHER OF HIS COMPLAINTS... AND DUSK, AND MIDNIGHT, IF HE WERE AWAKE. HE'D STILL BE AT ME.
WHY ARE WE STOPPING SO SOON? WE'VE HARDLY TRAVELED ANYWHERE. WE KEEP GOING AT THIS RATE, WE'LL NEVER GET TO A TOWN OF ANY SORT.
STAY MOUNTED, EULALIA. I NEED TO CHECK SOMETHING. I HOPE I WON'T SEE ANY-THING, AND WE CAN BE ON OUR WAY.
AND IF I SEE WHAT I FEAR...WELL, YOU HAVE SEEN ENOUGH THINGS TO WOUND THE EYE AND MIND, YOU DON'T NEED TO SEE ANYMORE.
WHAT IN THE WORLD ARE YOU TALKING ABOUT?

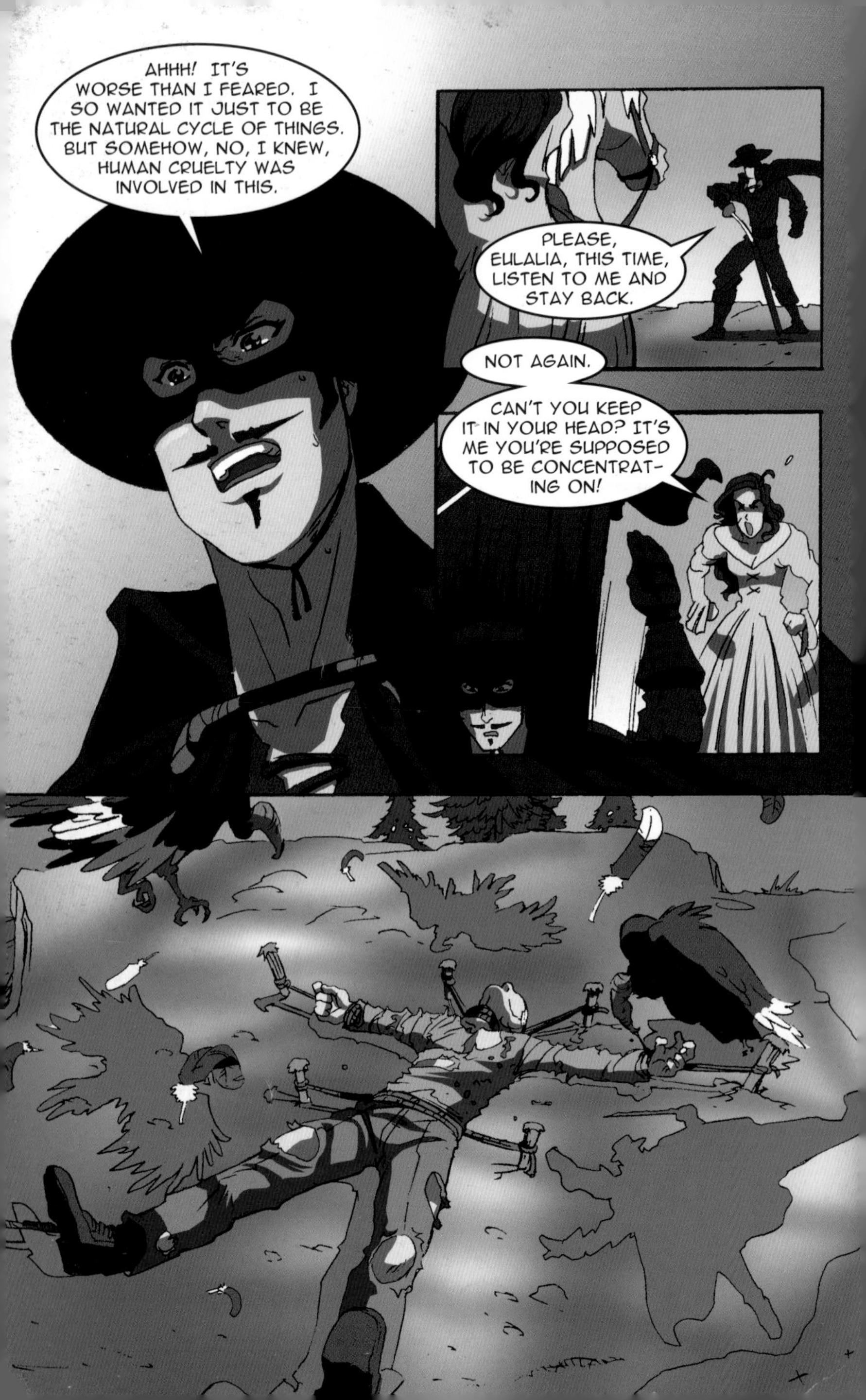
AHHH! IT'S WORSE THAN I FEARED. I SO WANTED IT JUST TO BE THE NATURAL CYCLE OF THINGS. BUT SOMEHOW, NO, I KNEW, HUMAN CRUELTY WAS INVOLVED IN THIS.
PLEASE, EULALIA, THIS TIME, LISTEN TO ME AND STAY BACK.
NOT AGAIN.
CAN'T YOU KEEP IT IN YOUR HEAD? IT'S ME YOU'RE SUPPOSED TO BE CONCENTRAT- ING ON!

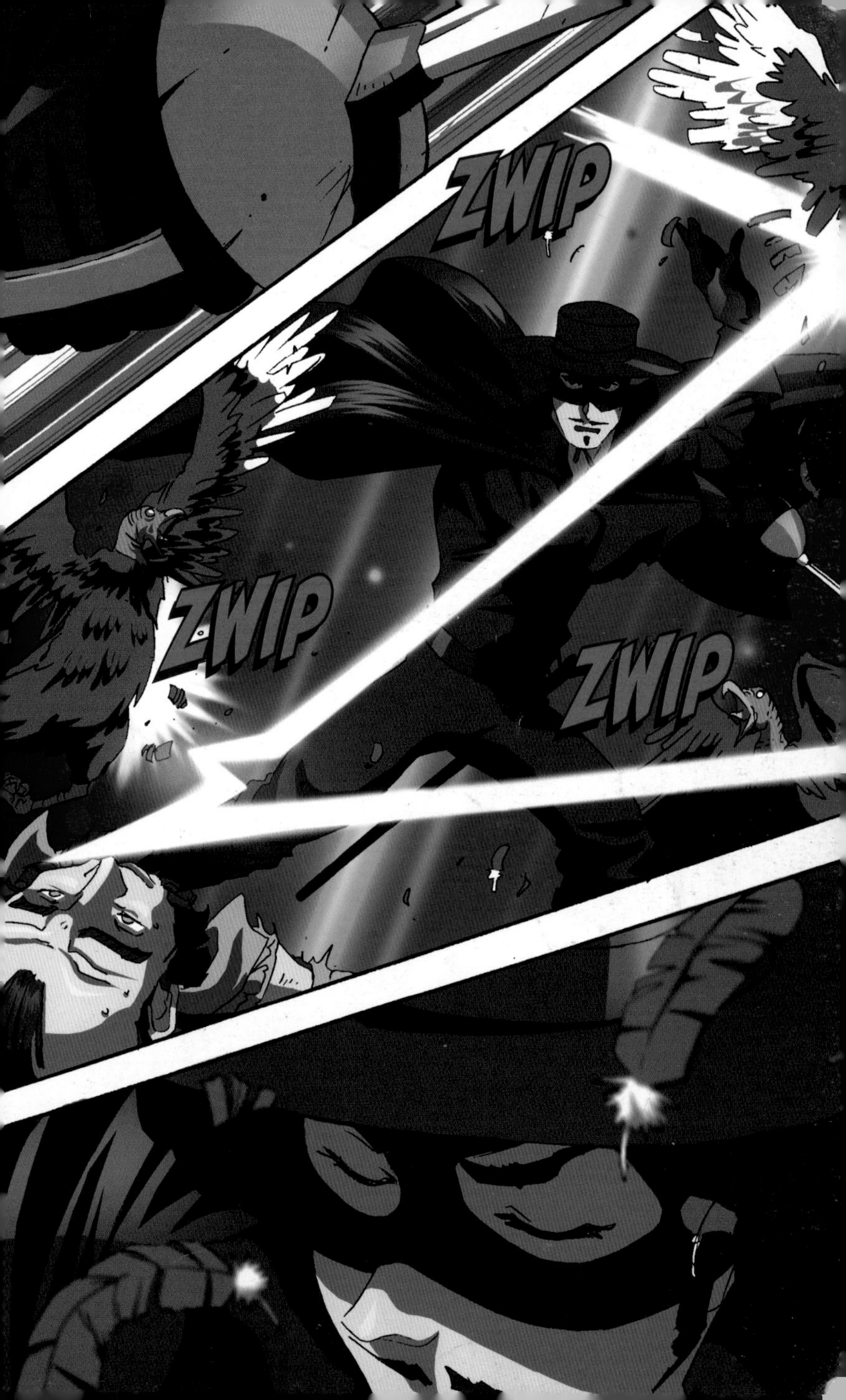
ZWIP
ZWIP
ZWIP

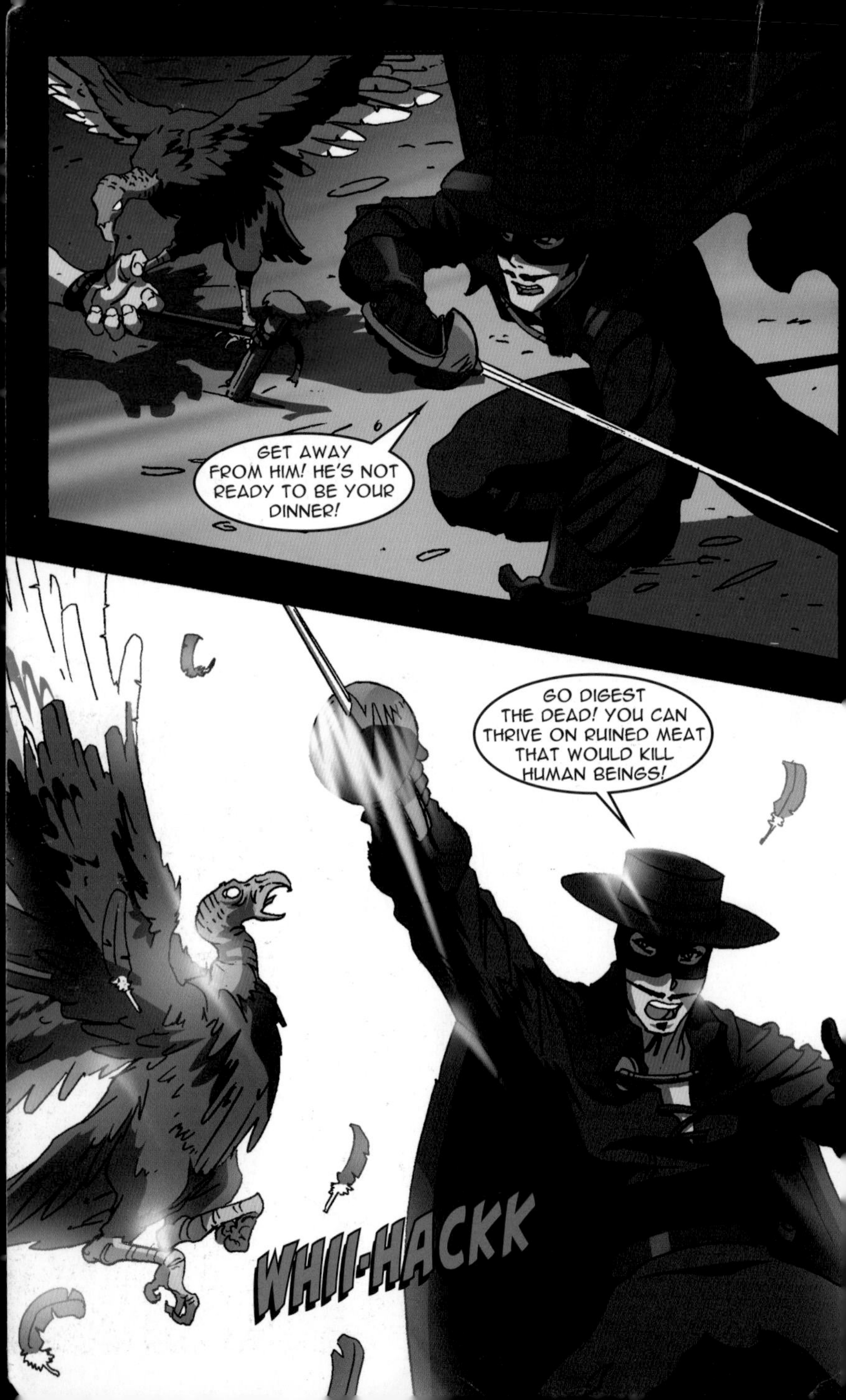
GET AWAY FROM HIM! HE'S NOT READY TO BE YOUR DINNER!
GO DIGEST THE DEAD! YOU CAN THRIVE ON RUINED MEAT THAT WOULD KILL HUMAN BEINGS!
WHII-HACKK

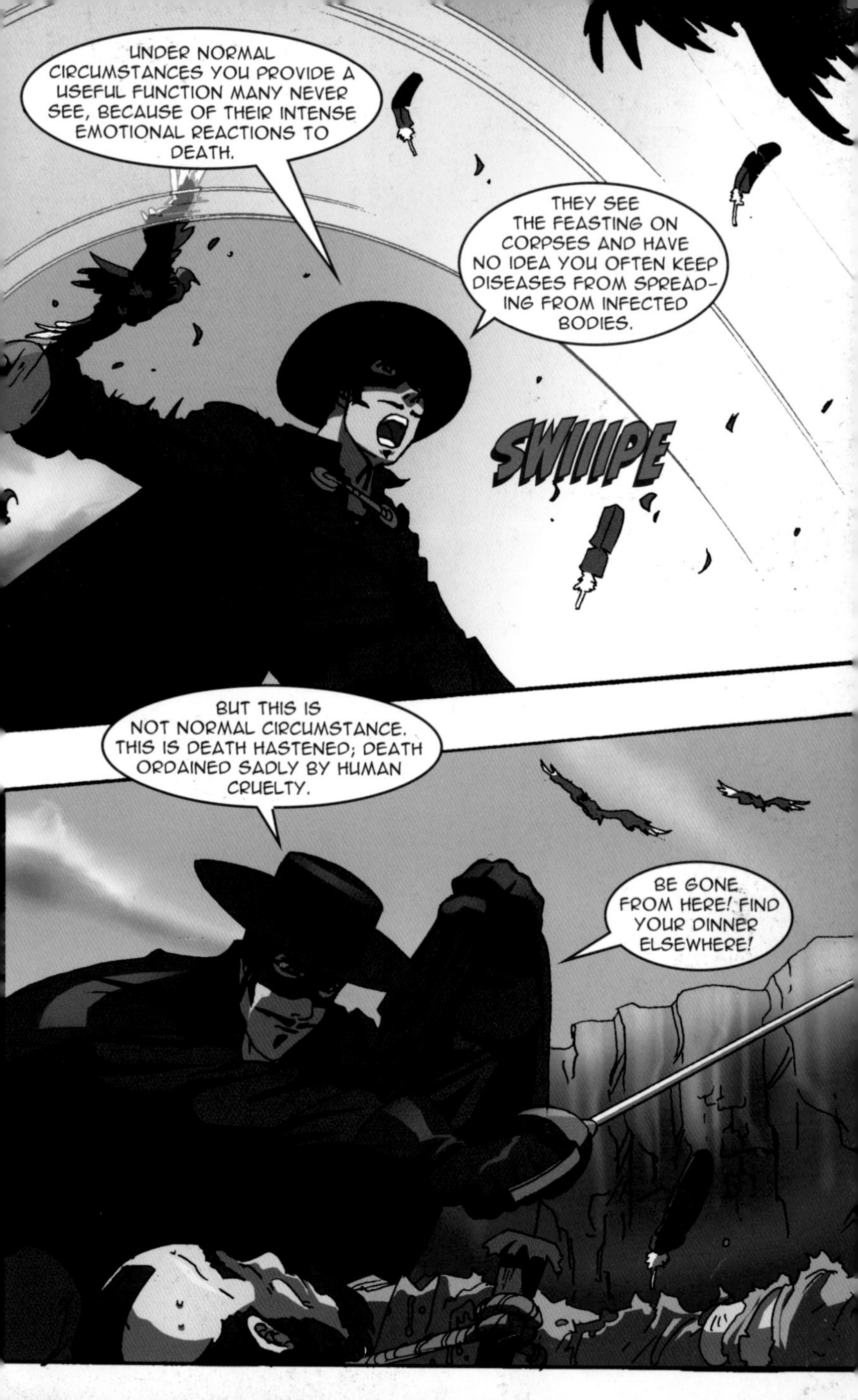
UNDER NORMAL CIRCUMSTANCES YOU PROVIDE A USEFUL FUNCTION MANY NEVER SEE, BECAUSE OF THEIR INTENSE EMOTIONAL REACTIONS TO DEATH.
THEY SEE THE FEASTING ON CORPSES AND HAVE NO IDEA YOU OFTEN KEEP DISEASES FROM SPREAD-ING FROM INFECTED BODIES.
SWIIIPE
BUT THIS IS NOT NORMAL CIRCUMSTANCE. THIS IS DEATH HASTENED; DEATH ORDAINED SADLY BY HUMAN CRUELTY.
BE GONE. FROM HERE! FIND YOUR DINNER ELSEWHERE!

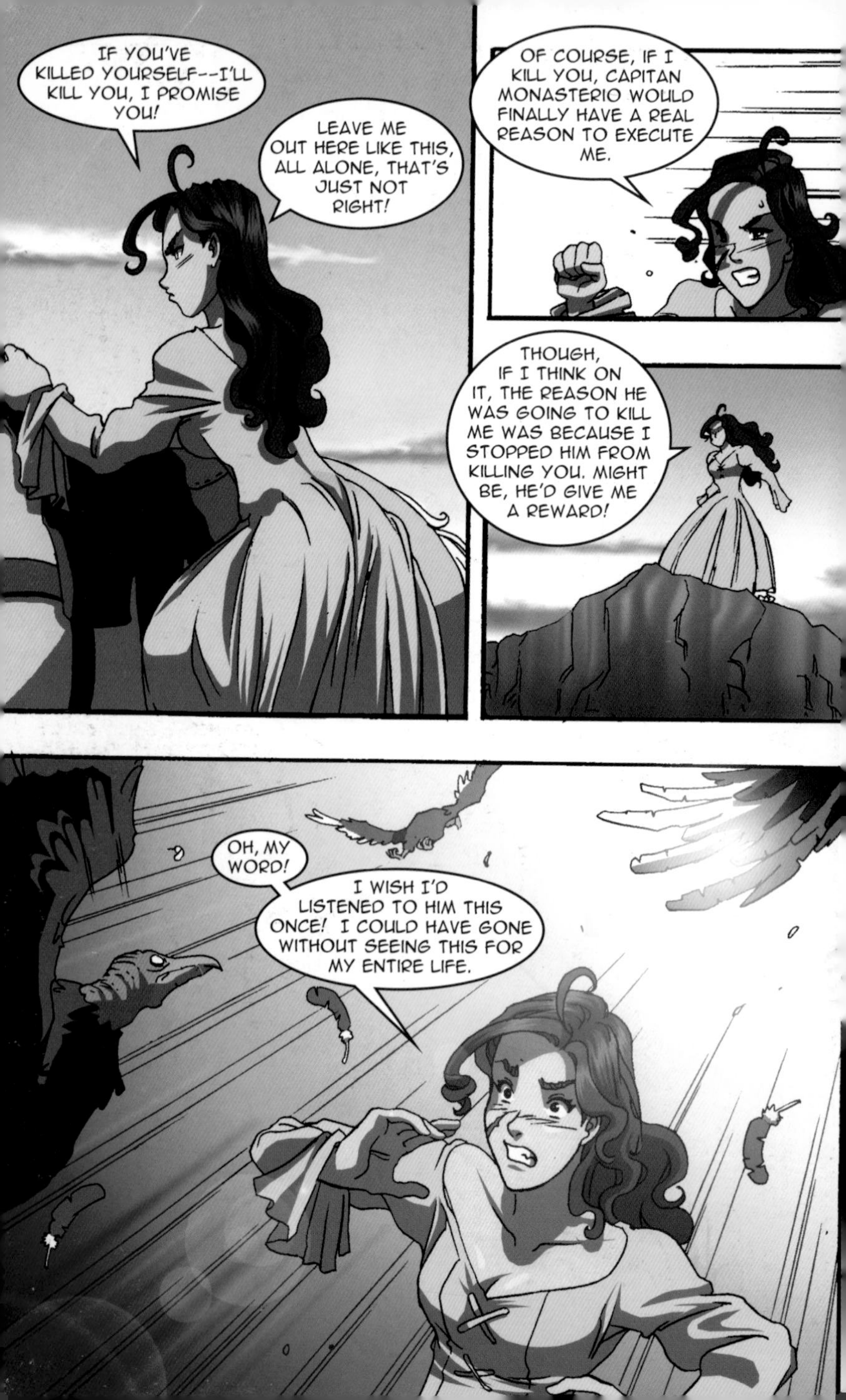
IF YOU'VE KILLED YOURSELF--I'LL KILL YOU, I PROMISE YOU!
LEAVE ME OUT HERE LIKE THIS, ALL ALONE, THAT'S JUST NOT RIGHT!
OF COURSE, IF I KILL YOU, CAPITAN MONASTERIO WOULD FINALLY HAVE A REAL REASON TO EXECUTE ME.
THOUGH, IF I THINK ON IT, THE REASON HE WAS GOING TO KILL ME WAS BECAUSE I STOPPED HIM FROM KILLING YOU. MIGHT BE, HE'D GIVE ME A REWARD!
OH, MY WORD!
I WISH I'D LISTENED TO HIM THIS ONCE! I COULD HAVE GONE WITHOUT SEEING THIS FOR MY ENTIRE LIFE.

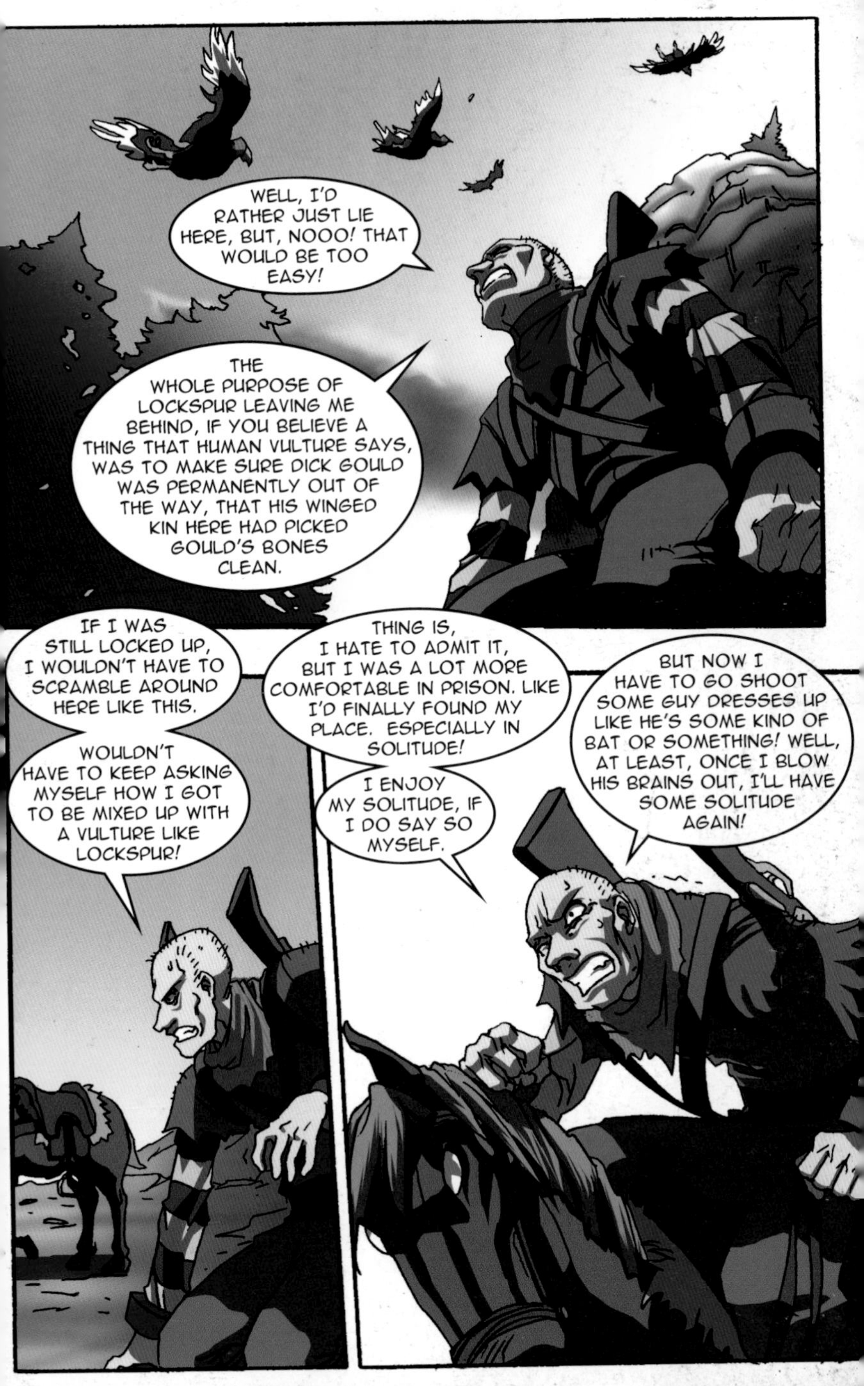
WELL, I'D RATHER JUST LIE HERE, BUT, NOOO! THAT WOULD BE TOO EASY!
THE WHOLE PURPOSE OF LOCKSPUR LEAVING ME BEHIND, IF YOU BELIEVE A THING THAT HUMAN VULTURE SAYS, WAS TO MAKE SURE DICK GOULD WAS PERMANENTLY OUT OF THE WAY, THAT HIS WINGED KIN HERE HAD PICKED GOULD'S BONES CLEAN.
IF I WAS STILL LOCKED UP, I WOULDN'T HAVE TO SCRAMBLE AROUND HERE LIKE THIS.
WOULDN'T HAVE TO KEEP ASKING MYSELF HOW I GOT TO BE MIXED UP WITH A VULTURE LIKE LOCKSPUR!
THING IS, I HATE TO ADMIT IT, BUT I WAS A LOT MORE COMFORTABLE IN PRISON. LIKE I'D FINALLY FOUND MY PLACE. ESPECIALLY IN SOLITUDE!
I ENJOY MY SOLITUDE, IF I DO SAY SO MYSELF.
BUT NOW I HAVE TO GO SHOOT SOME GUY DRESSES UP LIKE HE'S SOME KIND OF BAT OR SOMETHING! WELL, AT LEAST, ONCE I BLOW HIS BRAINS OUT, I'LL HAVE SOME SOLITUDE AGAIN!

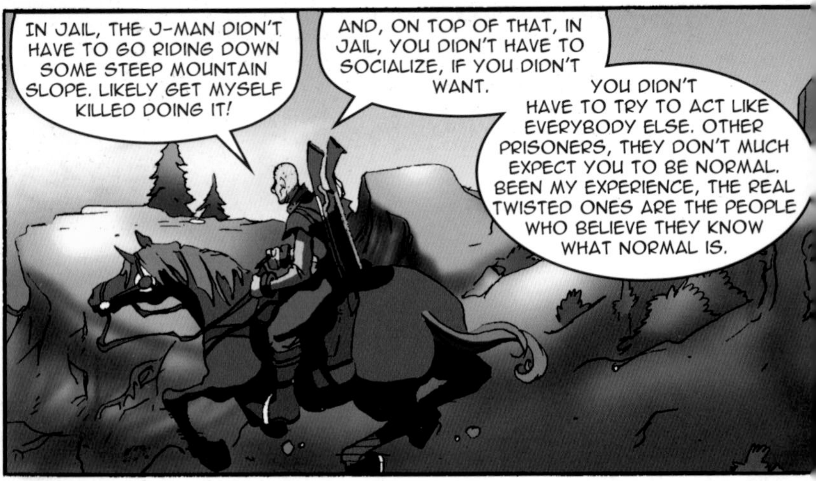
IN JAIL, THE J-MAN DIDN'T HAVE TO GO RIDING DOWN SOME STEEP MOUNTAIN SLOPE. LIKELY GET MYSELF KILLED DOING IT!
AND, ON TOP OF THAT, IN JAIL, YOU DIDN'T HAVE TO SOCIALIZE, IF YOU DIDN'T WANT.
YOU DIDN'T HAVE TO TRY TO ACT LIKE EVERYBODY ELSE. OTHER PRISONERS, THEY DON'T MUCH EXPECT YOU TO BE NORMAL. BEEN MY EXPERIENCE, THE REAL TWISTED ONES ARE THE PEOPLE WHO BELIEVE THEY KNOW WHAT NORMAL IS.

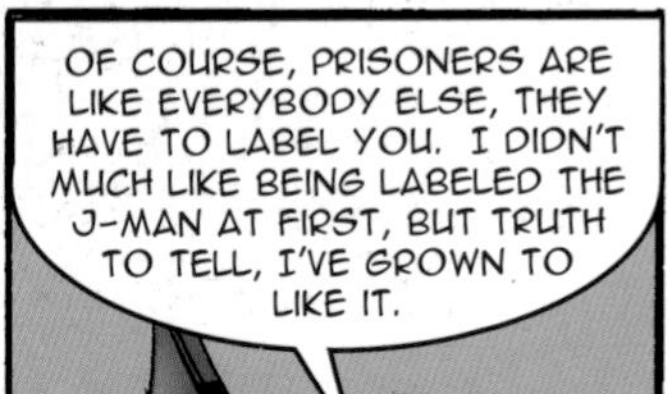
OF COURSE, PRISONERS ARE LIKE EVERYBODY ELSE, THEY HAVE TO LABEL YOU. I DIDN'T MUCH LIKE BEING LABELED THE J-MAN AT FIRST, BUT TRUTH TO TELL, I'VE GROWN TO LIKE IT.

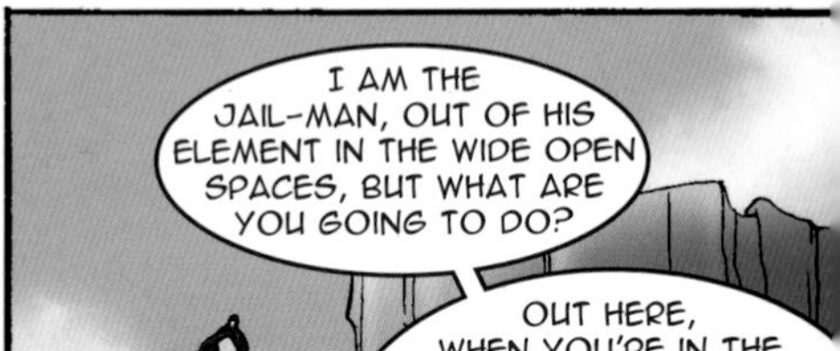
I AM THE JAIL-MAN, OUT OF HIS ELEMENT IN THE WIDE OPEN SPACES, BUT WHAT ARE YOU GOING TO DO?
OUT HERE, WHEN YOU'RE IN THE MIDDLE OF NOWHERE, ONE THING IS, NOT MANY PEOPL ARE GOING TO TELL YOU YOU'RE NUTS FOR TALKING TO YOURSELF.
I'D TELL ANY-BODY ANYHOW, THE BEST CONVERSATIONS THE J-MAN EVER HAD WAS WITH HIMSELF!

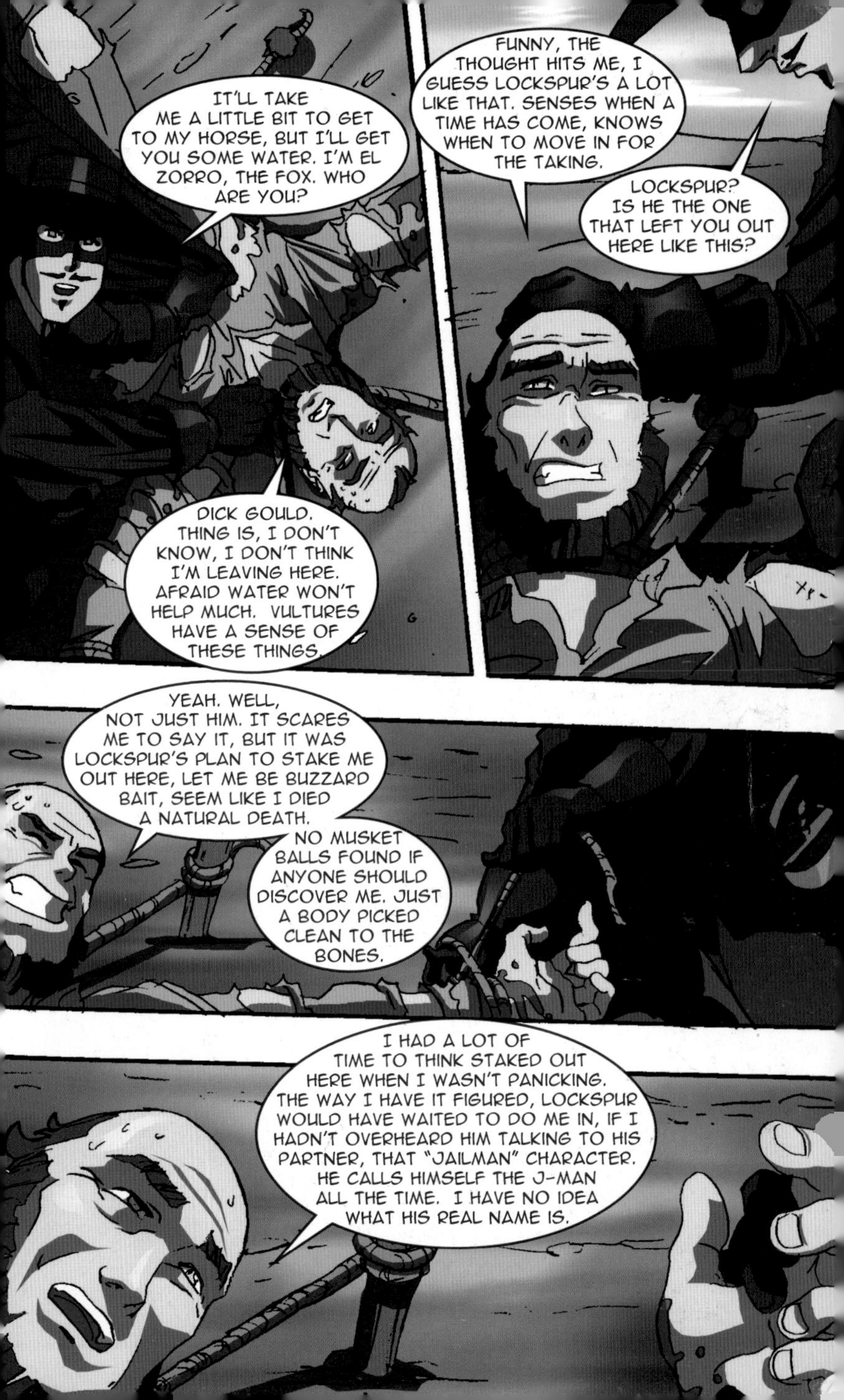
IT'LL TAKE ME A LITTLE BIT TO GET TO MY HORSE, BUT I'LL GET YOU SOME WATER. I'M EL ZORRO, THE FOX. WHO ARE YOU?
DICK GOULD. THING IS, I DON'T KNOW, I DON'T THINK I'M LEAVING HERE. AFRAID WATER WON'T HELP MUCH. VULTURES HAVE A SENSE OF THESE THINGS.
FUNNY, THE THOUGHT HITS ME, I GUESS LOCKSPUR'S A LOT LIKE THAT. SENSES WHEN A TIME HAS COME, KNOWS WHEN TO MOVE IN FOR THE TAKING.
LOCKSPUR? IS HE THE ONE THAT LEFT YOU OUT HERE LIKE THIS?
YEAH. WELL, NOT JUST HIM. IT SCARES ME TO SAY IT, BUT IT WAS LOCKSPUR'S PLAN TO STAKE ME OUT HERE, LET ME BE BUZZARD BAIT, SEEM LIKE I DIED A NATURAL DEATH.
NO MUSKET BALLS FOUND IF ANYONE SHOULD DISCOVER ME. JUST A BODY PICKED CLEAN TO THE BONES.
I HAD A LOT OF TIME TO THINK STAKED OUT HERE WHEN I WASN'T PANICKING. THE WAY I HAVE IT FIGURED, LOCKSPUR WOULD HAVE WAITED TO DO ME IN, IF I HADN'T OVERHEARD HIM TALKING TO HIS PARTNER, THAT "JAILMAN" CHARACTER. HE CALLS HIMSELF THE J-MAN ALL THE TIME. I HAVE NO IDEA WHAT HIS REAL NAME IS.

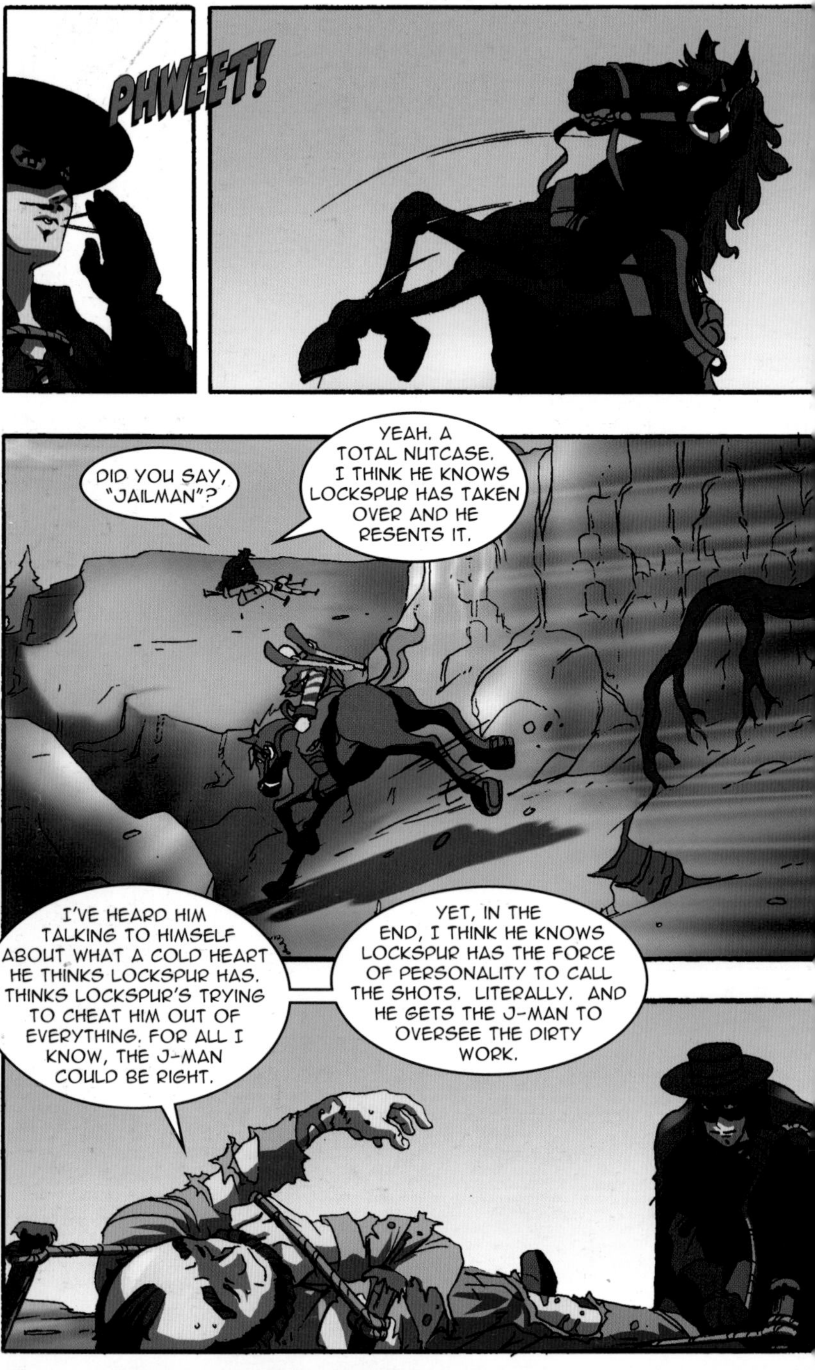
PHWEET!
DID YOU SAY, "JAILMAN"?
YEAH. A TOTAL NUTCASE. I THINK HE KNOWS LOCKSPUR HAS TAKEN OVER AND HE RESENTS IT.
I'VE HEARD HIM TALKING TO HIMSELF ABOUT WHAT A COLD HEART HE THINKS LOCKSPUR HAS. THINKS LOCKSPUR'S TRYING TO CHEAT HIM OUT OF EVERYTHING. FOR ALL I KNOW, THE J-MAN COULD BE RIGHT.
YET, IN THE END, I THINK HE KNOWS LOCKSPUR HAS THE FORCE OF PERSONALITY TO CALL THE SHOTS. LITERALLY. AND HE GETS THE J-MAN TO OVERSEE THE DIRTY WORK.

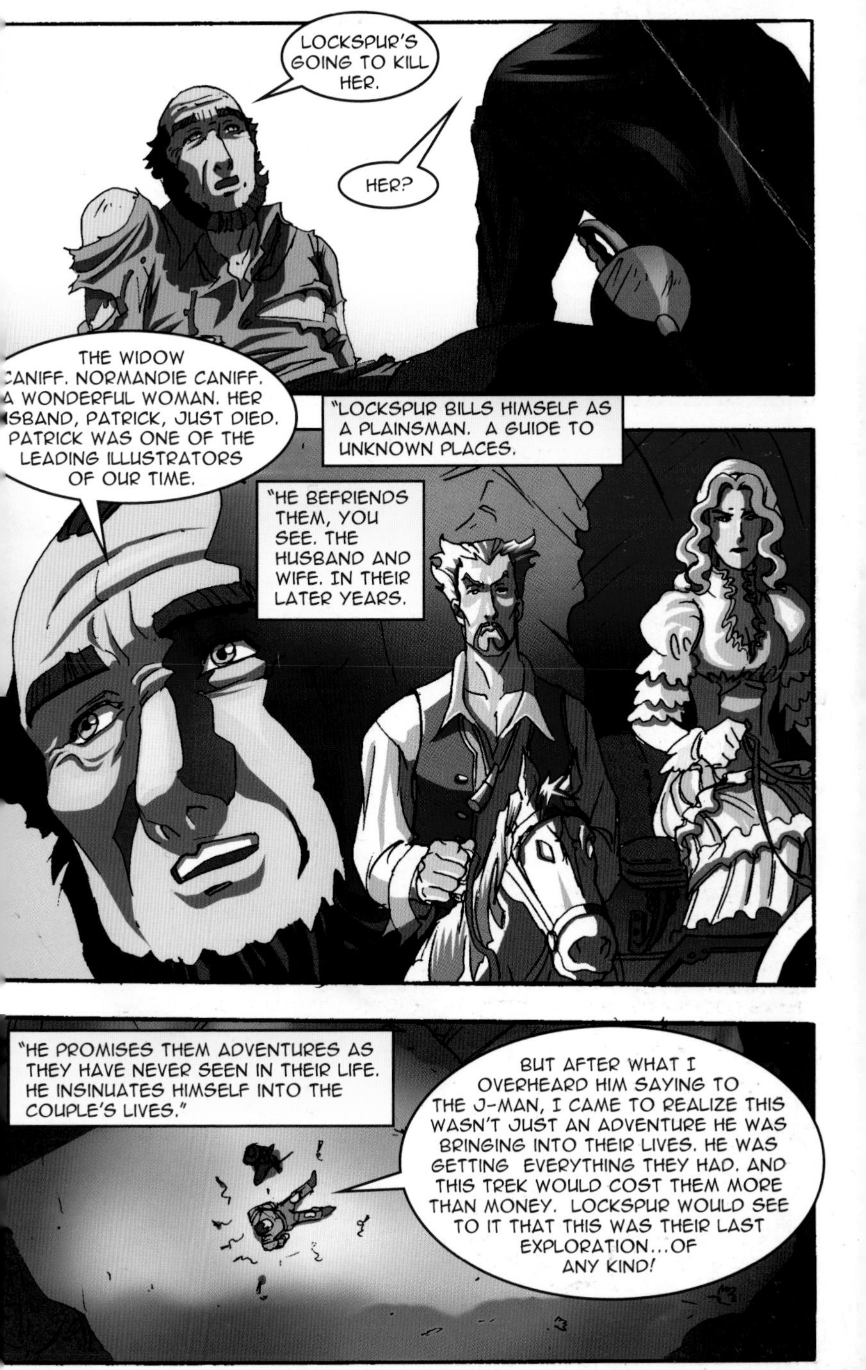

LOCKSPUR'S GOING TO KILL HER.
HER?
THE WIDOW CANIFF. NORMANDIE CANIFF. A WONDERFUL WOMAN. HER SBAND, PATRICK, JUST DIED. PATRICK WAS ONE OF THE LEADING ILLUSTRATORS OF OUR TIME.
"LOCKSPUR BILLS HIMSELF AS A PLAINSMAN. A GUIDE TO UNKNOWN PLACES.
"HE BEFRIENDS THEM, YOU SEE. THE HUSBAND AND WIFE. IN THEIR LATER YEARS.
"HE PROMISES THEM ADVENTURES AS THEY HAVE NEVER SEEN IN THEIR LIFE. HE INSINUATES HIMSELF INTO THE COUPLE'S LIVES."
BUT AFTER WHAT I OVERHEARD HIM SAYING TO THE J-MAN, I CAME TO REALIZE THIS WASN'T JUST AN ADVENTURE HE WAS BRINGING INTO THEIR LIVES. HE WAS GETTING EVERYTHING THEY HAD. AND THIS TREK WOULD COST THEM MORE THAN MONEY. LOCKSPUR WOULD SEE TO IT THAT THIS WAS THEIR LAST EXPLORATION...OF ANY KIND!

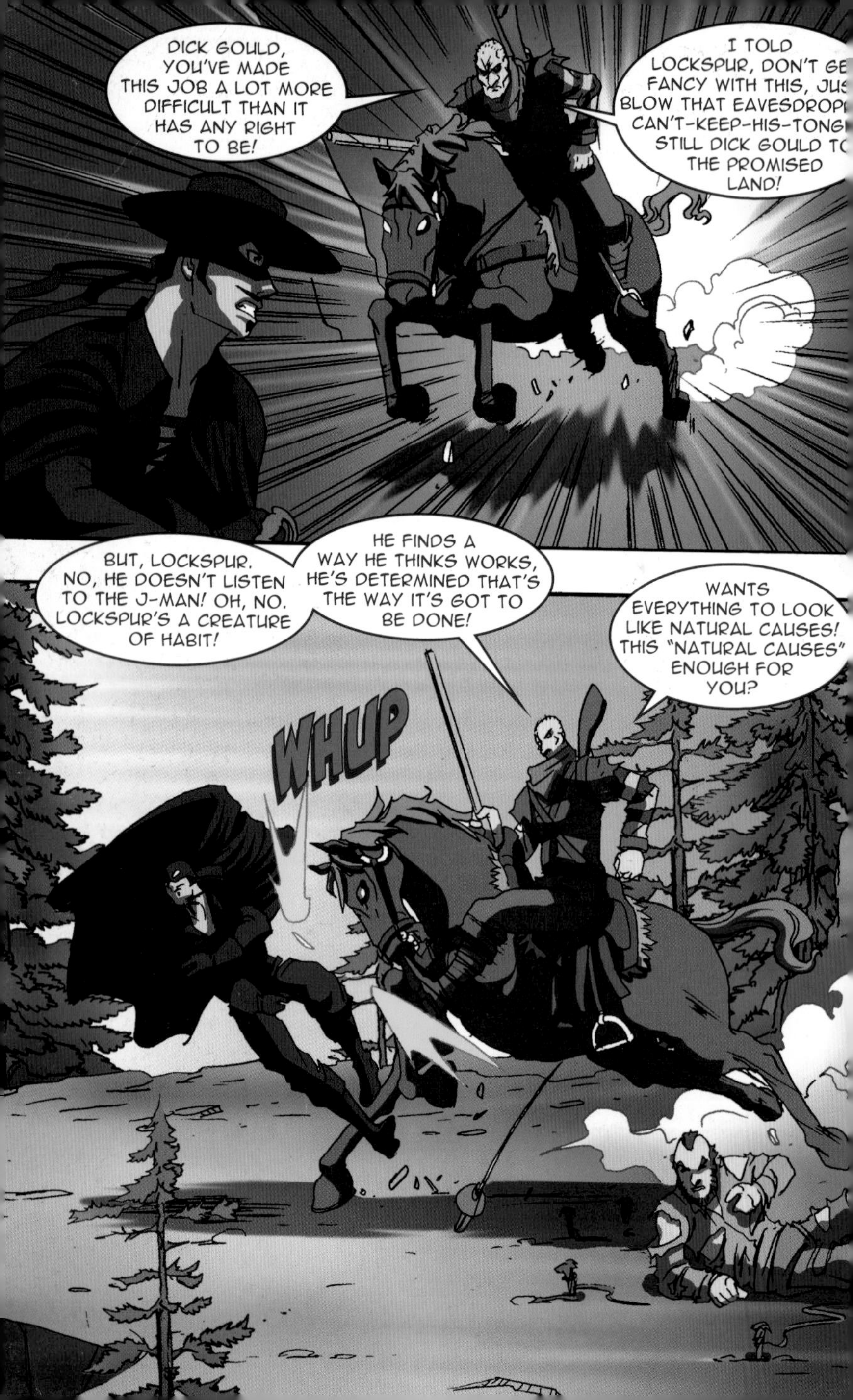
DICK GOULD, YOU'VE MADE THIS JOB A LOT MORE DIFFICULT THAN IT HAS ANY RIGHT TO BE!
I TOLD LOCKSPUR, DON'T GE FANCY WITH THIS, JUS BLOW THAT EAVESDROP CAN'T-KEEP-HIS-TONG STILL DICK GOULD T THE PROMISED LAND!
BUT, LOCKSPUR. NO, HE DOESN'T LISTEN TO THE J-MAN! OH, NO. LOCKSPUR'S A CREATURE OF HABIT!
HE FINDS A WAY HE THINKS WORKS, HE'S DETERMINED THAT'S THE WAY IT'S GOT TO BE DONE!
WANTS EVERYTHING TO LOOK LIKE NATURAL CAUSES! THIS "NATURAL CAUSES" ENOUGH FOR YOU?
WHUP

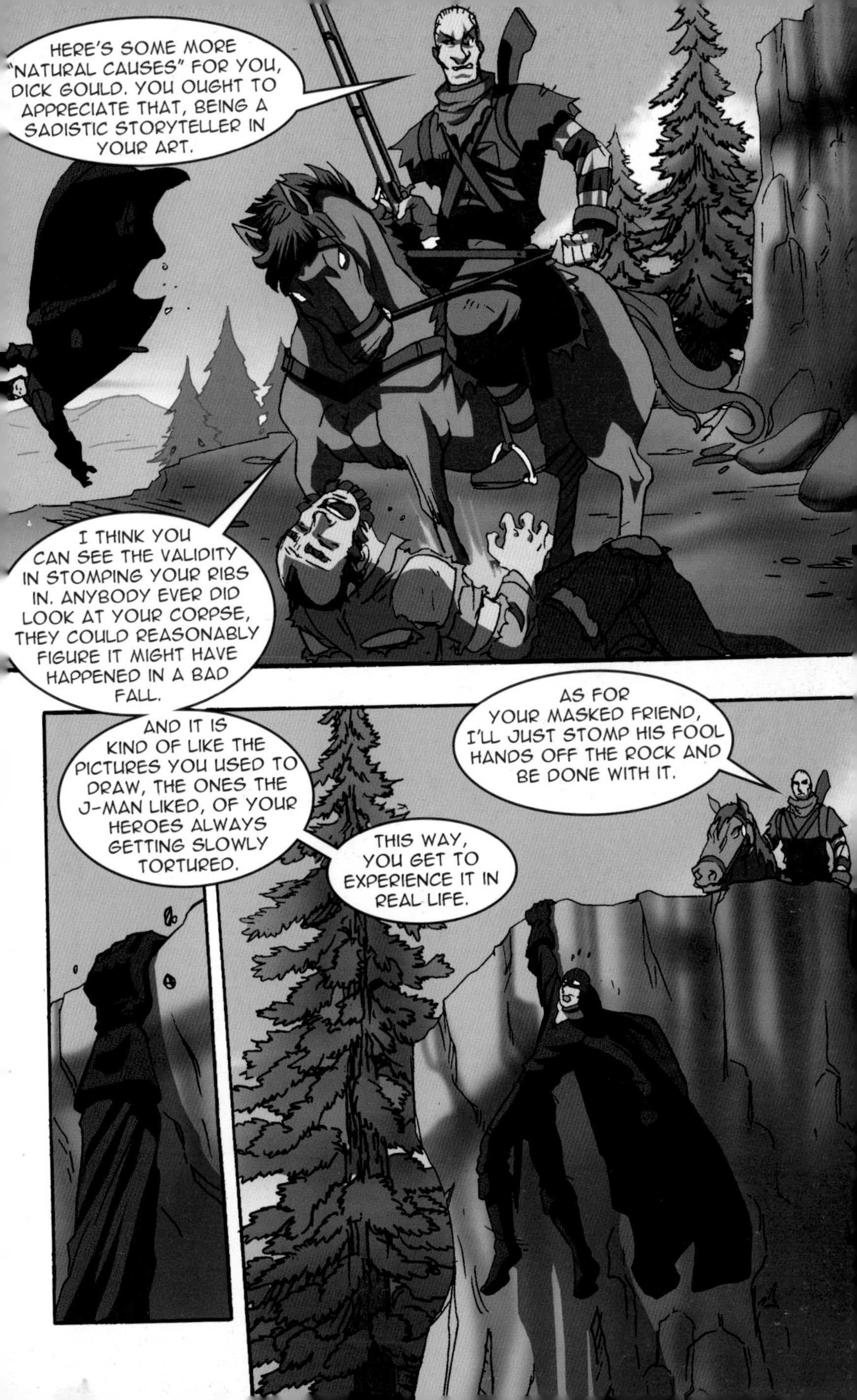
HERE'S SOME MORE "NATURAL CAUSES" FOR YOU, DICK GOULD. YOU OUGHT TO APPRECIATE THAT, BEING A SADISTIC STORYTELLER IN YOUR ART.
I THINK YOU CAN SEE THE VALIDITY IN STOMPING YOUR RIBS IN. ANYBODY EVER DID LOOK AT YOUR CORPSE, THEY COULD REASONABLY FIGURE IT MIGHT HAVE HAPPENED IN A BAD FALL.
AND IT IS KIND OF LIKE THE PICTURES YOU USED TO DRAW, THE ONES THE J-MAN LIKED, OF YOUR HEROES ALWAYS GETTING SLOWLY TORTURED.
THIS WAY, YOU GET TO EXPERIENCE IT IN REAL LIFE.
AS FOR YOUR MASKED FRIEND, I'LL JUST STOMP HIS FOOL HANDS OFF THE ROCK AND BE DONE WITH IT.

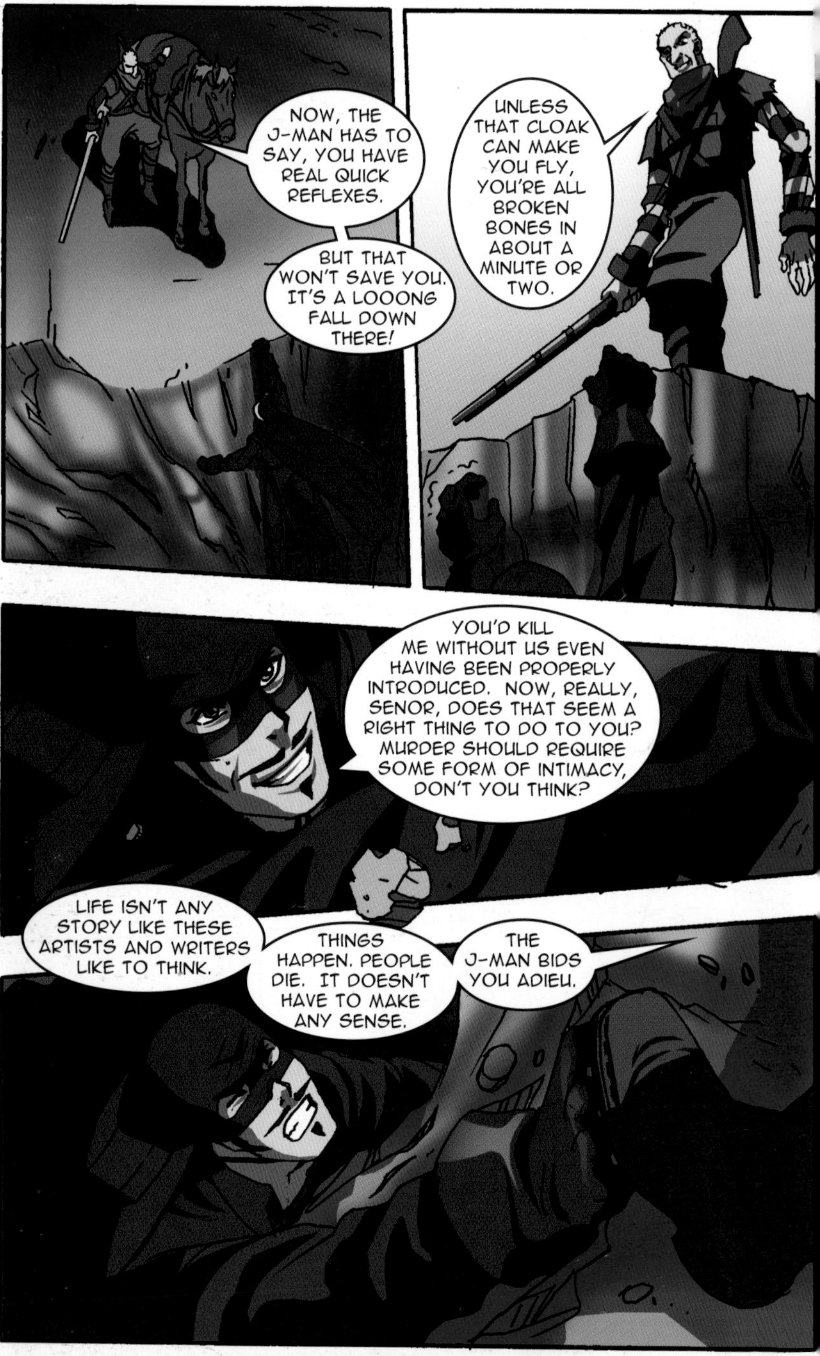
NOW, THE J-MAN HAS TO SAY, YOU HAVE REAL QUICK REFLEXES.
BUT THAT WON'T SAVE YOU. IT'S A LOOONG FALL DOWN THERE!
UNLESS THAT CLOAK CAN MAKE YOU FLY, YOU'RE ALL BROKEN BONES IN ABOUT A MINUTE OR TWO.
YOU'D KILL ME WITHOUT US EVEN HAVING BEEN PROPERLY INTRODUCED. NOW, REALLY, SENOR, DOES THAT SEEM A RIGHT THING TO DO TO YOU? MURDER SHOULD REQUIRE SOME FORM OF INTIMACY, DON'T YOU THINK?
LIFE ISN'T ANY STORY LIKE THESE ARTISTS AND WRITERS LIKE TO THINK.
THINGS HAPPEN. PEOPLE DIE. IT DOESN'T HAVE TO MAKE ANY SENSE.
THE J-MAN BIDS YOU ADIEU.

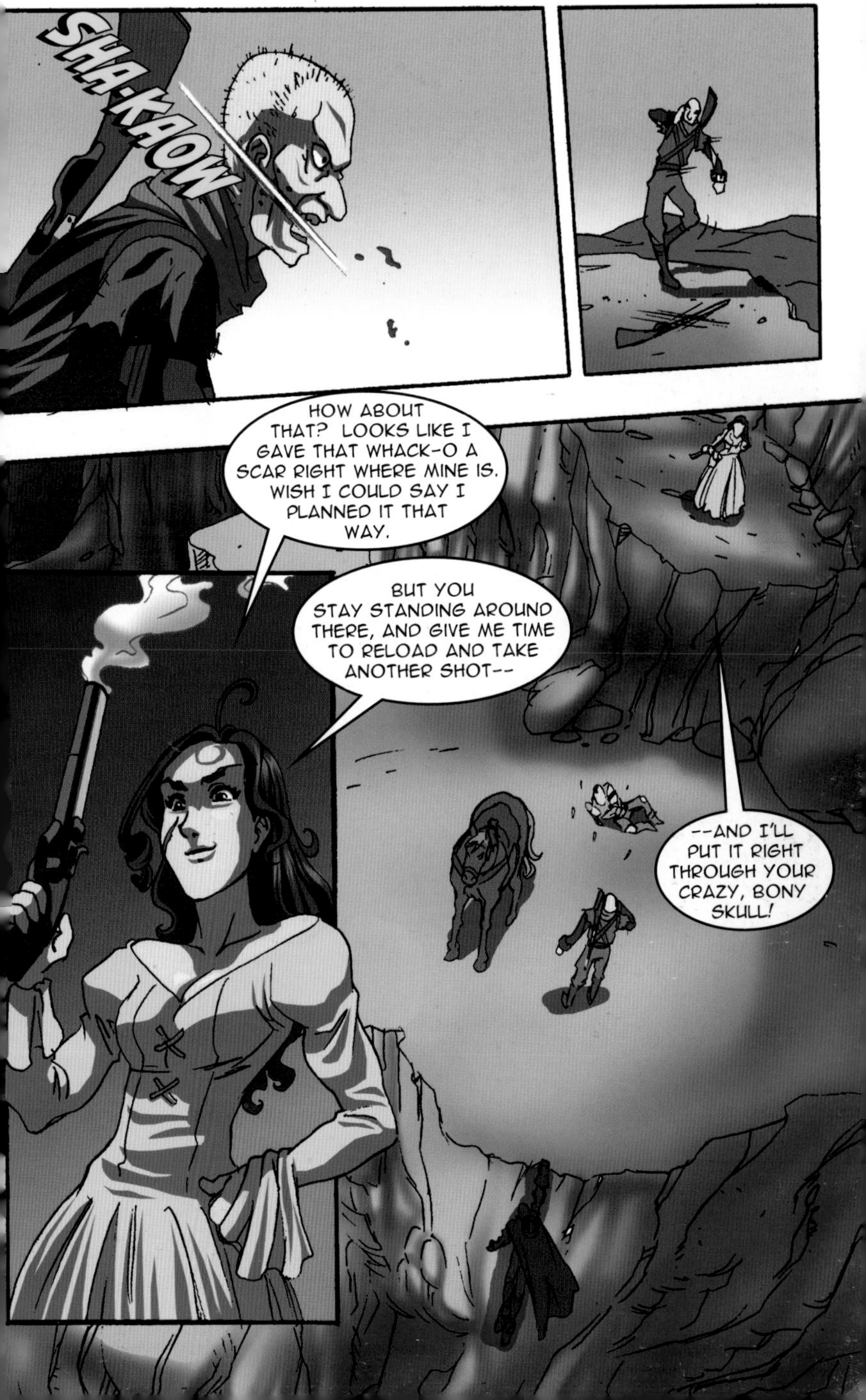
SHA-KAOW
HOW ABOUT THAT? LOOKS LIKE I GAVE THAT WHACK-O A SCAR RIGHT WHERE MINE IS. WISH I COULD SAY I PLANNED IT THAT WAY.
BUT YOU STAY STANDING AROUND THERE, AND GIVE ME TIME TO RELOAD AND TAKE ANOTHER SHOT--
--AND I'LL PUT IT RIGHT THROUGH YOUR CRAZY, BONY SKULL!

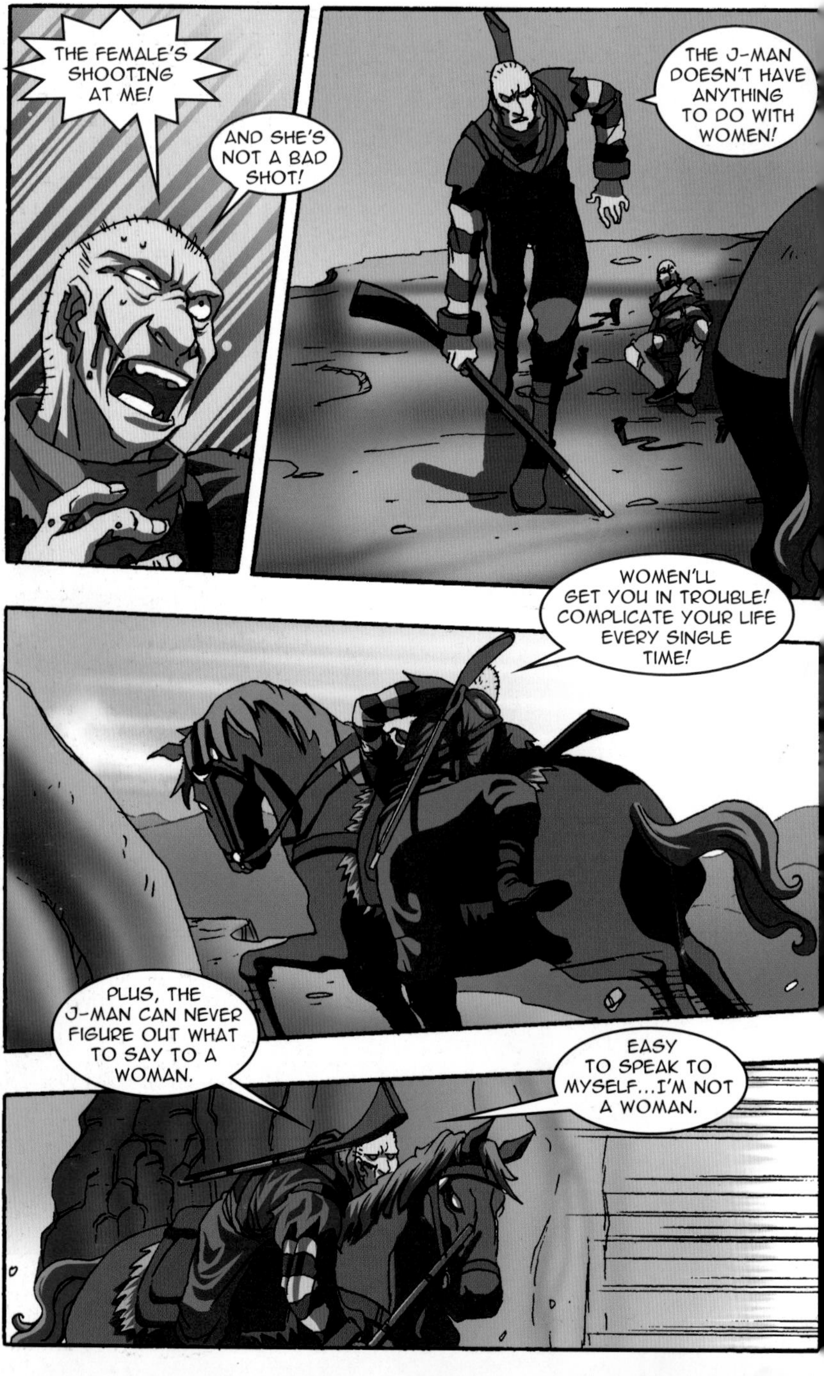
THE FEMALE'S SHOOTING AT ME!
AND SHE'S NOT A BAD SHOT!
THE J-MAN DOESN'T HAVE ANYTHING TO DO WITH WOMEN!
WOMEN'LL GET YOU IN TROUBLE! COMPLICATE YOUR LIFE EVERY SINGLE TIME!
PLUS, THE J-MAN CAN NEVER FIGURE OUT WHAT TO SAY TO A WOMAN.
EASY TO SPEAK TO MYSELF...I'M NOT A WOMAN.

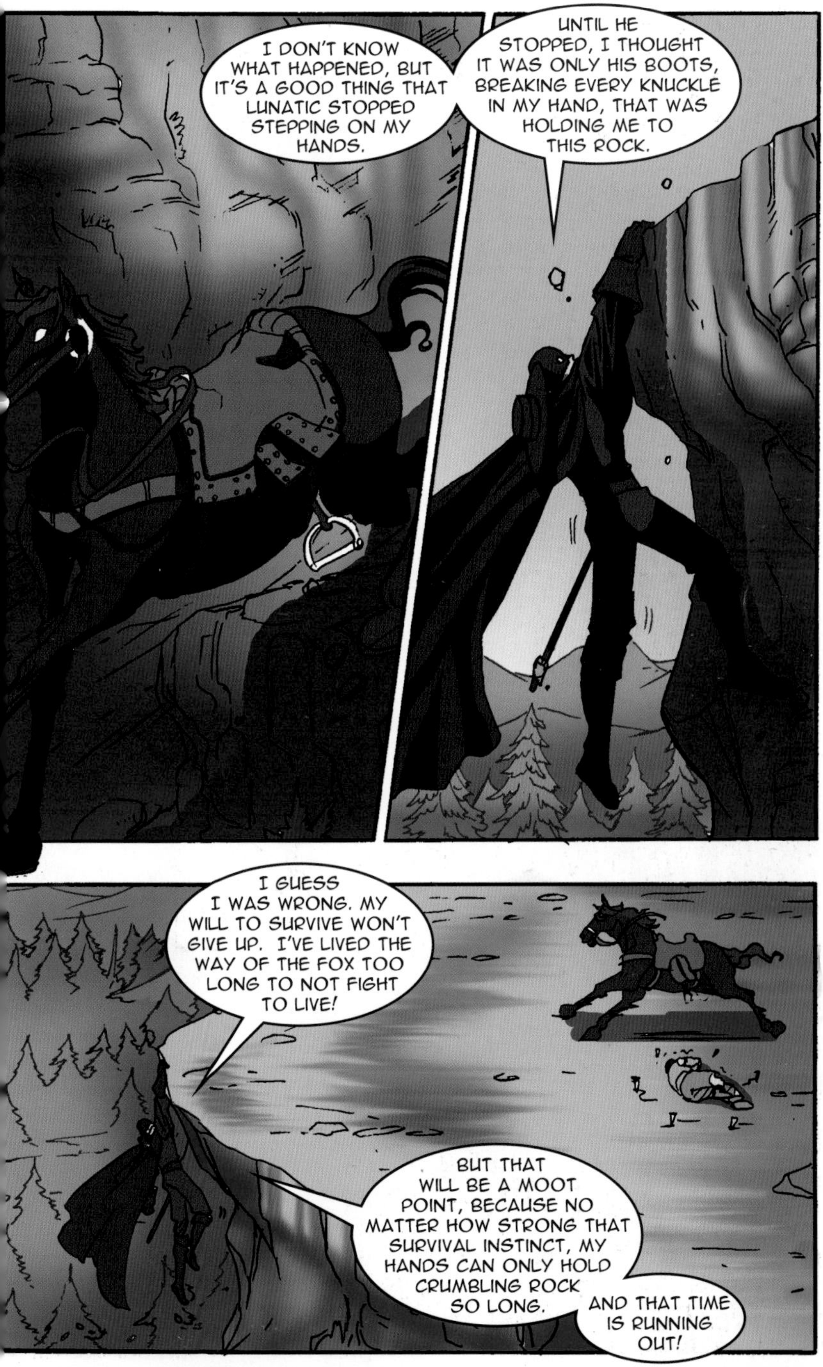

I DON'T KNOW WHAT HAPPENED, BUT IT'S A GOOD THING THAT LUNATIC STOPPED STEPPING ON MY HANDS.
UNTIL HE STOPPED, I THOUGHT IT WAS ONLY HIS BOOTS, BREAKING EVERY KNUCKLE IN MY HAND, THAT WAS HOLDING ME TO THIS ROCK.
I GUESS I WAS WRONG. MY WILL TO SURVIVE WON'T GIVE UP. I'VE LIVED THE WAY OF THE FOX TOO LONG TO NOT FIGHT TO LIVE!
BUT THAT WILL BE A MOOT POINT, BECAUSE NO MATTER HOW STRONG THAT SURVIVAL INSTINCT, MY HANDS CAN ONLY HOLD CRUMBLING ROCK SO LONG.
AND THAT TIME IS RUNNING OUT!

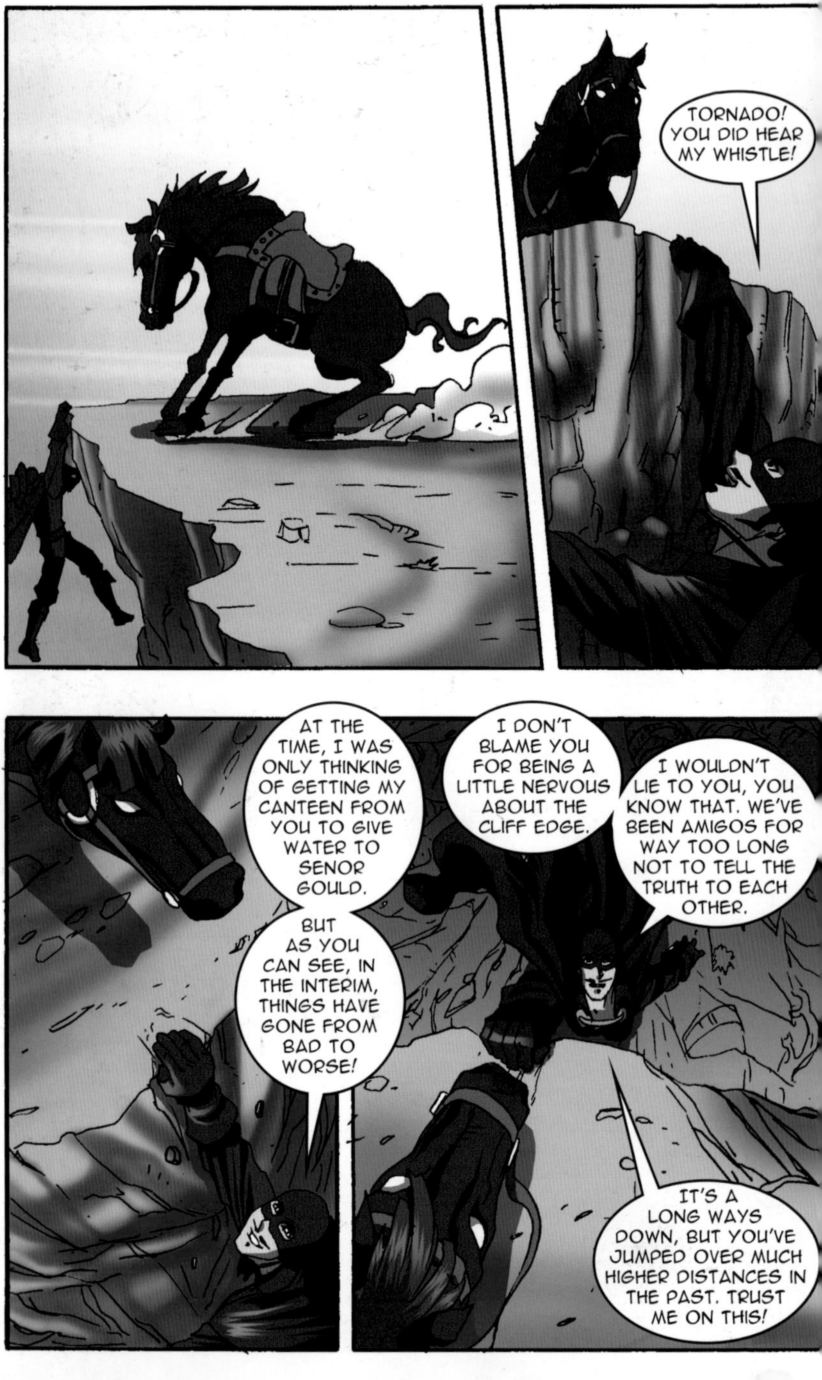
TORNADO! YOU DID HEAR MY WHISTLE!
AT THE TIME, I WAS ONLY THINKING OF GETTING MY CANTEEN FROM YOU TO GIVE WATER TO SENOR GOULD.
BUT AS YOU CAN SEE, IN THE INTERIM, THINGS HAVE GONE FROM BAD TO WORSE!
I DON'T BLAME YOU FOR BEING A LITTLE NERVOUS ABOUT THE CLIFF EDGE.
I WOULDN'T LIE TO YOU, YOU KNOW THAT. WE'VE BEEN AMIGOS FOR WAY TOO LONG NOT TO TELL THE TRUTH TO EACH OTHER.
IT'S A LONG WAYS DOWN, BUT YOU'VE JUMPED OVER MUCH HIGHER DISTANCES IN THE PAST. TRUST ME ON THIS!

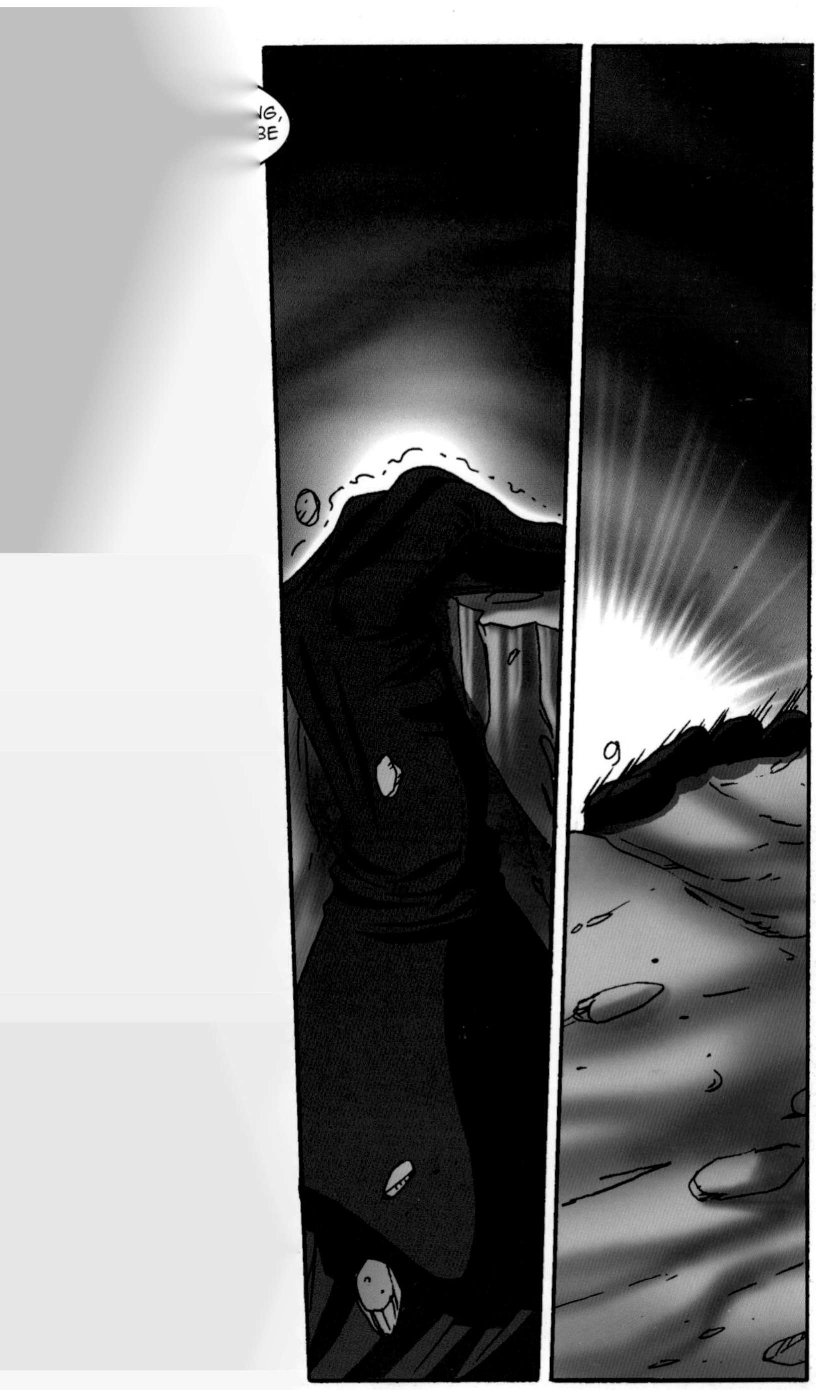

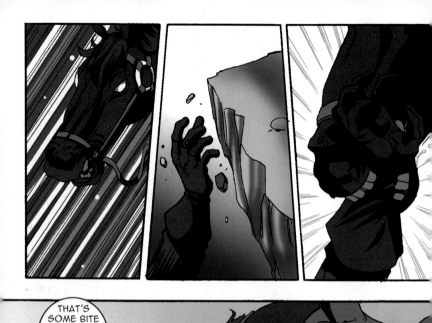

THAT'S SOME BITE YOU HAVE, TORNADO. I NEVER REALIZED.

I DIDN'T REALIZE MY HEART COULD... BEAT SO HARD... IT FEELS LIKE IT MIGHT... BURST...OUT OF MY CHEST!

NOT...THAT I DOUBTED...FOR A SECOND...THAT YOU'D COME THROUGH!

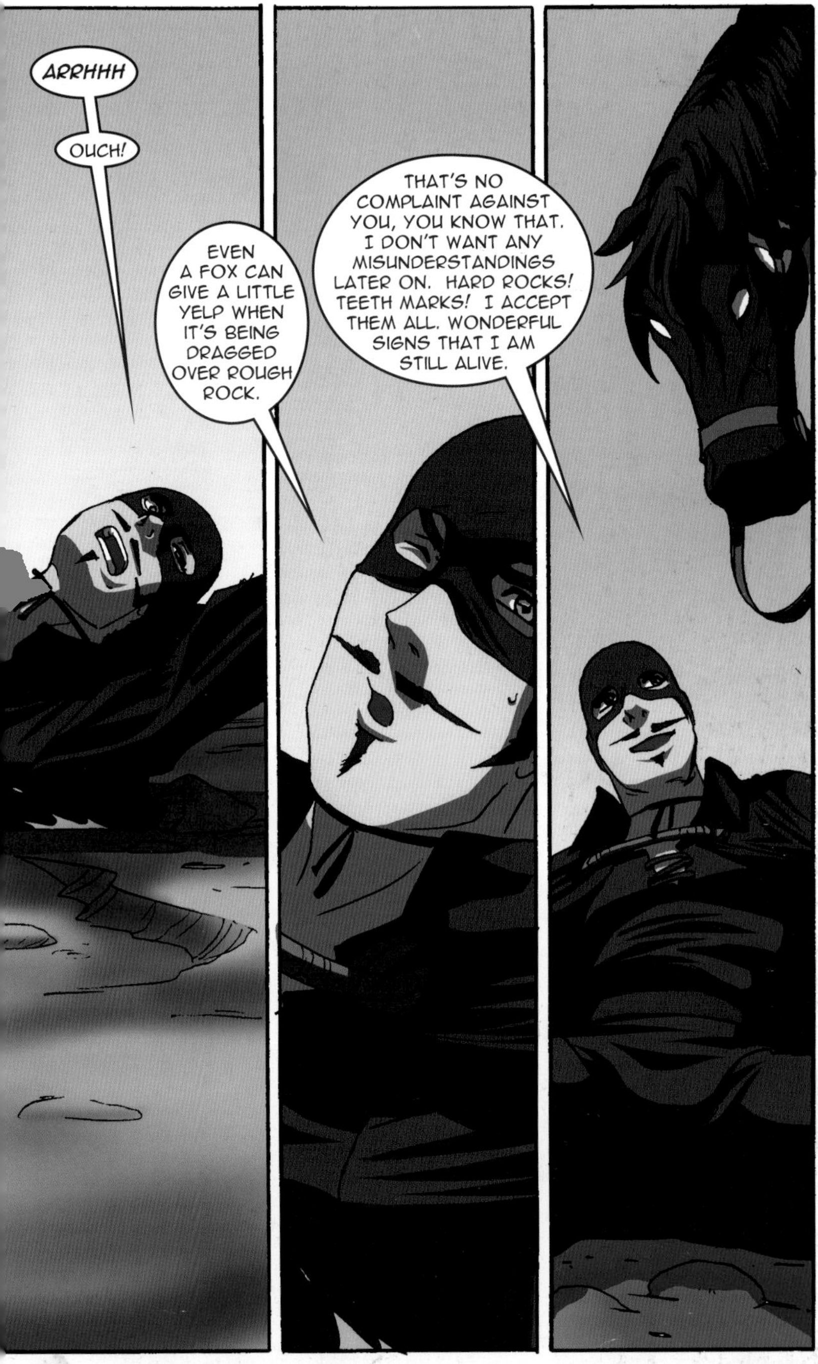
ARRHHH
OUCH!
EVEN A FOX CAN GIVE A LITTLE YELP WHEN IT'S BEING DRAGGED OVER ROUGH ROCK.
THAT'S NO COMPLAINT AGAINST YOU, YOU KNOW THAT. I DON'T WANT ANY MISUNDERSTANDINGS LATER ON. HARD ROCKS! TEETH MARKS! I ACCEPT THEM ALL. WONDERFUL SIGNS THAT I AM STILL ALIVE.

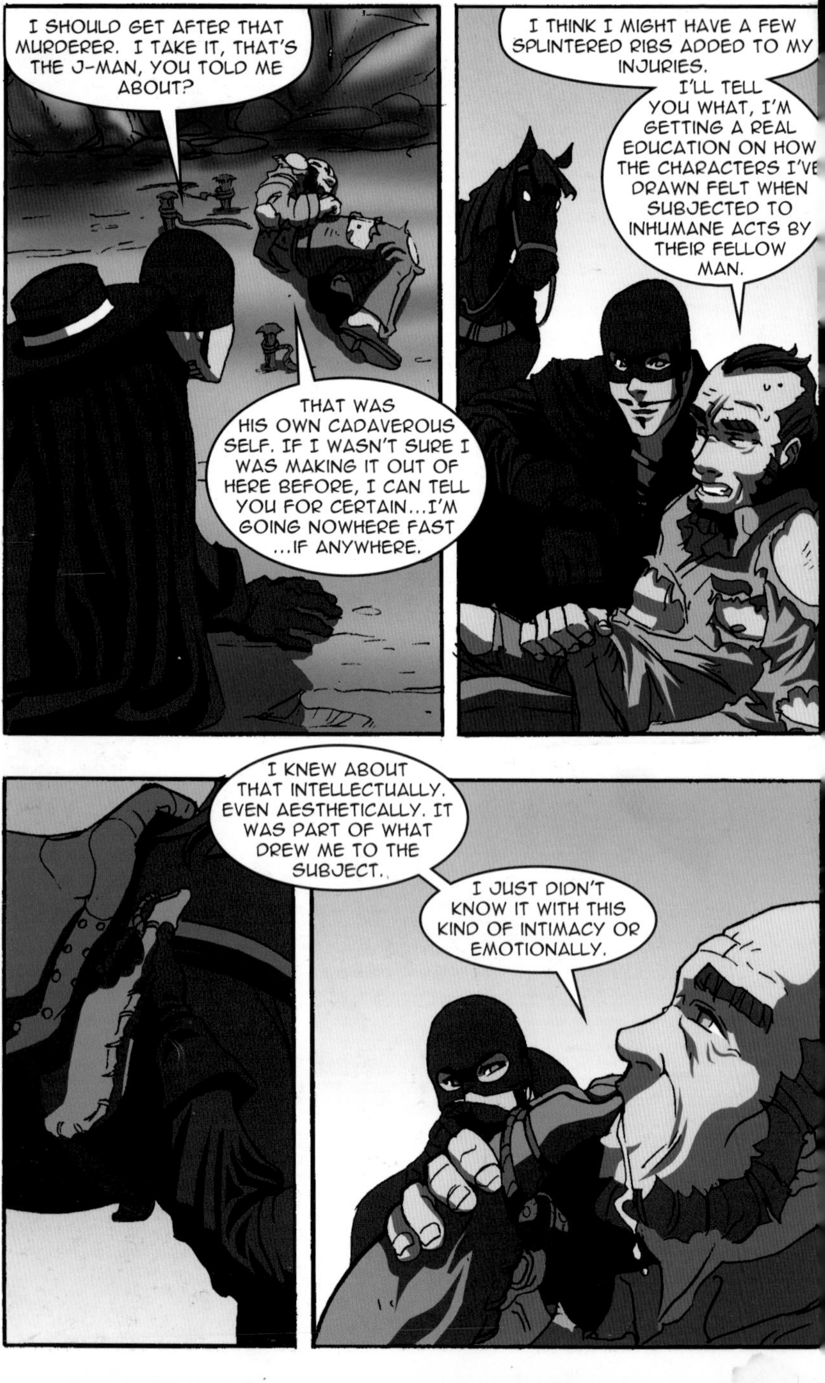

I SHOULD GET AFTER THAT MURDERER. I TAKE IT, THAT'S THE J-MAN, YOU TOLD ME ABOUT?
THAT WAS HIS OWN CADAVEROUS SELF. IF I WASN'T SURE I WAS MAKING IT OUT OF HERE BEFORE, I CAN TELL YOU FOR CERTAIN...I'M GOING NOWHERE FAST ...IF ANYWHERE.
I THINK I MIGHT HAVE A FEW SPLINTERED RIBS ADDED TO MY INJURIES.
I'LL TELL YOU WHAT, I'M GETTING A REAL EDUCATION ON HOW THE CHARACTERS I'VE DRAWN FELT WHEN SUBJECTED TO INHUMANE ACTS BY THEIR FELLOW MAN.
I KNEW ABOUT THAT INTELLECTUALLY. EVEN AESTHETICALLY. IT WAS PART OF WHAT DREW ME TO THE SUBJECT.
I JUST DIDN'T KNOW IT WITH THIS KIND OF INTIMACY OR EMOTIONALLY.

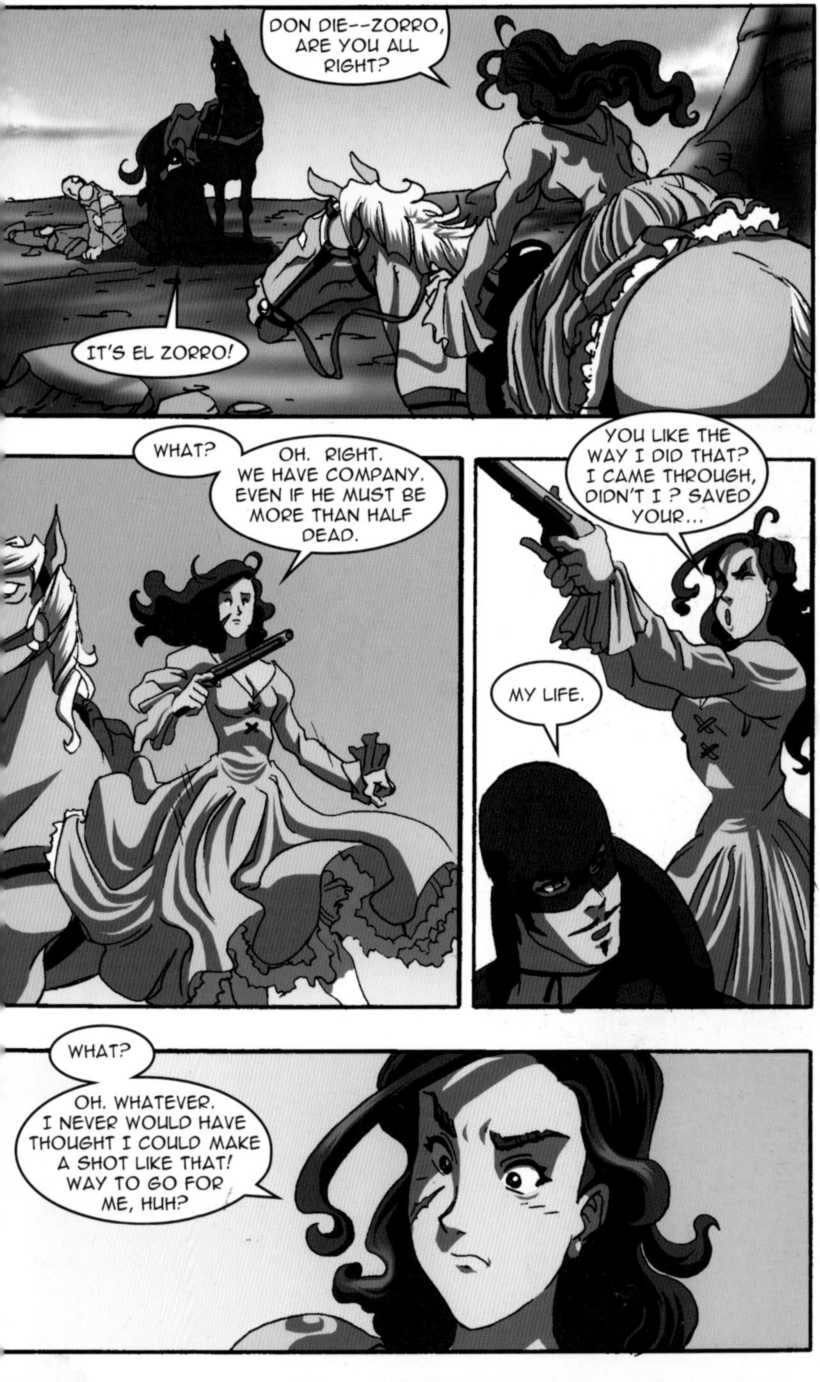

DON DIE--ZORRO, ARE YOU ALL RIGHT?
IT'S EL ZORRO!
WHAT?
OH. RIGHT. WE HAVE COMPANY. EVEN IF HE MUST BE MORE THAN HALF DEAD.
YOU LIKE THE WAY I DID THAT? I CAME THROUGH, DIDN'T I ? SAVED YOUR...
MY LIFE.
WHAT?
OH. WHATEVER. I NEVER WOULD HAVE THOUGHT I COULD MAKE A SHOT LIKE THAT! WAY TO GO FOR ME, HUH?

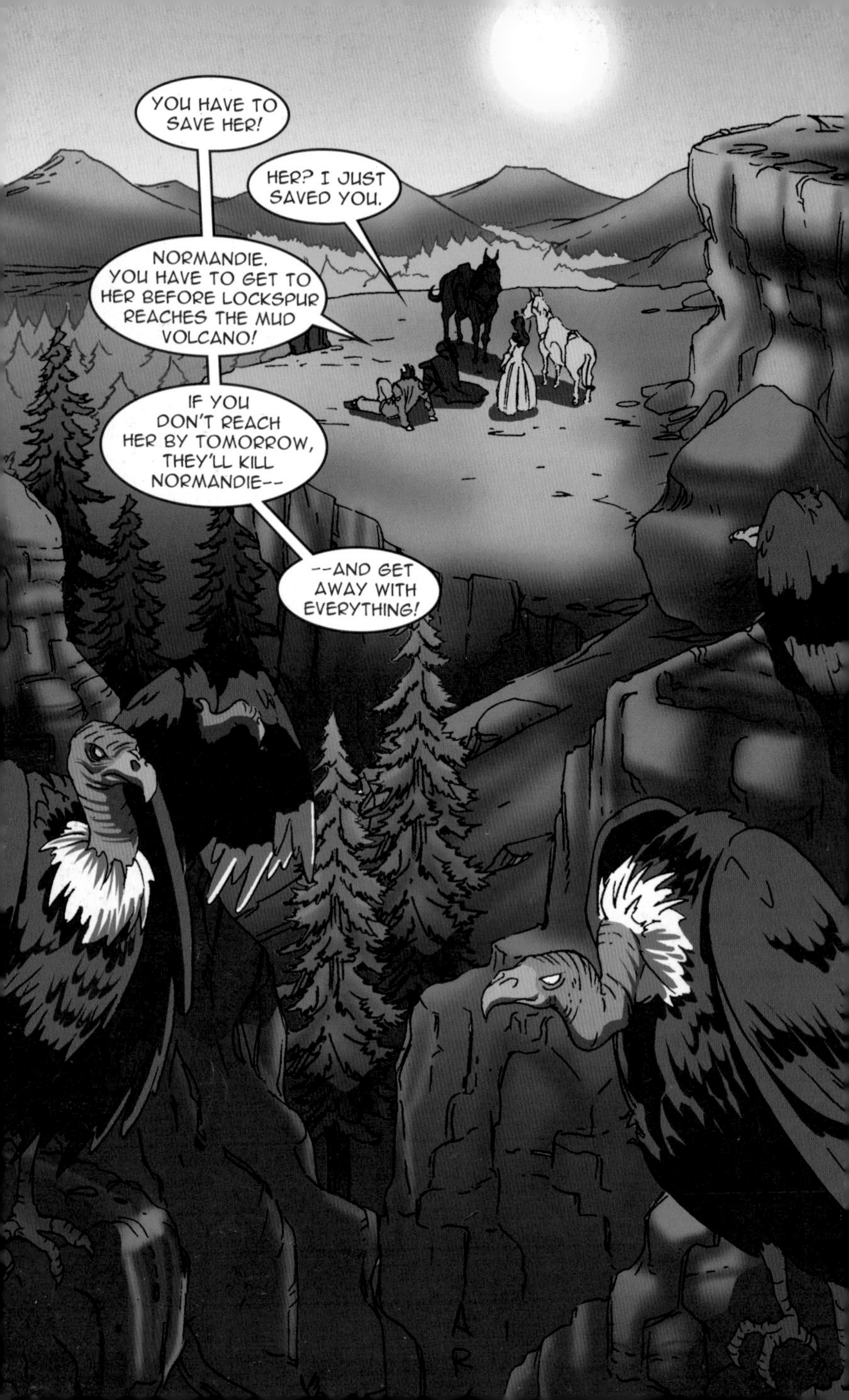
YOU HAVE TO SAVE HER!
HER? I JUST SAVED YOU.
NORMANDIE. YOU HAVE TO GET TO HER BEFORE LOCKSPUR REACHES THE MUD VOLCANO!
IF YOU DON'T REACH HER BY TOMORROW, THEY'LL KILL NORMANDIE--
--AND GET AWAY WITH EVERYTHING!

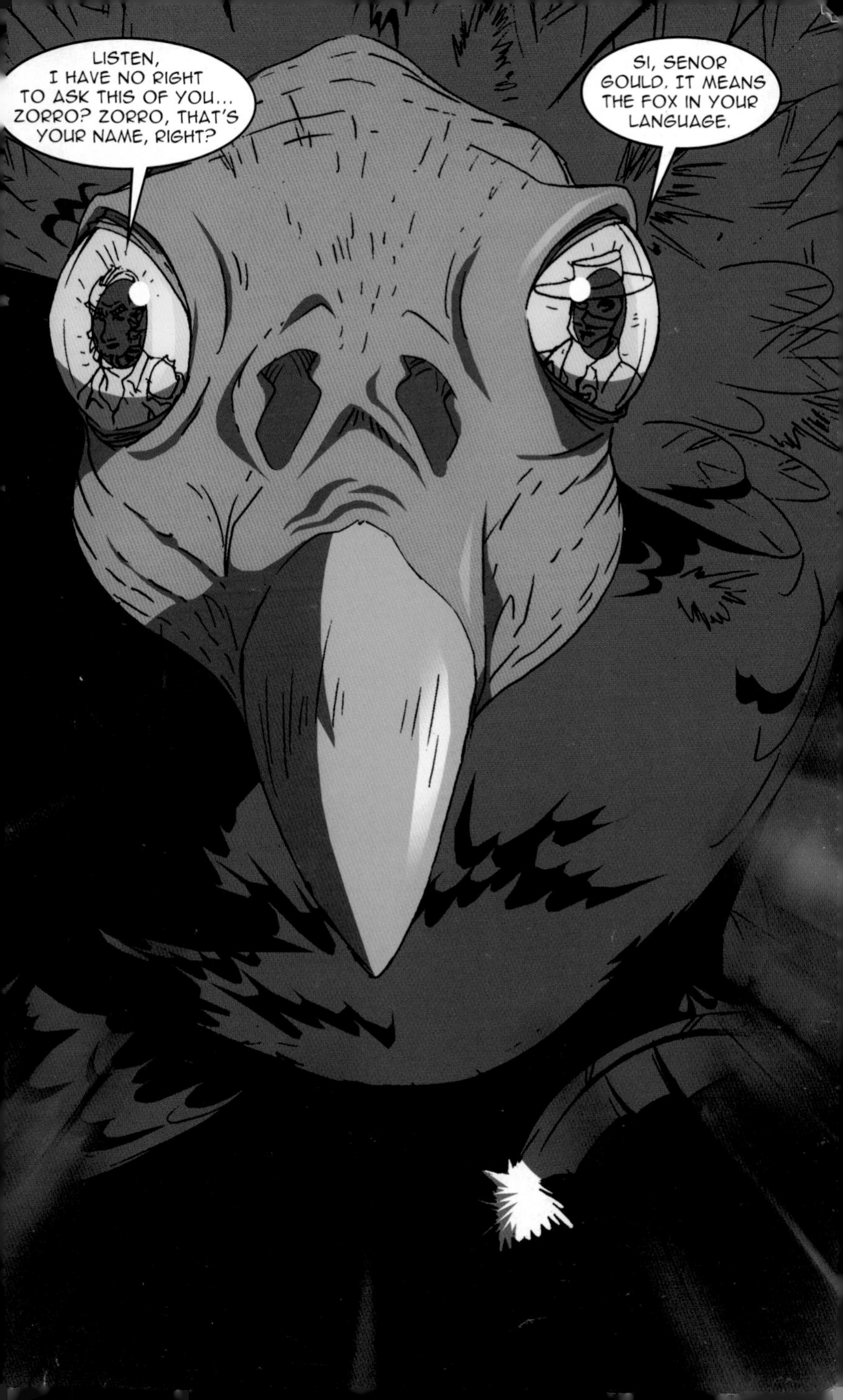
LISTEN, I HAVE NO RIGHT TO ASK THIS OF YOU... ZORRO? ZORRO, THAT'S YOUR NAME, RIGHT?
SI, SENOR GOULD. IT MEANS THE FOX IN YOUR LANGUAGE.

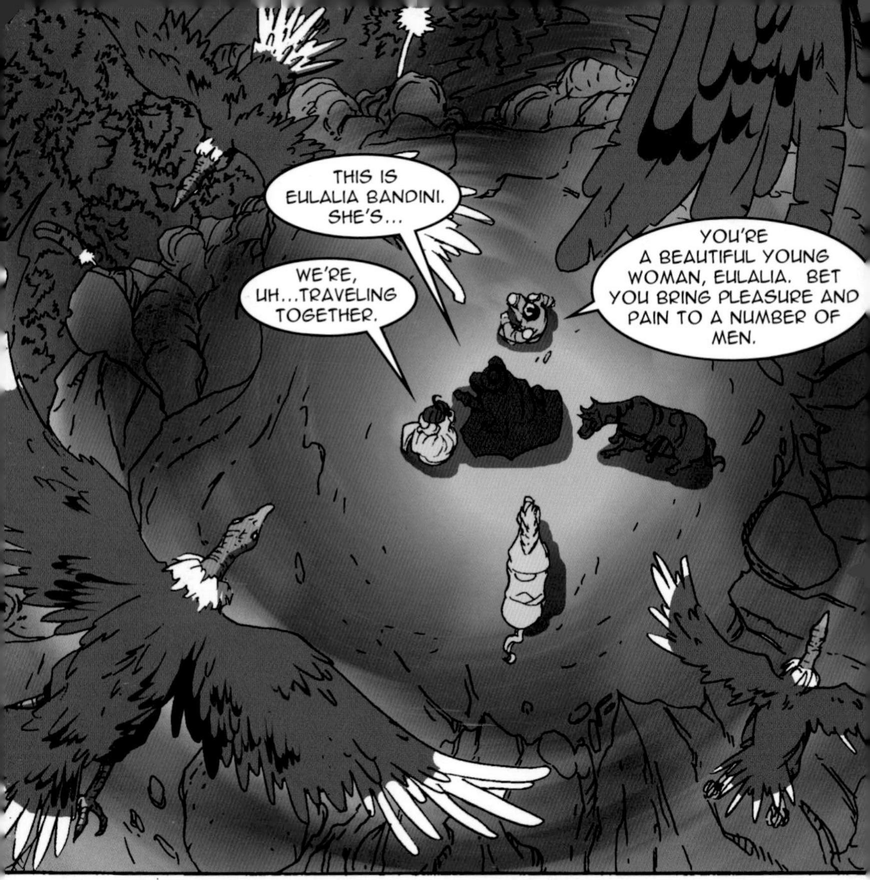
THIS IS EULALIA BANDINI. SHE'S...
WE'RE, UH...TRAVELING TOGETHER.
YOU'RE A BEAUTIFUL YOUNG WOMAN, EULALIA. BET YOU BRING PLEASURE AND PAIN TO A NUMBER OF MEN.

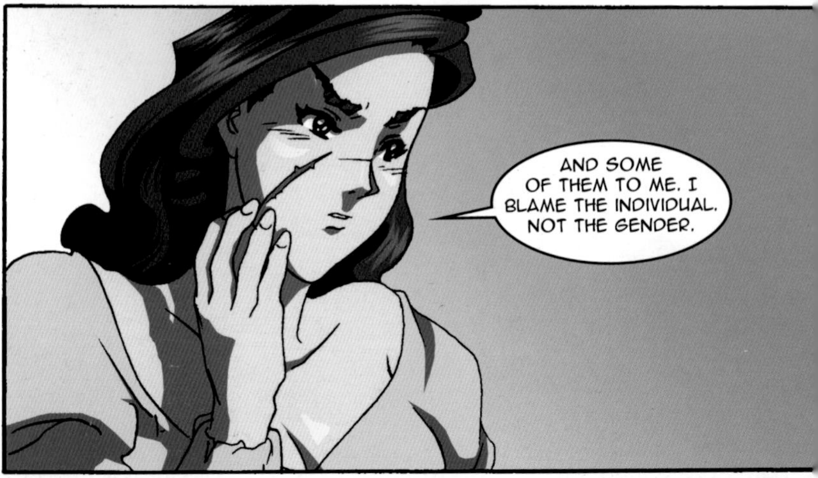
AND SOME OF THEM TO ME. I BLAME THE INDIVIDUAL. NOT THE GENDER.

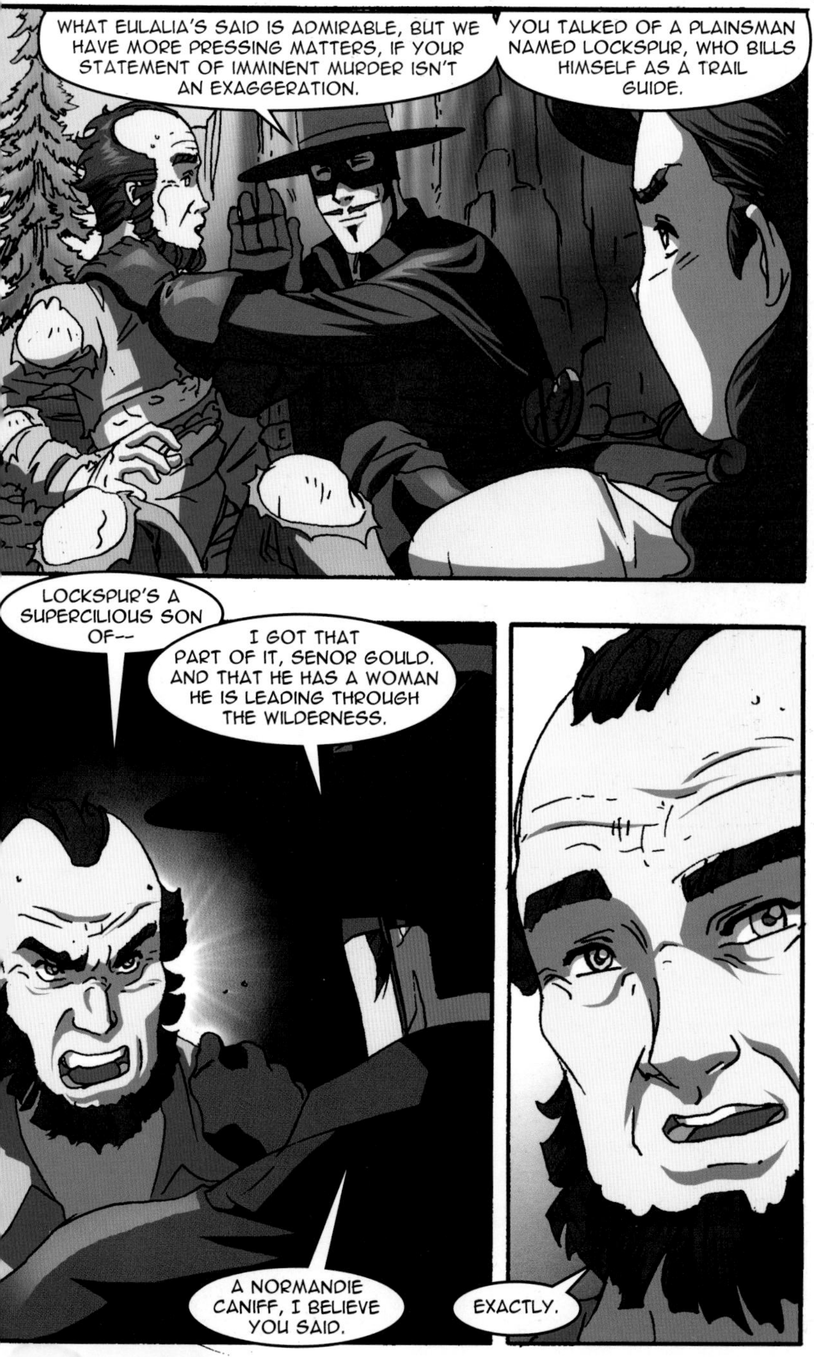
WHAT EULALIA'S SAID IS ADMIRABLE, BUT WE HAVE MORE PRESSING MATTERS, IF YOUR STATEMENT OF IMMINENT MURDER ISN'T AN EXAGGERATION.
YOU TALKED OF A PLAINSMAN NAMED LOCKSPUR, WHO BILLS HIMSELF AS A TRAIL GUIDE.
LOCKSPUR'S A SUPERCILIOUS SON OF--
I GOT THAT PART OF IT, SENOR GOULD. AND THAT HE HAS A WOMAN HE IS LEADING THROUGH THE WILDERNESS.
A NORMANDIE CANIFF, I BELIEVE YOU SAID.
EXACTLY.

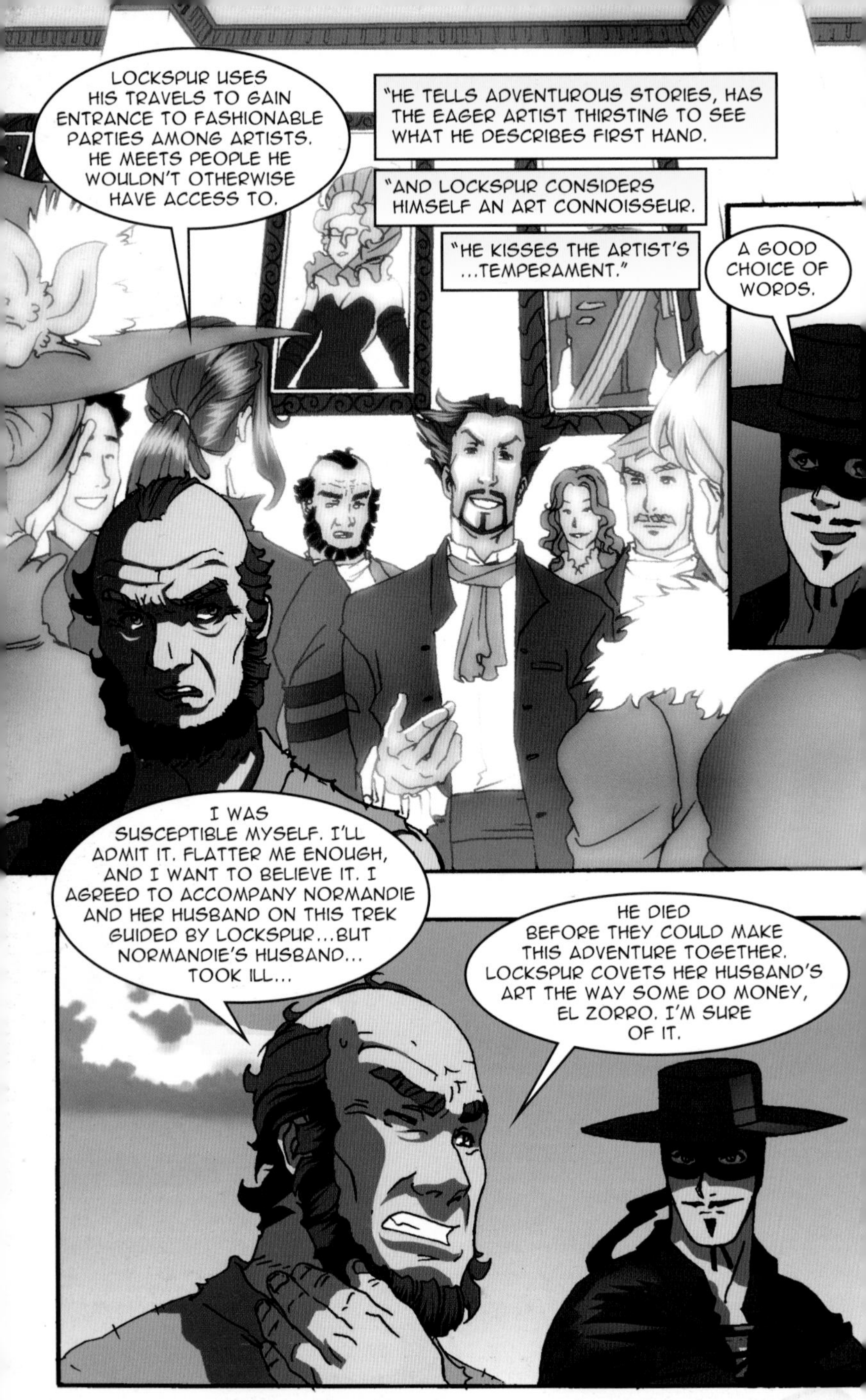
LOCKSPUR USES HIS TRAVELS TO GAIN ENTRANCE TO FASHIONABLE PARTIES AMONG ARTISTS. HE MEETS PEOPLE HE WOULDN'T OTHERWISE HAVE ACCESS TO.
"HE TELLS ADVENTUROUS STORIES, HAS THE EAGER ARTIST THIRSTING TO SEE WHAT HE DESCRIBES FIRST HAND.
"AND LOCKSPUR CONSIDERS HIMSELF AN ART CONNOISSEUR.
"HE KISSES THE ARTIST'S ...TEMPERAMENT."
A GOOD CHOICE OF WORDS.
I WAS SUSCEPTIBLE MYSELF. I'LL ADMIT IT. FLATTER ME ENOUGH, AND I WANT TO BELIEVE IT. I AGREED TO ACCOMPANY NORMANDIE AND HER HUSBAND ON THIS TREK GUIDED BY LOCKSPUR...BUT NORMANDIE'S HUSBAND... TOOK ILL...
HE DIED BEFORE THEY COULD MAKE THIS ADVENTURE TOGETHER. LOCKSPUR COVETS HER HUSBAND'S ART THE WAY SOME DO MONEY, EL ZORRO. I'M SURE OF IT.

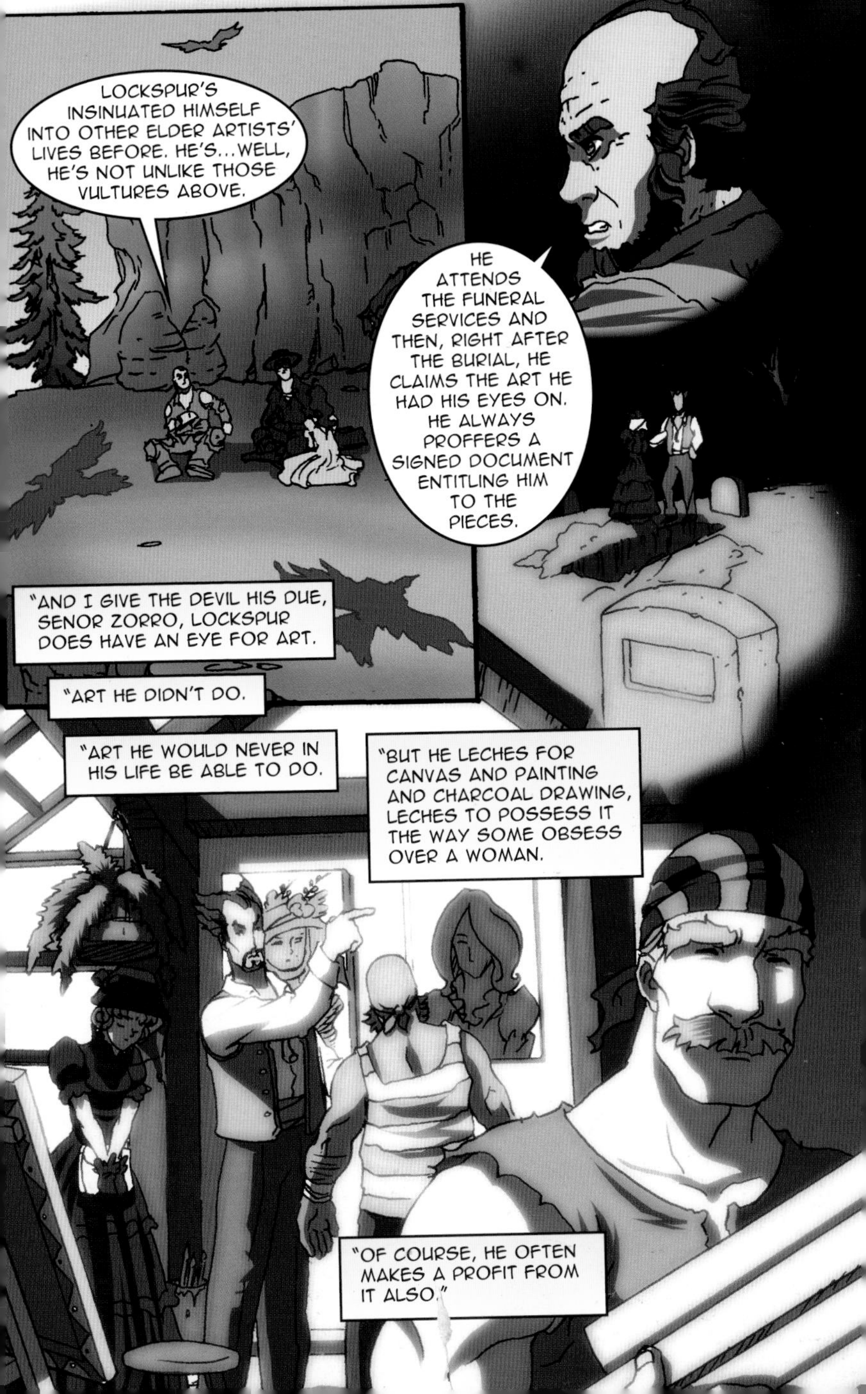
LOCKSPUR'S INSINUATED HIMSELF INTO OTHER ELDER ARTISTS' LIVES BEFORE. HE'S...WELL, HE'S NOT UNLIKE THOSE VULTURES ABOVE.
HE ATTENDS THE FUNERAL SERVICES AND THEN, RIGHT AFTER THE BURIAL, HE CLAIMS THE ART HE HAD HIS EYES ON. HE ALWAYS PROFFERS A SIGNED DOCUMENT ENTITLING HIM TO THE PIECES.
"AND I GIVE THE DEVIL HIS DUE, SENOR ZORRO, LOCKSPUR DOES HAVE AN EYE FOR ART.
"ART HE DIDN'T DO.
"ART HE WOULD NEVER IN HIS LIFE BE ABLE TO DO.
"BUT HE LECHES FOR CANVAS AND PAINTING AND CHARCOAL DRAWING, LECHES TO POSSESS IT THE WAY SOME OBSESS OVER A WOMAN.
"OF COURSE, HE OFTEN MAKES A PROFIT FROM IT ALSO."

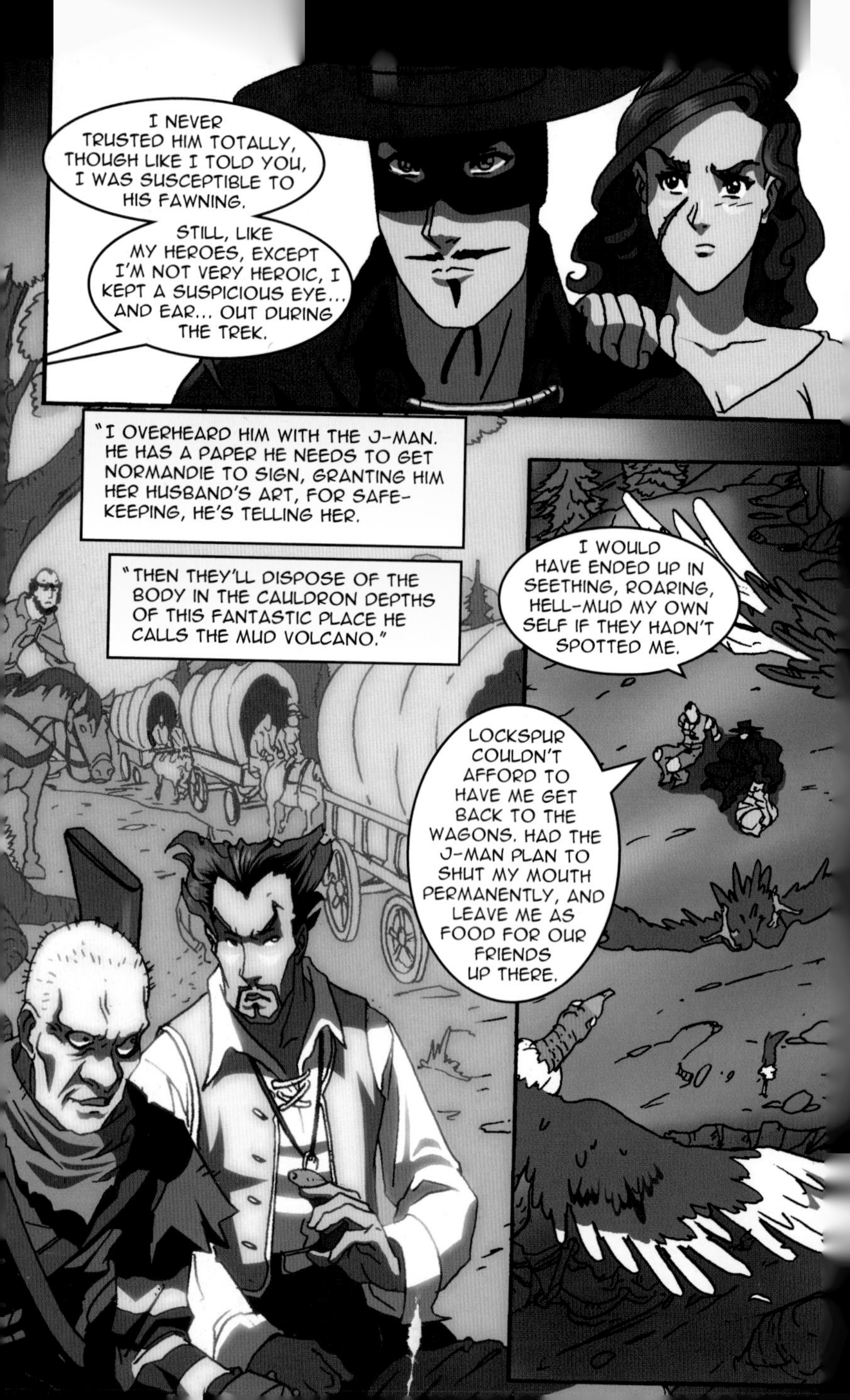
I NEVER TRUSTED HIM TOTALLY, THOUGH LIKE I TOLD YOU, I WAS SUSCEPTIBLE TO HIS FAWNING.
STILL, LIKE MY HEROES, EXCEPT I'M NOT VERY HEROIC, I KEPT A SUSPICIOUS EYE... AND EAR... OUT DURING THE TREK.
"I OVERHEARD HIM WITH THE J-MAN. HE HAS A PAPER HE NEEDS TO GET NORMANDIE TO SIGN, GRANTING HIM HER HUSBAND'S ART, FOR SAFE-KEEPING, HE'S TELLING HER.
"THEN THEY'LL DISPOSE OF THE BODY IN THE CAULDRON DEPTHS OF THIS FANTASTIC PLACE HE CALLS THE MUD VOLCANO."
I WOULD HAVE ENDED UP IN SEETHING, ROARING, HELL-MUD MY OWN SELF IF THEY HADN'T SPOTTED ME.
LOCKSPUR COULDN'T AFFORD TO HAVE ME GET BACK TO THE WAGONS. HAD THE J-MAN PLAN TO SHUT MY MOUTH PERMANENTLY, AND LEAVE ME AS FOOD FOR OUR FRIENDS UP THERE.

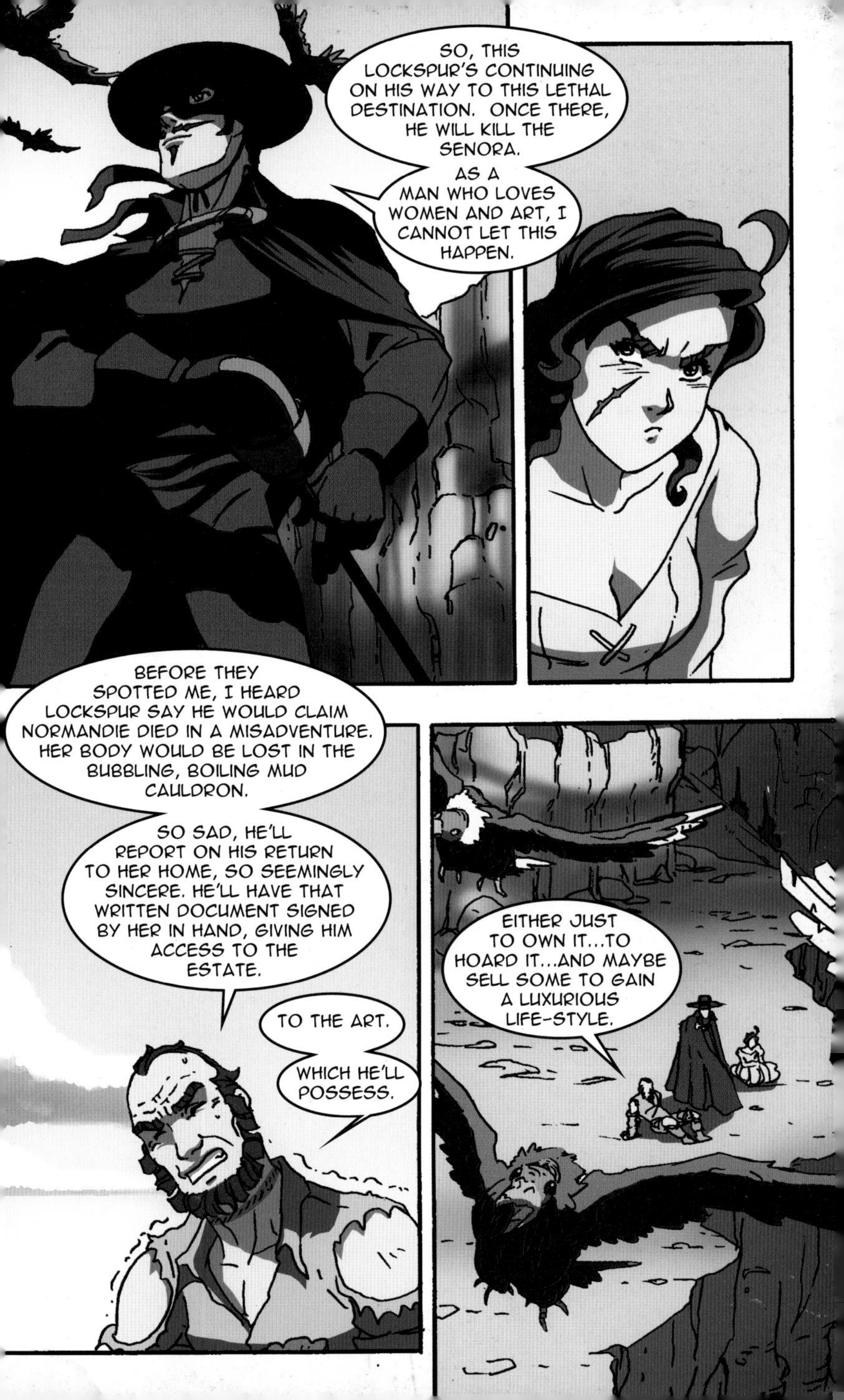
SO, THIS LOCKSPUR'S CONTINUING ON HIS WAY TO THIS LETHAL DESTINATION. ONCE THERE, HE WILL KILL THE SENORA.
AS A MAN WHO LOVES WOMEN AND ART, I CANNOT LET THIS HAPPEN.
BEFORE THEY SPOTTED ME, I HEARD LOCKSPUR SAY HE WOULD CLAIM NORMANDIE DIED IN A MISADVENTURE. HER BODY WOULD BE LOST IN THE BUBBLING, BOILING MUD CAULDRON.
SO SAD, HE'LL REPORT ON HIS RETURN TO HER HOME, SO SEEMINGLY SINCERE. HE'LL HAVE THAT WRITTEN DOCUMENT SIGNED BY HER IN HAND, GIVING HIM ACCESS TO THE ESTATE.
TO THE ART.
WHICH HE'LL POSSESS.
EITHER JUST TO OWN IT...TO HOARD IT...AND MAYBE SELL SOME TO GAIN A LUXURIOUS LIFE-STYLE.

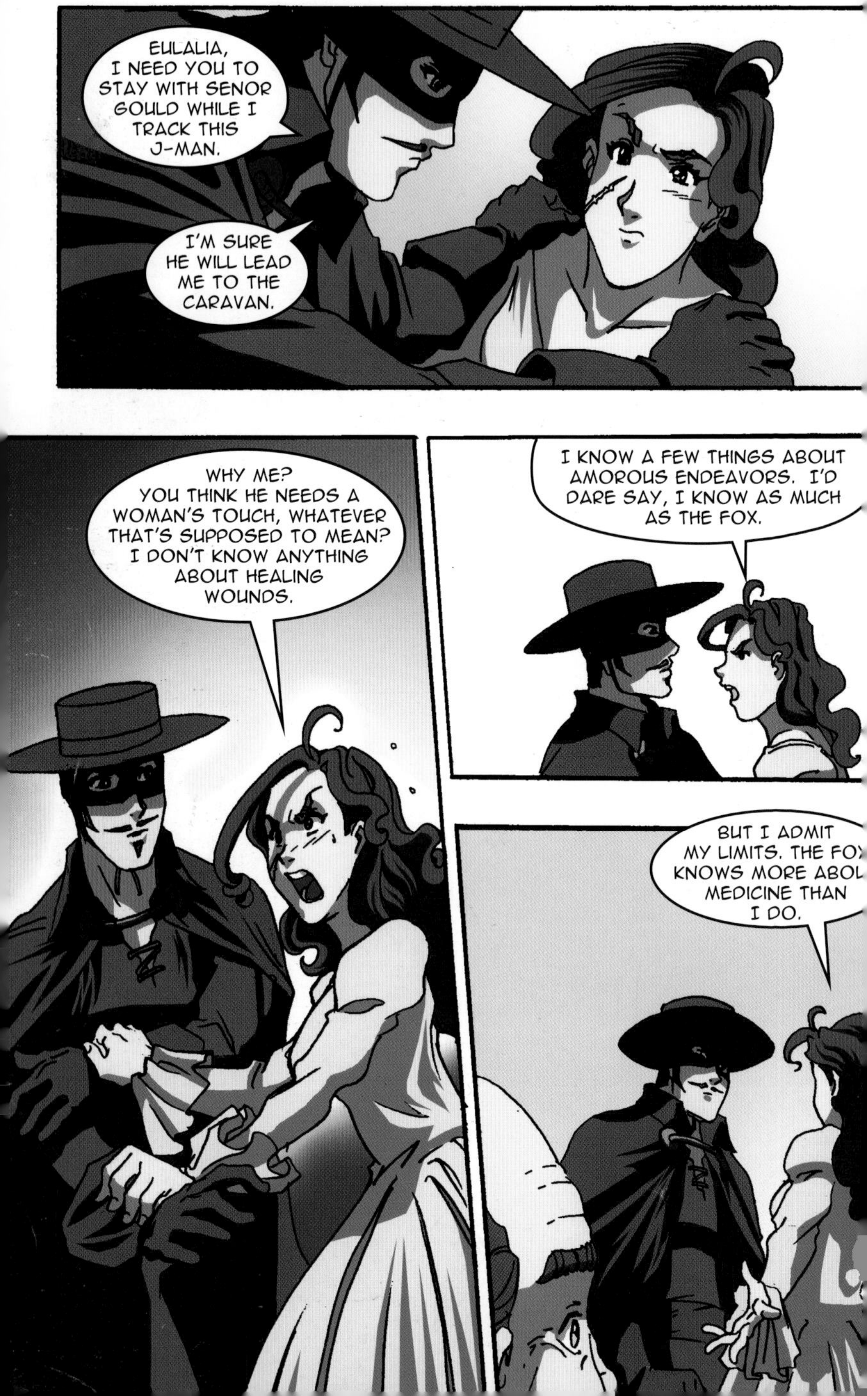
EULALIA, I NEED YOU TO STAY WITH SENOR GOULD WHILE I TRACK THIS J-MAN.
I'M SURE HE WILL LEAD ME TO THE CARAVAN.
WHY ME? YOU THINK HE NEEDS A WOMAN'S TOUCH, WHATEVER THAT'S SUPPOSED TO MEAN? I DON'T KNOW ANYTHING ABOUT HEALING WOUNDS.
I KNOW A FEW THINGS ABOUT AMOROUS ENDEAVORS. I'D DARE SAY, I KNOW AS MUCH AS THE FOX.
BUT I ADMIT MY LIMITS. THE FO KNOWS MORE ABOU MEDICINE THAN I DO.

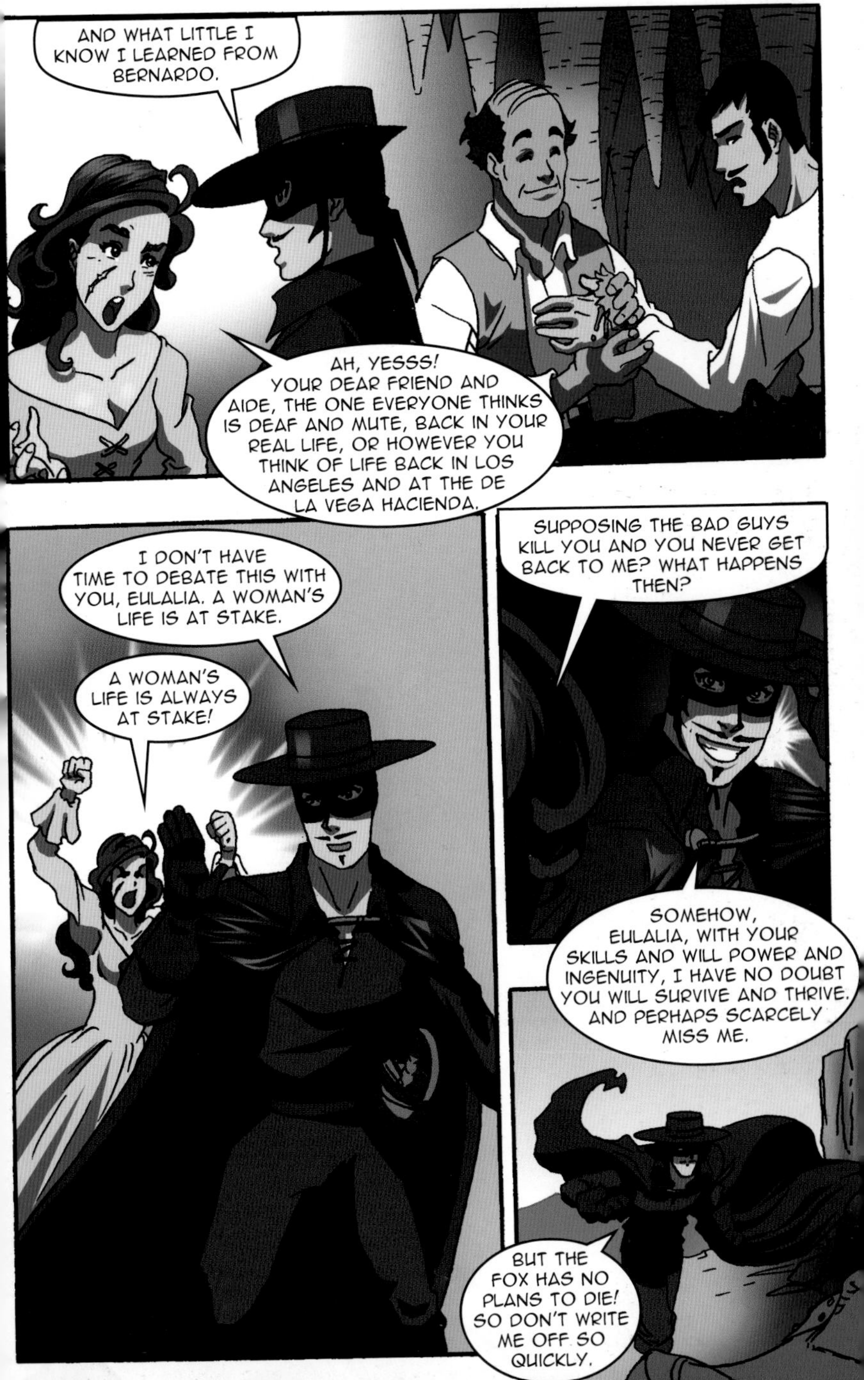
AND WHAT LITTLE I KNOW I LEARNED FROM BERNARDO.
AH, YESSS! YOUR DEAR FRIEND AND AIDE, THE ONE EVERYONE THINKS IS DEAF AND MUTE, BACK IN YOUR REAL LIFE, OR HOWEVER YOU THINK OF LIFE BACK IN LOS ANGELES AND AT THE DE LA VEGA HACIENDA.
I DON'T HAVE TIME TO DEBATE THIS WITH YOU, EULALIA. A WOMAN'S LIFE IS AT STAKE.
A WOMAN'S LIFE IS ALWAYS AT STAKE!
SUPPOSING THE BAD GUYS KILL YOU AND YOU NEVER GET BACK TO ME? WHAT HAPPENS THEN?
SOMEHOW, EULALIA, WITH YOUR SKILLS AND WILL POWER AND INGENUITY, I HAVE NO DOUBT YOU WILL SURVIVE AND THRIVE. AND PERHAPS SCARCELY MISS ME.
BUT THE FOX HAS NO PLANS TO DIE! SO DON'T WRITE ME OFF SO QUICKLY.

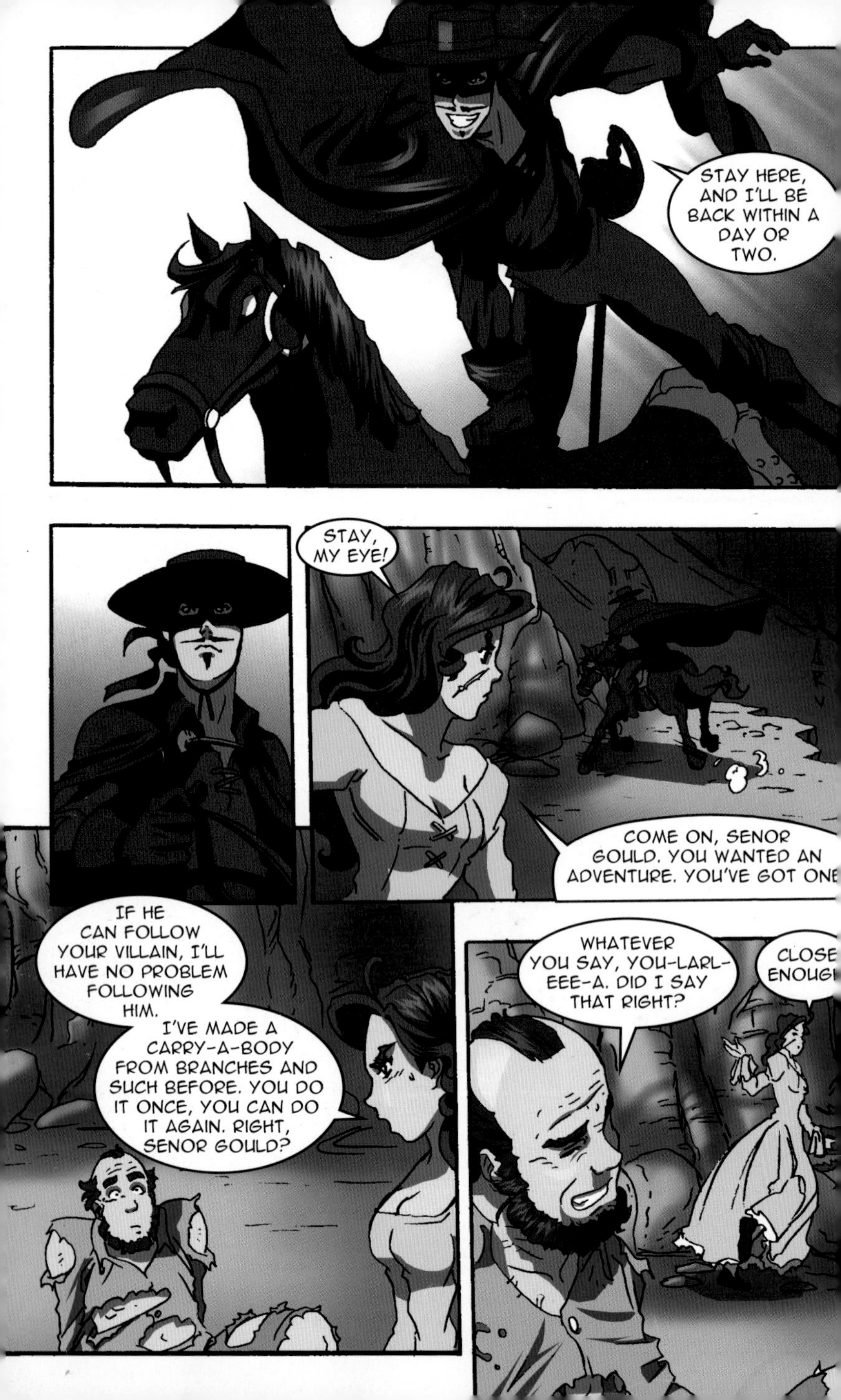
STAY HERE, AND I'LL BE BACK WITHIN A DAY OR TWO.
STAY, MY EYE!
COME ON, SENOR GOULD. YOU WANTED AN ADVENTURE. YOU'VE GOT ONE
IF HE CAN FOLLOW YOUR VILLAIN, I'LL HAVE NO PROBLEM FOLLOWING HIM.
I'VE MADE A CARRY-A-BODY FROM BRANCHES AND SUCH BEFORE. YOU DO IT ONCE, YOU CAN DO IT AGAIN. RIGHT, SENOR GOULD?
WHATEVER YOU SAY, YOU-LARL-EEE-A. DID I SAY THAT RIGHT?
CLOSE ENOUG

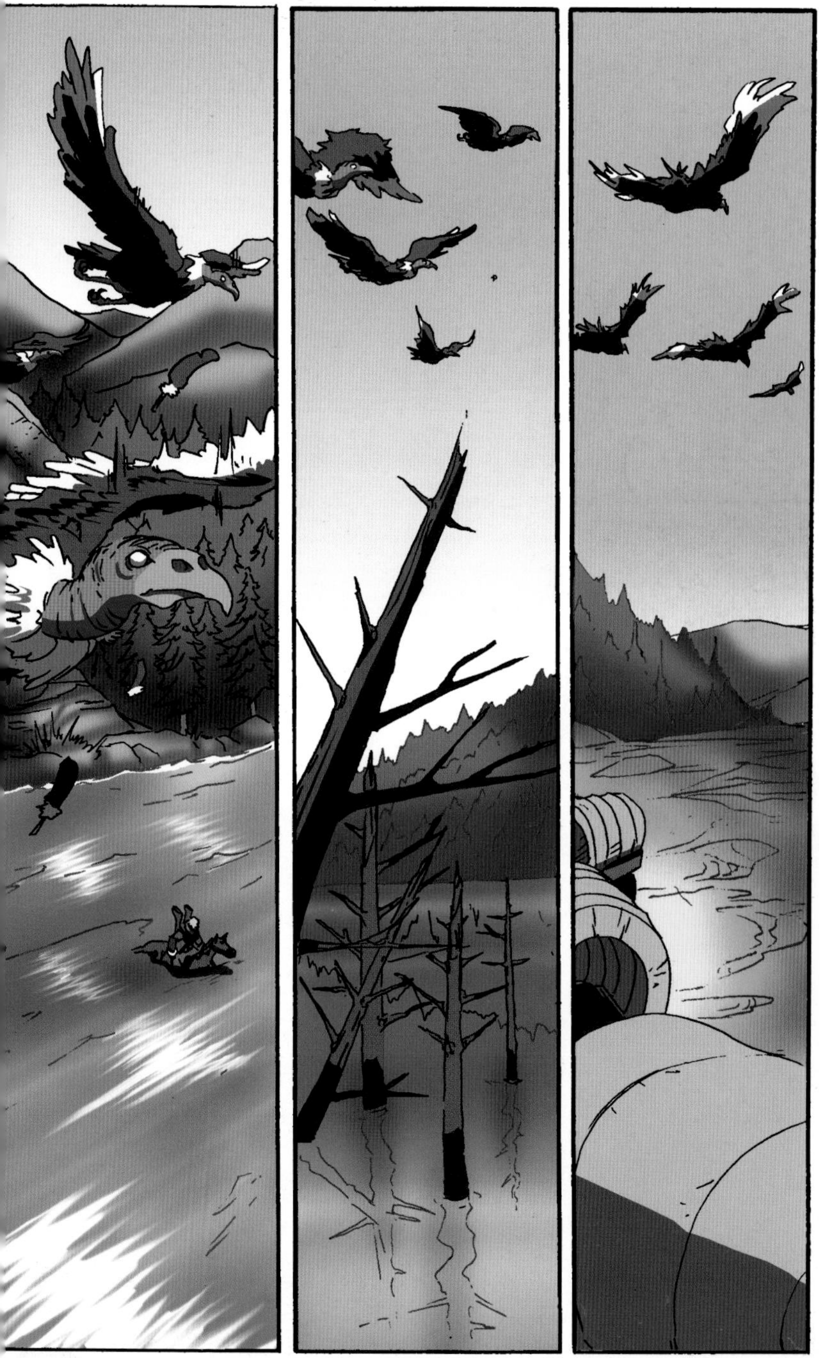

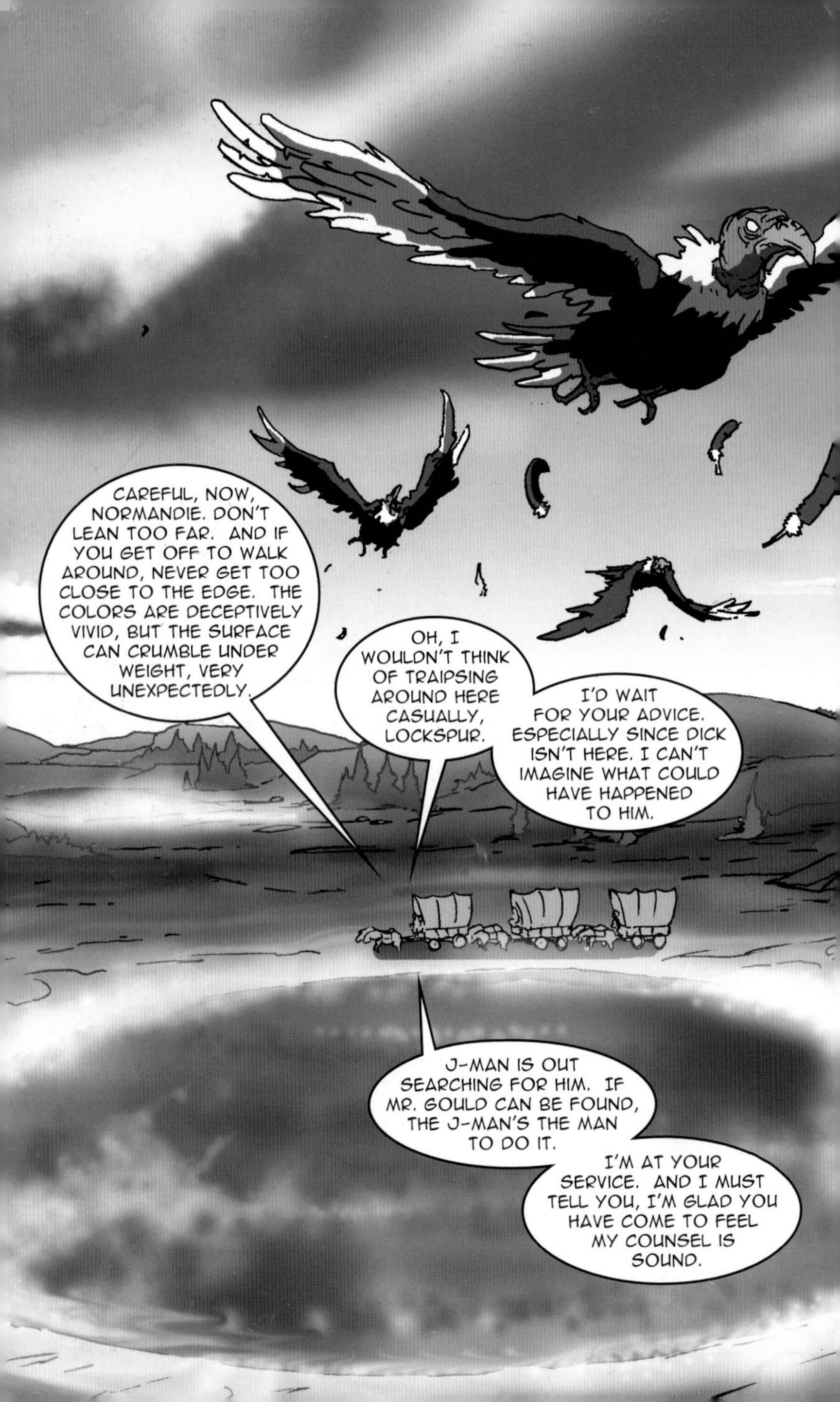
CAREFUL, NOW, NORMANDIE. DON'T LEAN TOO FAR. AND IF YOU GET OFF TO WALK AROUND, NEVER GET TOO CLOSE TO THE EDGE. THE COLORS ARE DECEPTIVELY VIVID, BUT THE SURFACE CAN CRUMBLE UNDER WEIGHT, VERY UNEXPECTEDLY.
OH, I WOULDN'T THINK OF TRAIPSING AROUND HERE CASUALLY, LOCKSPUR.
I'D WAIT FOR YOUR ADVICE. ESPECIALLY SINCE DICK ISN'T HERE. I CAN'T IMAGINE WHAT COULD HAVE HAPPENED TO HIM.
J-MAN IS OUT SEARCHING FOR HIM. IF MR. GOULD CAN BE FOUND, THE J-MAN'S THE MAN TO DO IT.
I'M AT YOUR SERVICE. AND I MUST TELL YOU, I'M GLAD YOU HAVE COME TO FEEL MY COUNSEL IS SOUND.

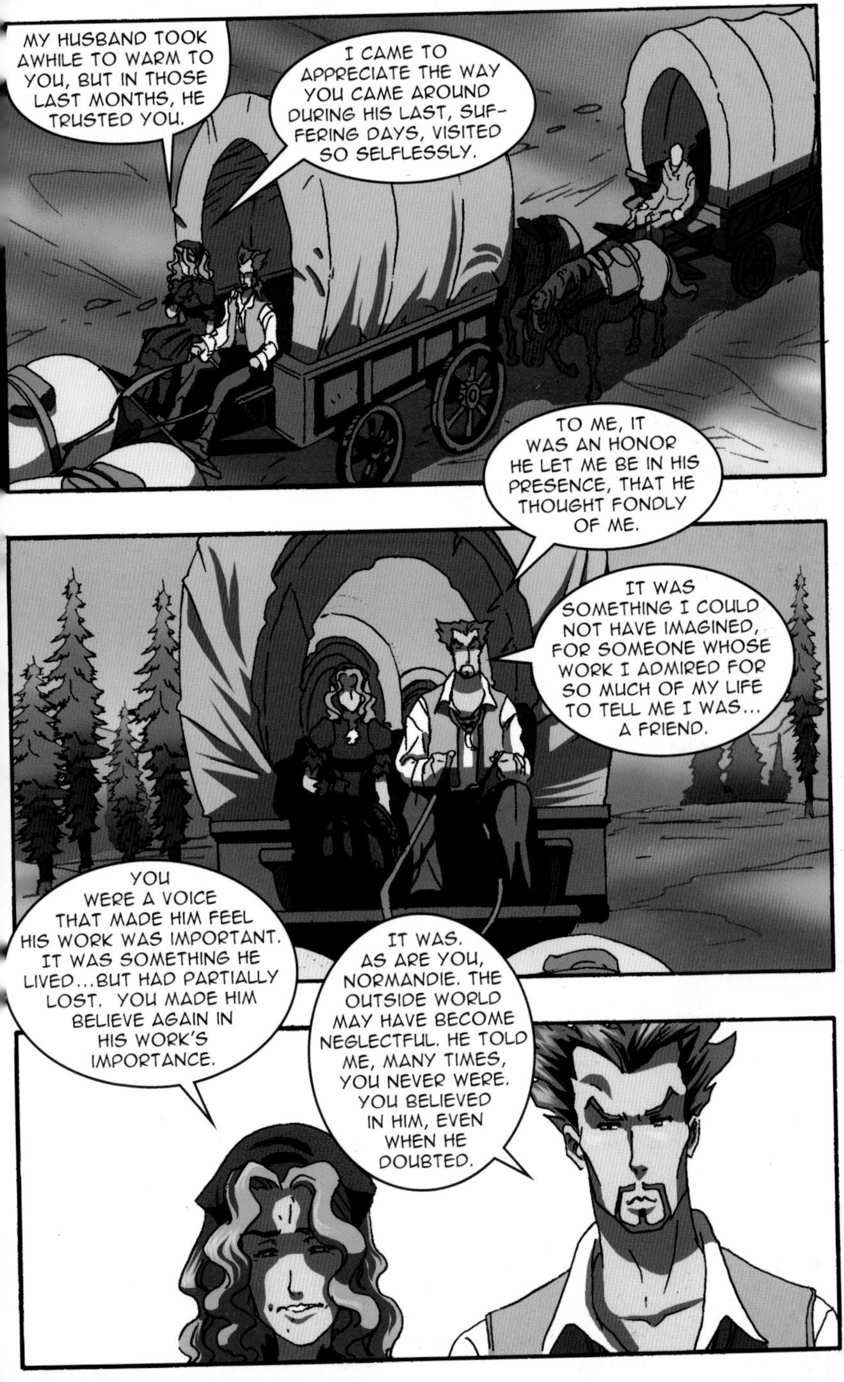
MY HUSBAND TOOK AWHILE TO WARM TO YOU, BUT IN THOSE LAST MONTHS, HE TRUSTED YOU.
I CAME TO APPRECIATE THE WAY YOU CAME AROUND DURING HIS LAST, SUFFERING DAYS, VISITED SO SELFLESSLY.
TO ME, IT WAS AN HONOR HE LET ME BE IN HIS PRESENCE, THAT HE THOUGHT FONDLY OF ME.
IT WAS SOMETHING I COULD NOT HAVE IMAGINED, FOR SOMEONE WHOSE WORK I ADMIRED FOR SO MUCH OF MY LIFE TO TELL ME I WAS... A FRIEND.
YOU WERE A VOICE THAT MADE HIM FEEL HIS WORK WAS IMPORTANT. IT WAS SOMETHING HE LIVED...BUT HAD PARTIALLY LOST. YOU MADE HIM BELIEVE AGAIN IN HIS WORK'S IMPORTANCE.
IT WAS. AS ARE YOU, NORMANDIE. THE OUTSIDE WORLD MAY HAVE BECOME NEGLECTFUL. HE TOLD ME, MANY TIMES, YOU NEVER WERE. YOU BELIEVED IN HIM, EVEN WHEN HE DOUBTED.

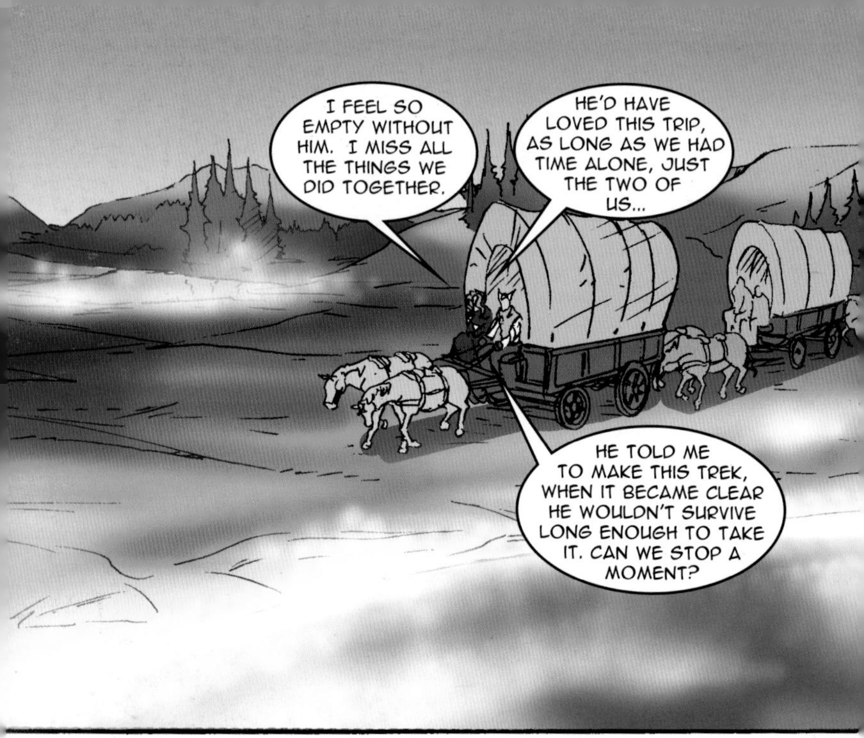
I FEEL SO EMPTY WITHOUT HIM. I MISS ALL THE THINGS WE DID TOGETHER.
HE'D HAVE LOVED THIS TRIP, AS LONG AS WE HAD TIME ALONE, JUST THE TWO OF US...
HE TOLD ME TO MAKE THIS TREK, WHEN IT BECAME CLEAR HE WOULDN'T SURVIVE LONG ENOUGH TO TAKE IT. CAN WE STOP A MOMENT?

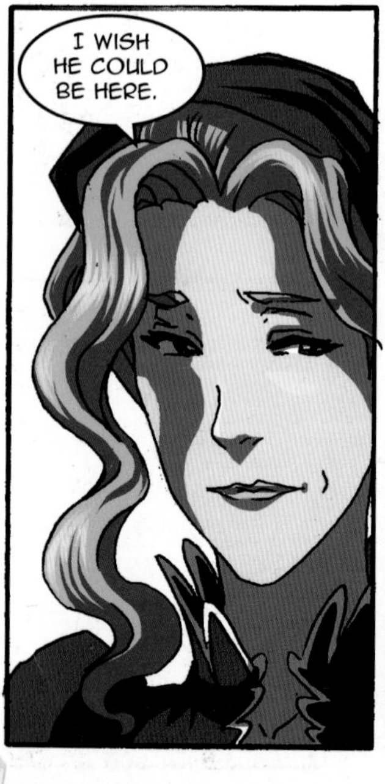
I WISH HE COULD BE HERE.

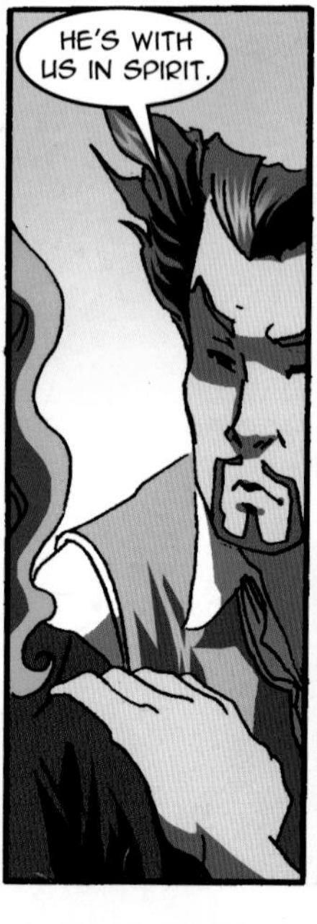
HE'S WITH US IN SPIRIT.

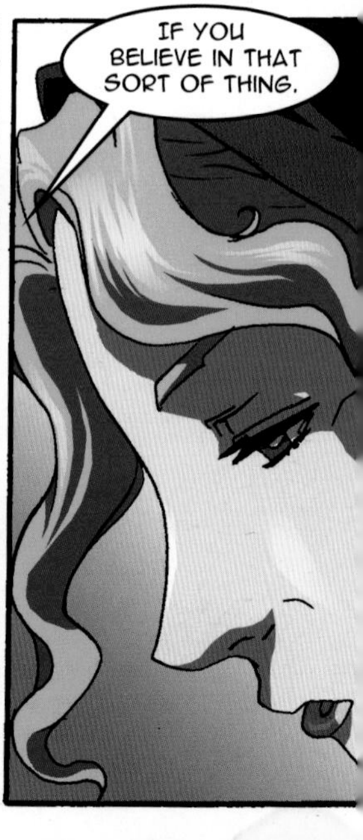
IF YOU BELIEVE IN THAT SORT OF THING.

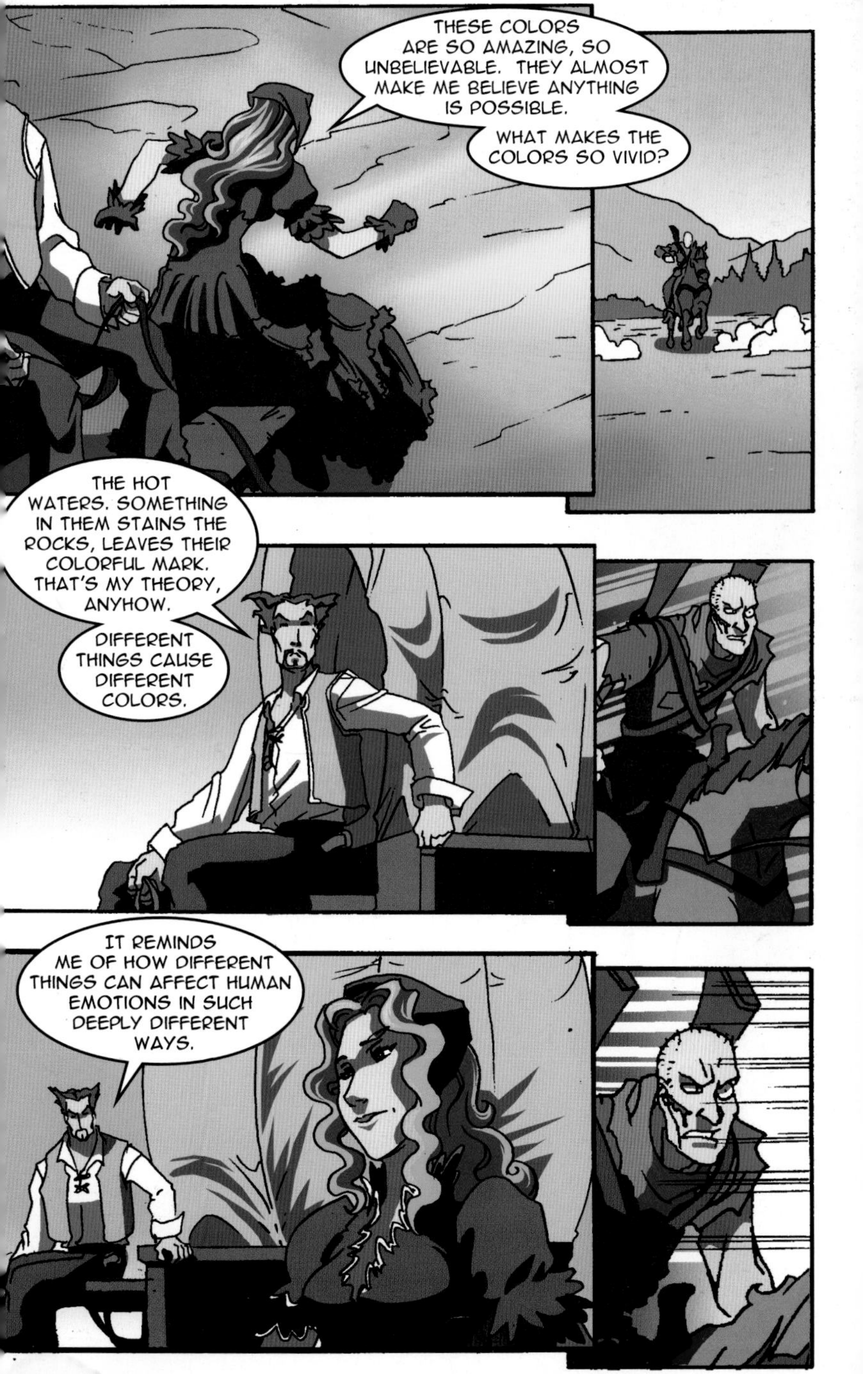
THESE COLORS ARE SO AMAZING, SO UNBELIEVABLE. THEY ALMOST MAKE ME BELIEVE ANYTHING IS POSSIBLE.
WHAT MAKES THE COLORS SO VIVID?
THE HOT WATERS. SOMETHING IN THEM STAINS THE ROCKS, LEAVES THEIR COLORFUL MARK. THAT'S MY THEORY, ANYHOW.
DIFFERENT THINGS CAUSE DIFFERENT COLORS.
IT REMINDS ME OF HOW DIFFERENT THINGS CAN AFFECT HUMAN EMOTIONS IN SUCH DEEPLY DIFFERENT WAYS.

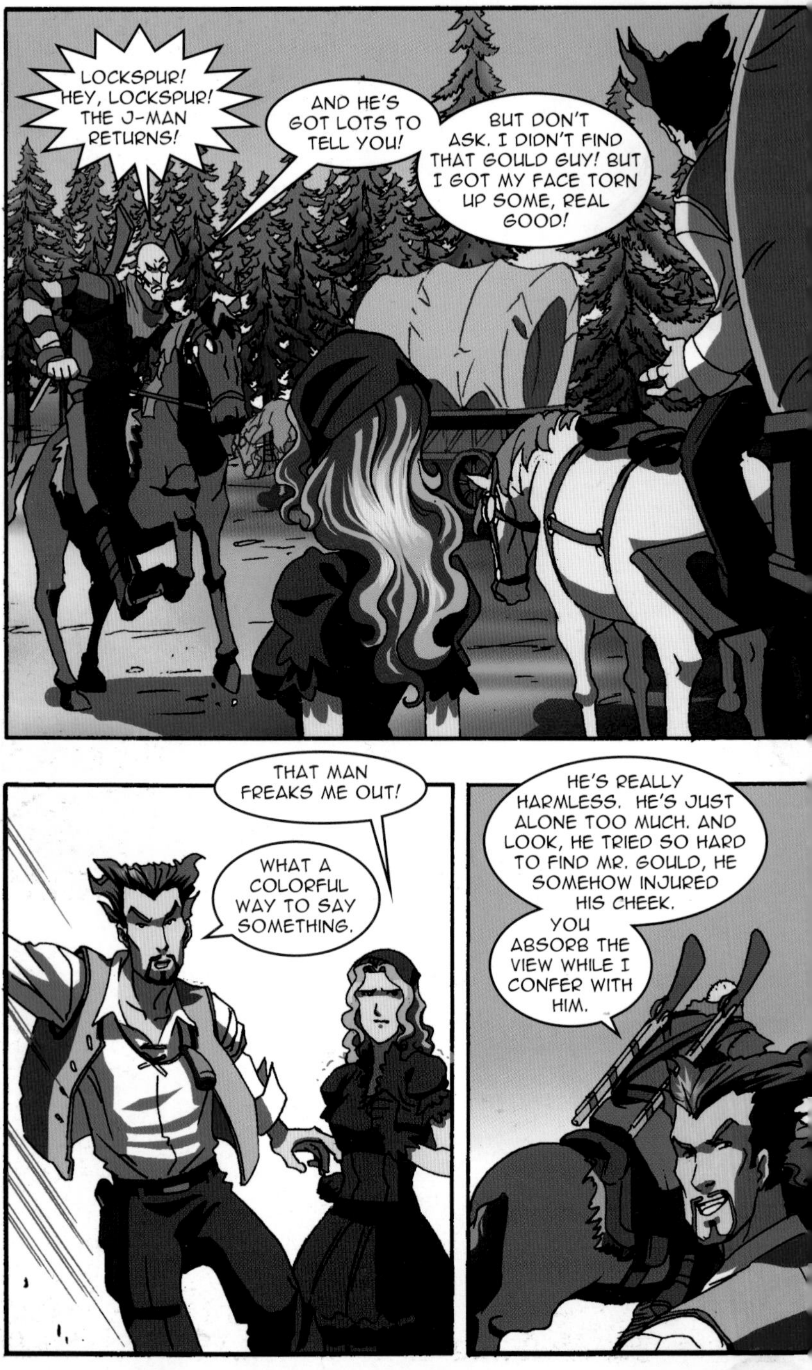

LOCKSPUR! HEY, LOCKSPUR! THE J-MAN RETURNS!
AND HE'S GOT LOTS TO TELL YOU!
BUT DON'T ASK. I DIDN'T FIND THAT GOULD GUY! BUT I GOT MY FACE TORN UP SOME, REAL GOOD!
THAT MAN FREAKS ME OUT!
WHAT A COLORFUL WAY TO SAY SOMETHING.
HE'S REALLY HARMLESS. HE'S JUST ALONE TOO MUCH. AND LOOK, HE TRIED SO HARD TO FIND MR. GOULD, HE SOMEHOW INJURED HIS CHEEK.
YOU ABSORB THE VIEW WHILE I CONFER WITH HIM.

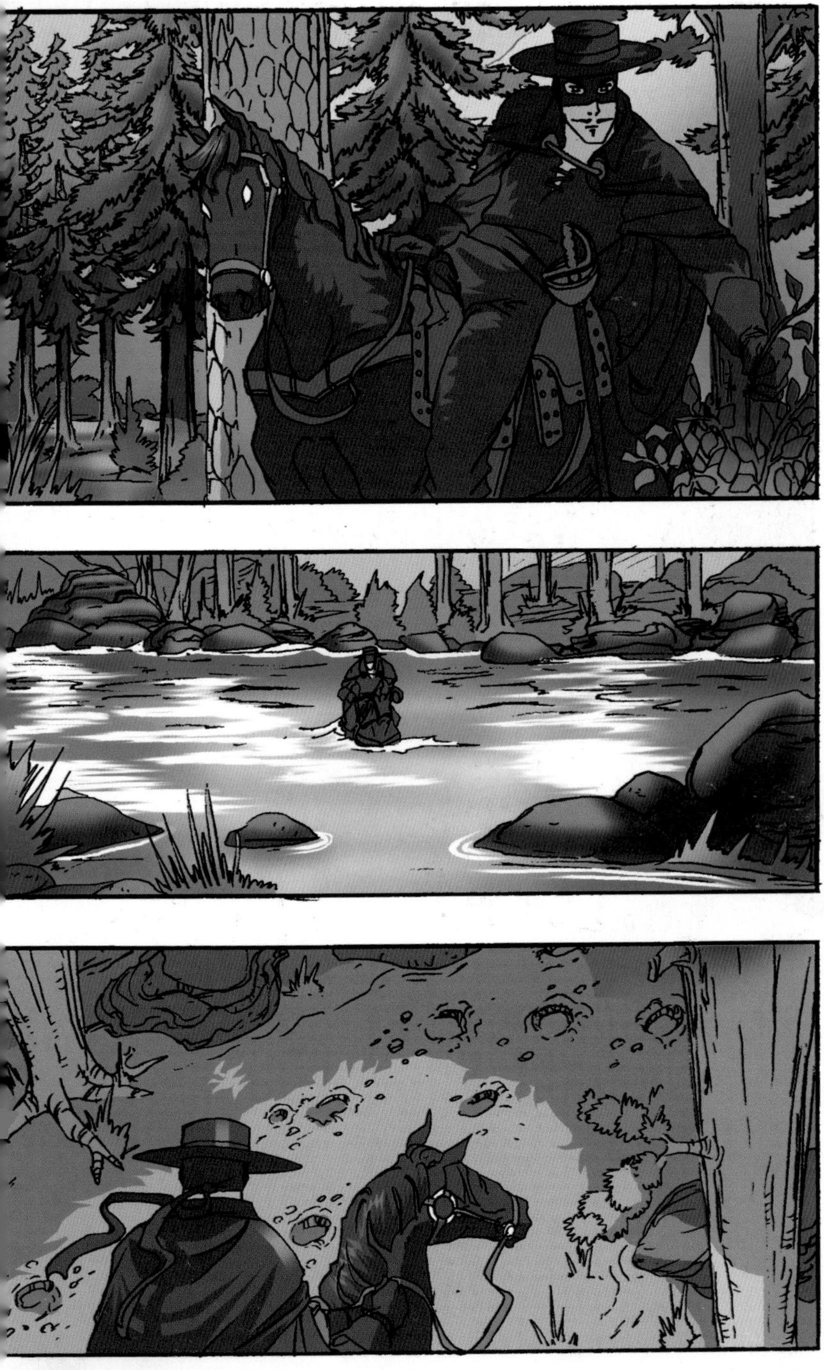

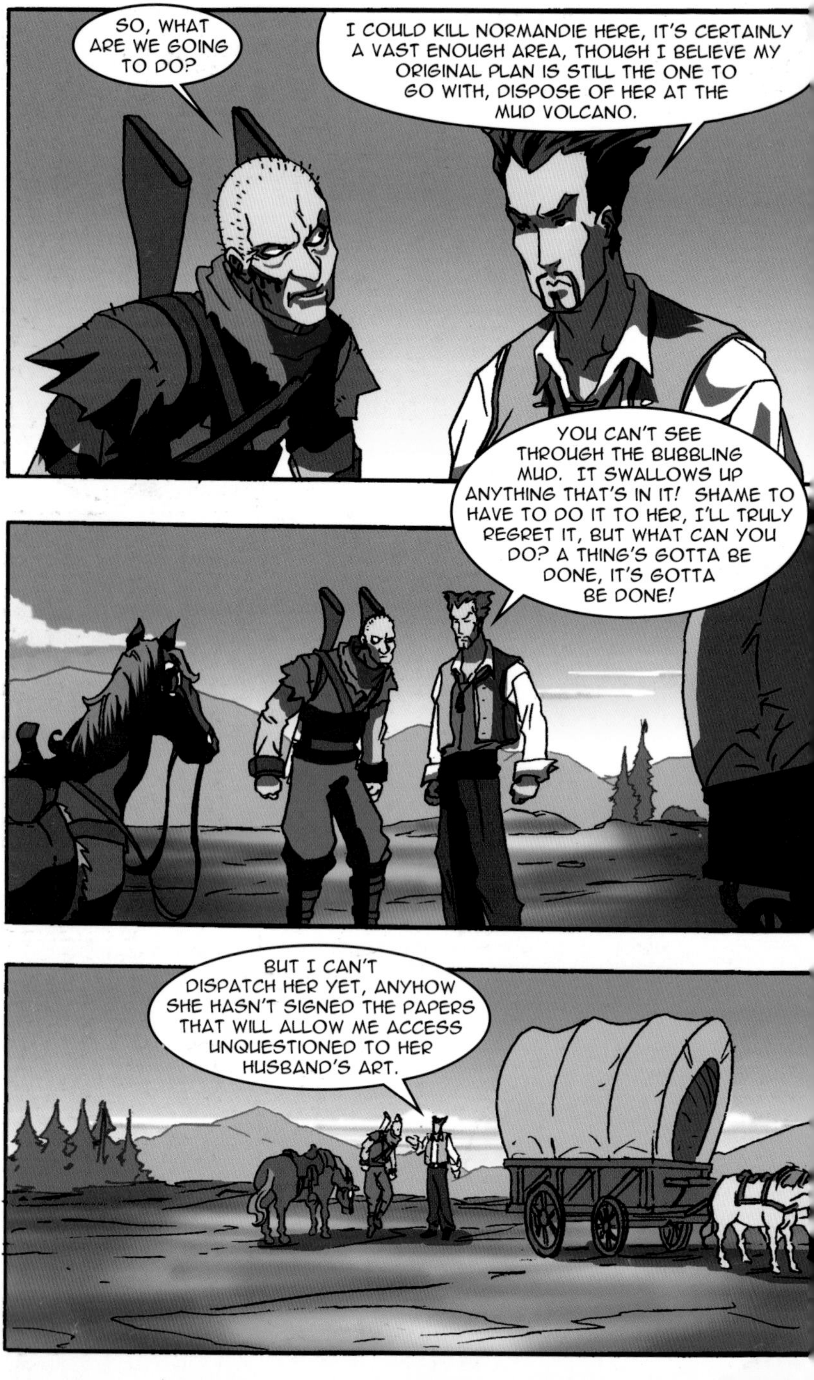

SO, WHAT ARE WE GOING TO DO?
I COULD KILL NORMANDIE HERE, IT'S CERTAINLY A VAST ENOUGH AREA, THOUGH I BELIEVE MY ORIGINAL PLAN IS STILL THE ONE TO GO WITH, DISPOSE OF HER AT THE MUD VOLCANO.
YOU CAN'T SEE THROUGH THE BUBBLING MUD. IT SWALLOWS UP ANYTHING THAT'S IN IT! SHAME TO HAVE TO DO IT TO HER, I'LL TRULY REGRET IT, BUT WHAT CAN YOU DO? A THING'S GOTTA BE DONE, IT'S GOTTA BE DONE!
BUT I CAN'T DISPATCH HER YET, ANYHOW SHE HASN'T SIGNED THE PAPERS THAT WILL ALLOW ME ACCESS UNQUESTIONED TO HER HUSBAND'S ART.

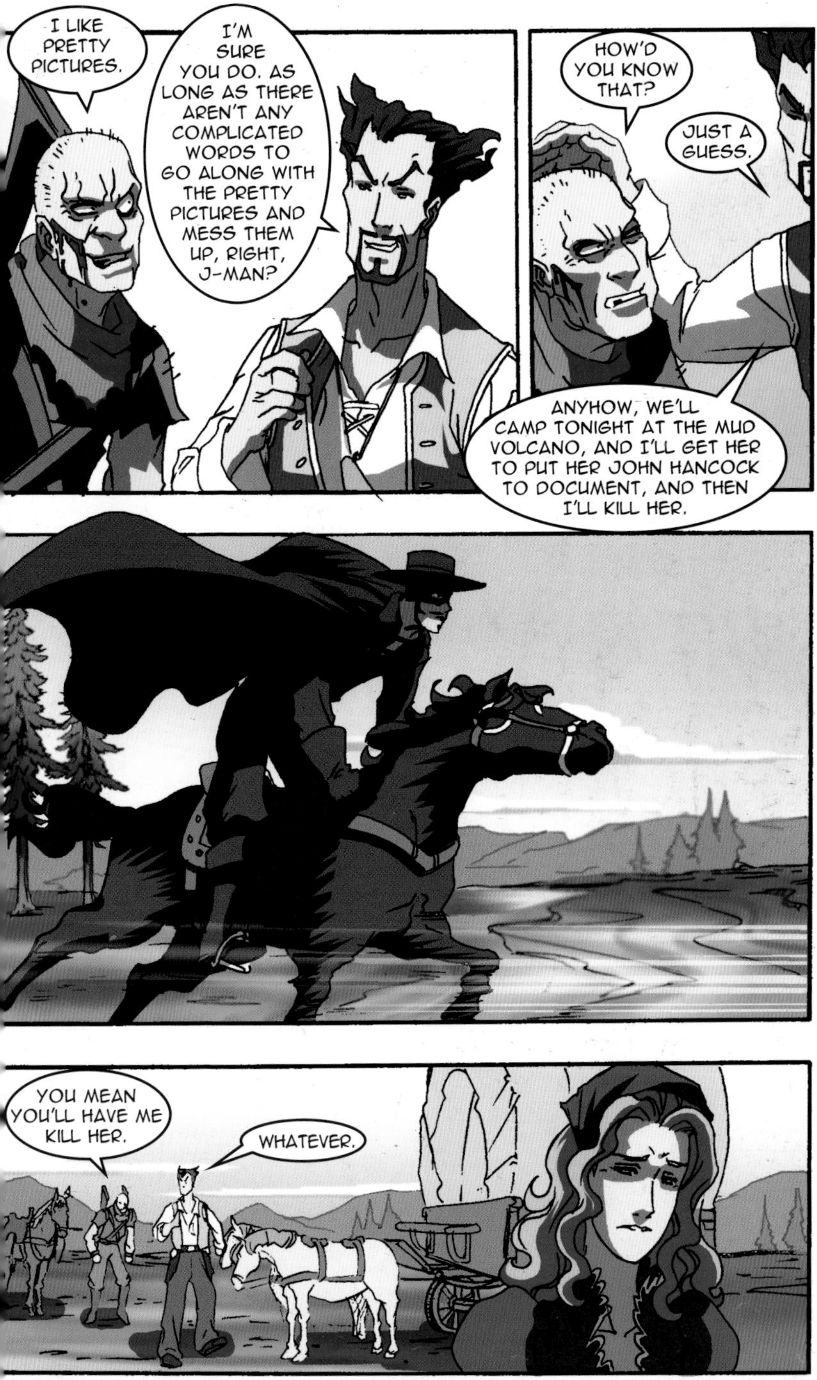
I LIKE PRETTY PICTURES.
I'M SURE YOU DO. AS LONG AS THERE AREN'T ANY COMPLICATED WORDS TO GO ALONG WITH THE PRETTY PICTURES AND MESS THEM UP, RIGHT, J-MAN?
HOW'D YOU KNOW THAT?
JUST A GUESS.
ANYHOW, WE'LL CAMP TONIGHT AT THE MUD VOLCANO, AND I'LL GET HER TO PUT HER JOHN HANCOCK TO DOCUMENT, AND THEN I'LL KILL HER.
YOU MEAN YOU'LL HAVE ME KILL HER.
WHATEVER.

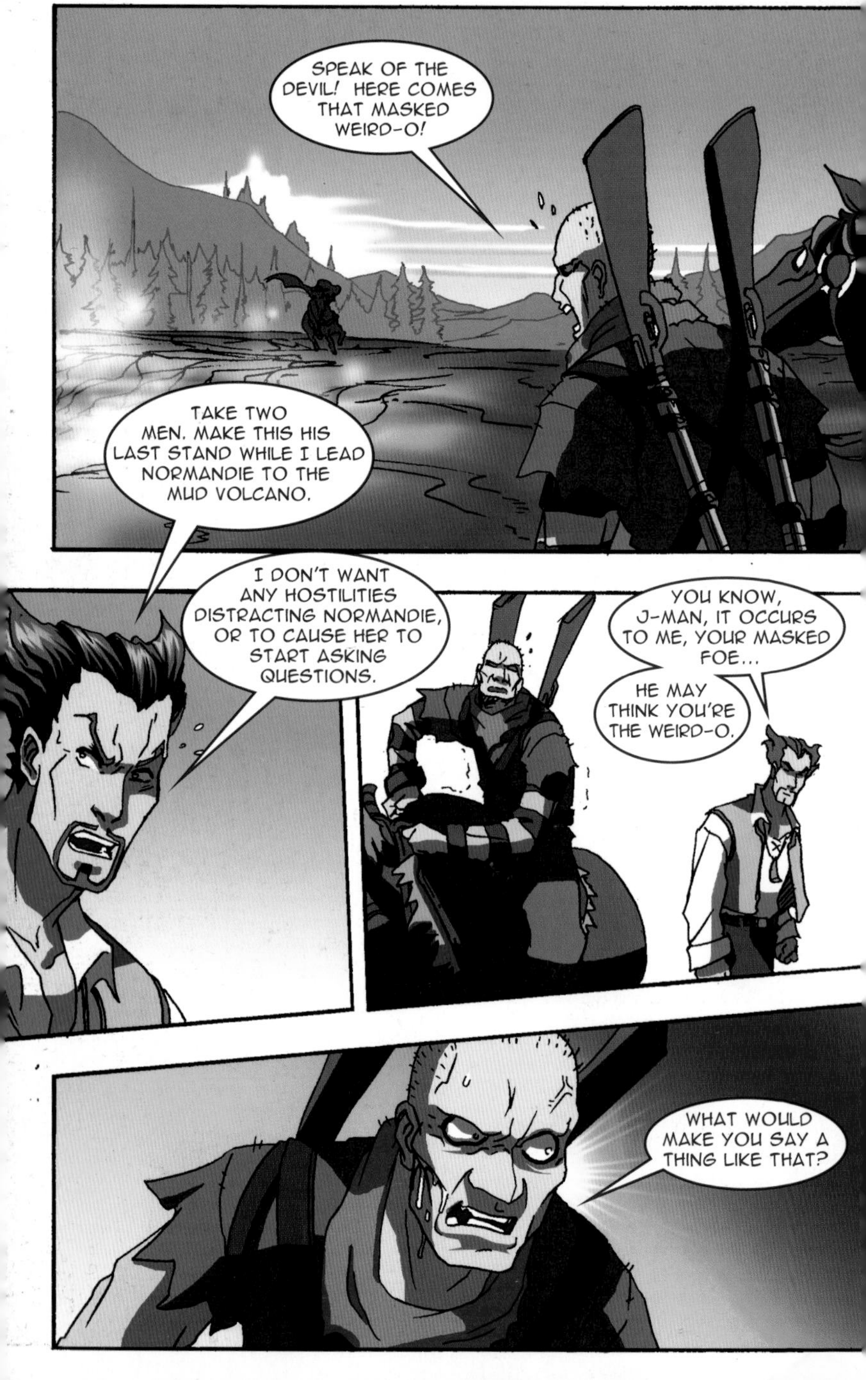

SPEAK OF THE DEVIL! HERE COMES THAT MASKED WEIRD-O!
TAKE TWO MEN. MAKE THIS HIS LAST STAND WHILE I LEAD NORMANDIE TO THE MUD VOLCANO.
I DON'T WANT ANY HOSTILITIES DISTRACTING NORMANDIE, OR TO CAUSE HER TO START ASKING QUESTIONS.
YOU KNOW, J-MAN, IT OCCURS TO ME, YOUR MASKED FOE...
HE MAY THINK YOU'RE THE WEIRD-O.
WHAT WOULD MAKE YOU SAY A THING LIKE THAT?

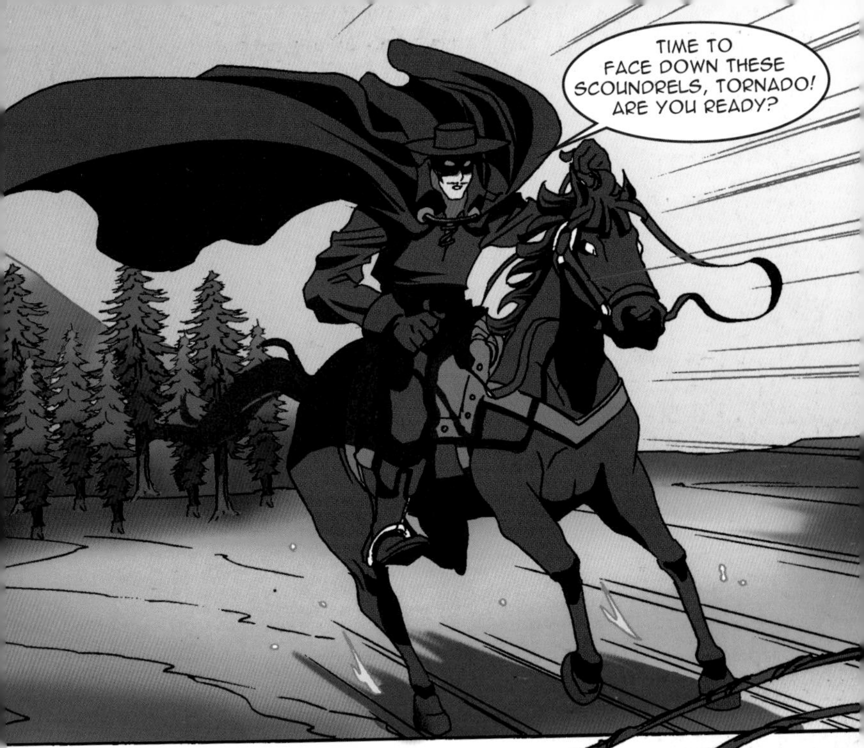
TIME TO FACE DOWN THESE SCOUNDRELS, TORNADO! ARE YOU READY?

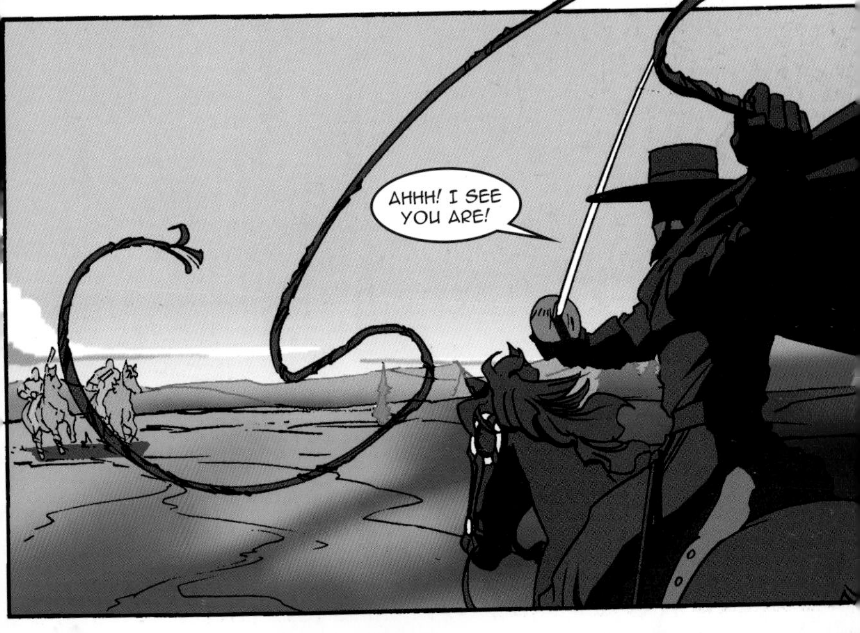
AHHH! I SEE YOU ARE!

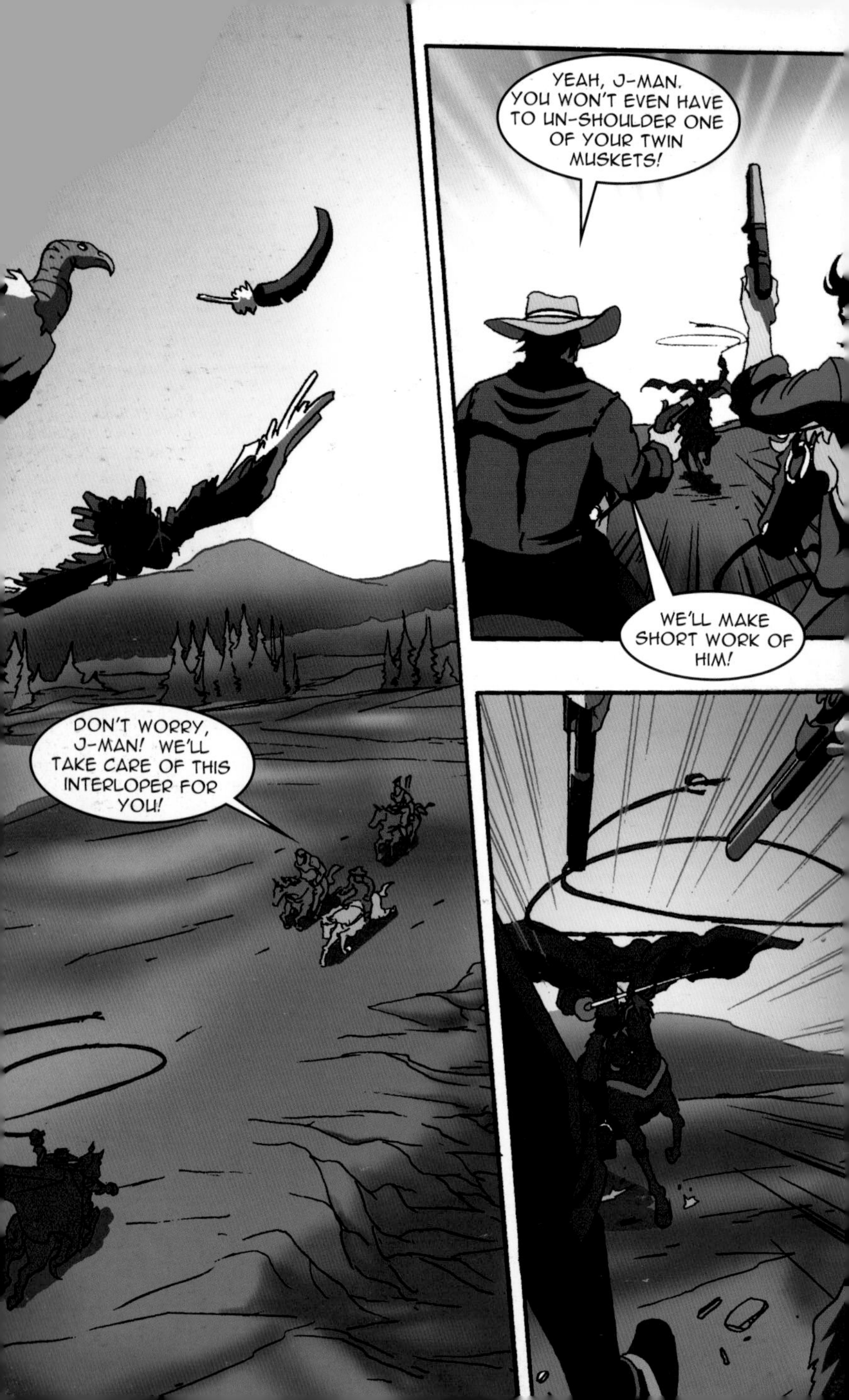
DON'T WORRY, J-MAN! WE'LL TAKE CARE OF THIS INTERLOPER FOR YOU!
YEAH, J-MAN. YOU WON'T EVEN HAVE TO UN-SHOULDER ONE OF YOUR TWIN MUSKETS!
WE'LL MAKE SHORT WORK OF HIM!

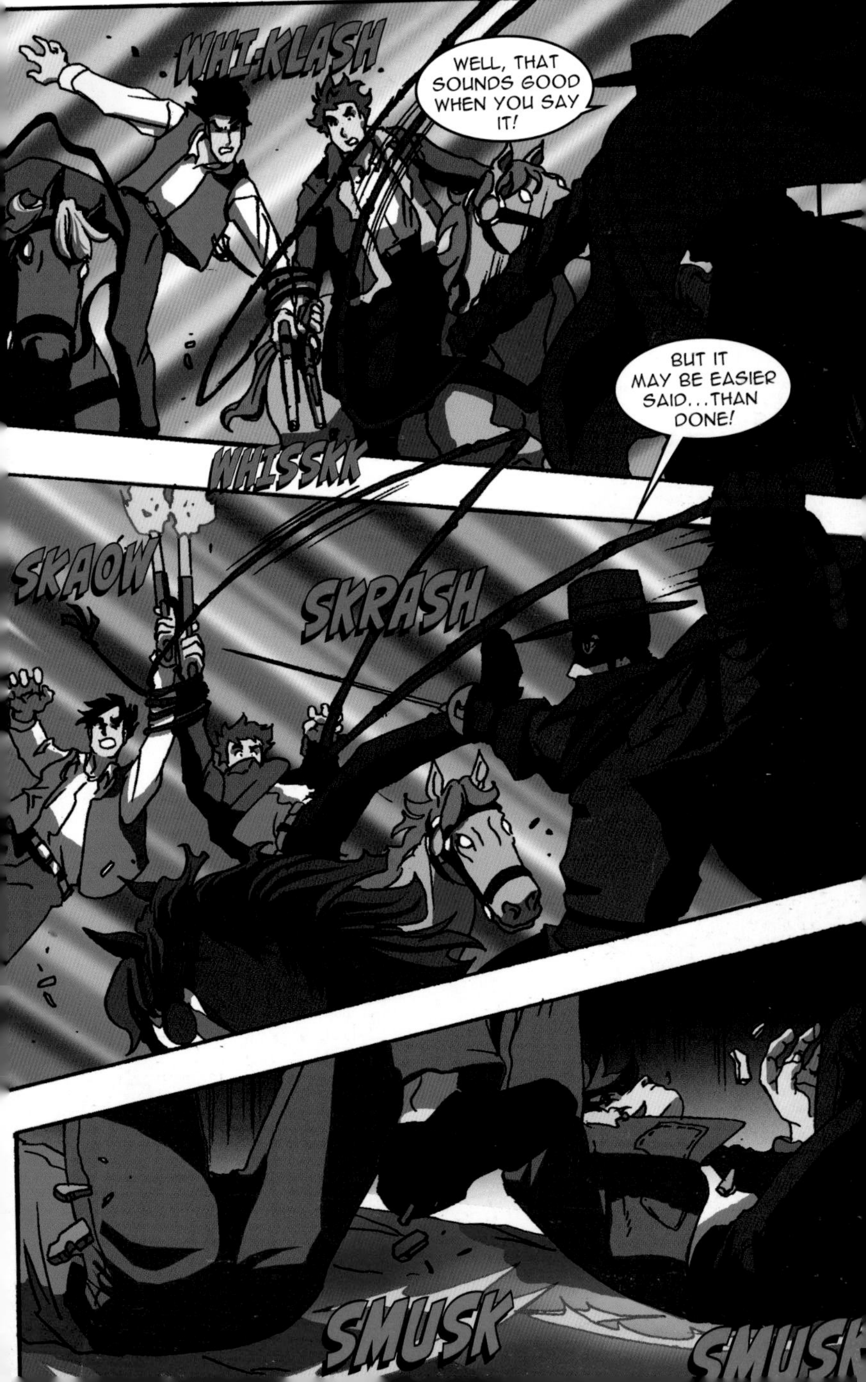
WHI-KLASH
WELL, THAT SOUNDS GOOD WHEN YOU SAY IT!
BUT IT MAY BE EASIER SAID...THAN DONE!
WHISSKK
SKAOW
SKRASH
SMUSK
SMUSK

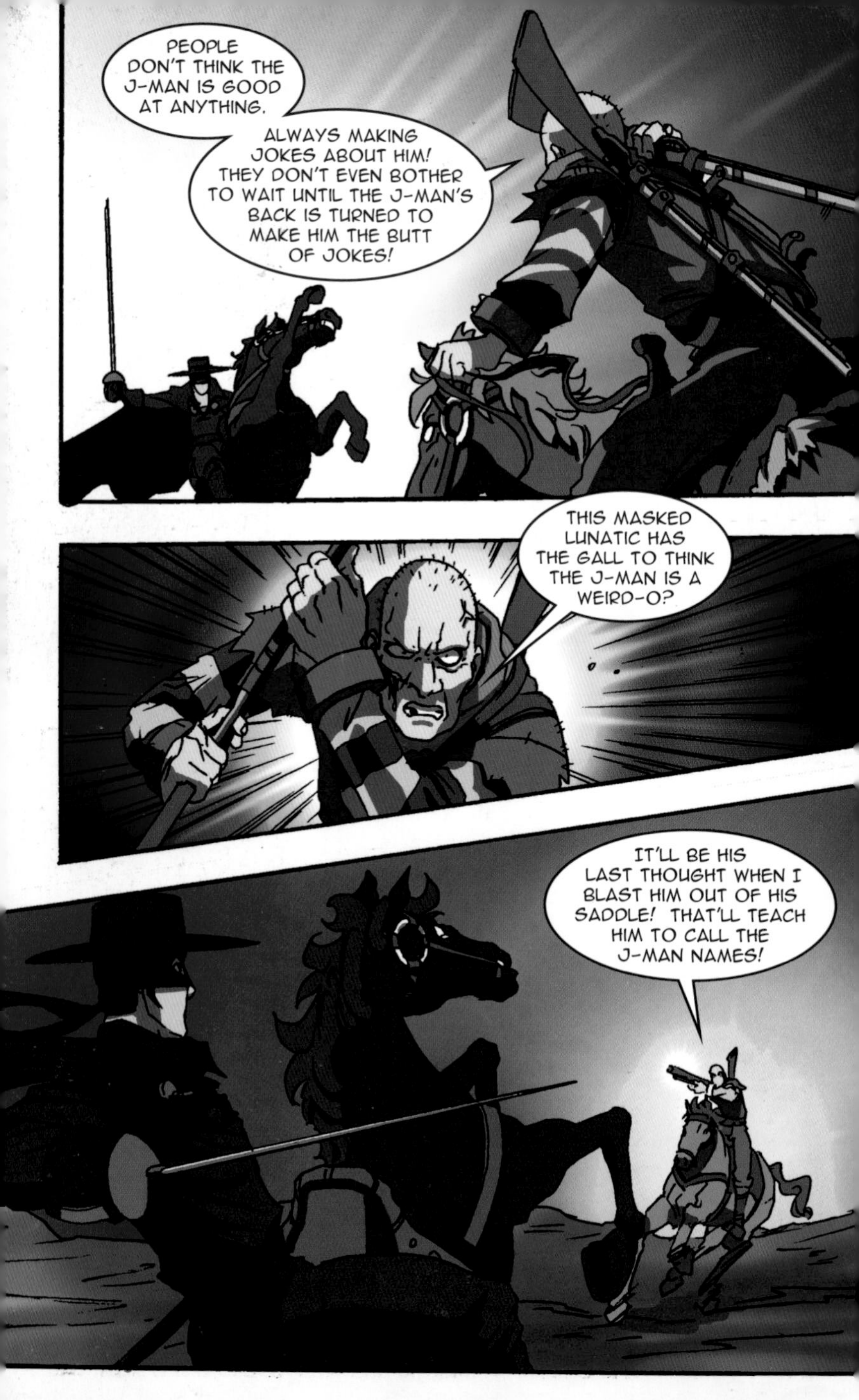
PEOPLE DON'T THINK THE J-MAN IS GOOD AT ANYTHING.
ALWAYS MAKING JOKES ABOUT HIM! THEY DON'T EVEN BOTHER TO WAIT UNTIL THE J-MAN'S BACK IS TURNED TO MAKE HIM THE BUTT OF JOKES!
THIS MASKED LUNATIC HAS THE GALL TO THINK THE J-MAN IS A WEIRD-O?
IT'LL BE HIS LAST THOUGHT WHEN I BLAST HIM OUT OF HIS SADDLE! THAT'LL TEACH HIM TO CALL THE J-MAN NAMES!

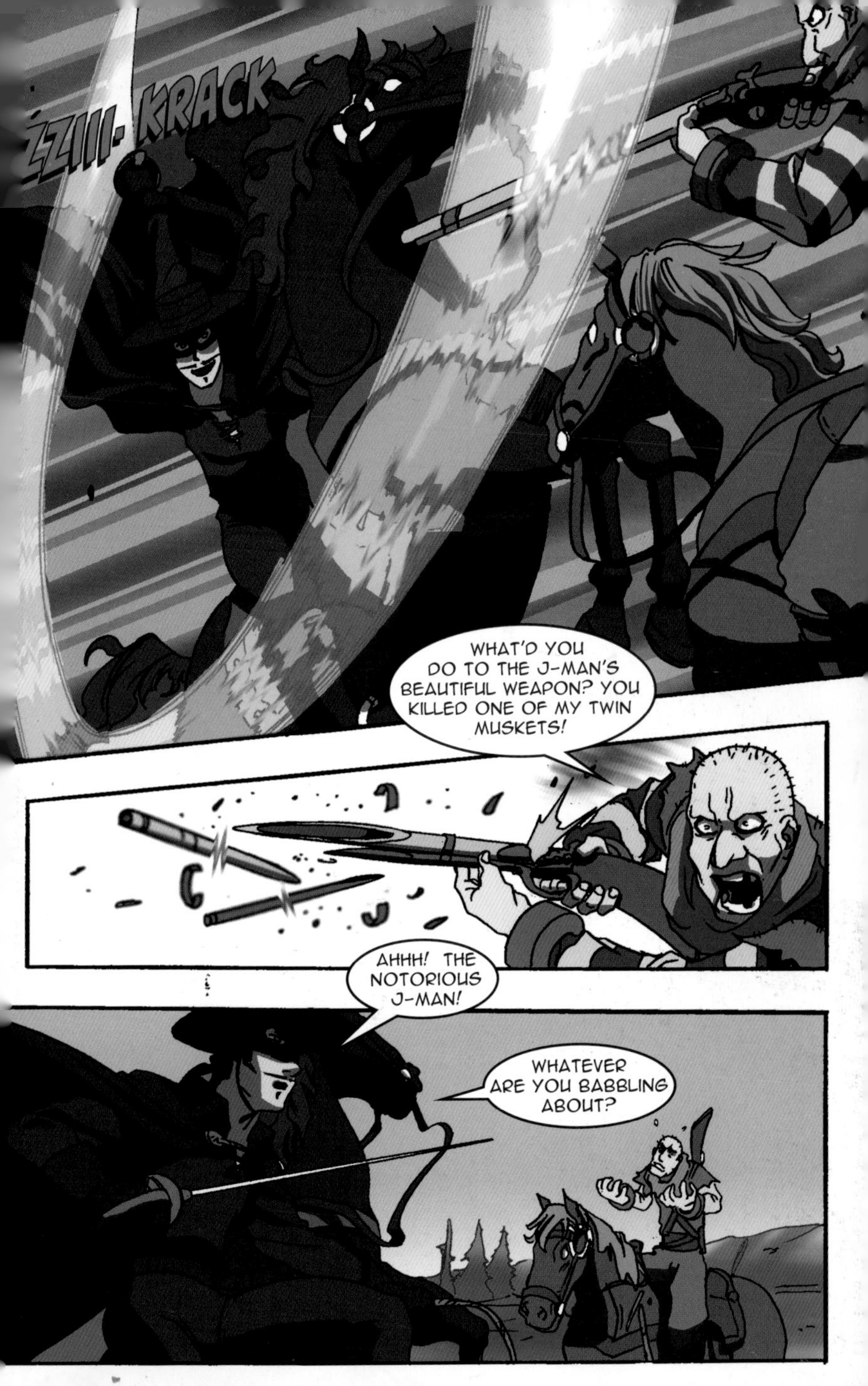
ZZIIII- KRACK
WHAT'D YOU DO TO THE J-MAN'S BEAUTIFUL WEAPON? YOU KILLED ONE OF MY TWIN MUSKETS!
AHHH! THE NOTORIOUS J-MAN!
WHATEVER ARE YOU BABBLING ABOUT?

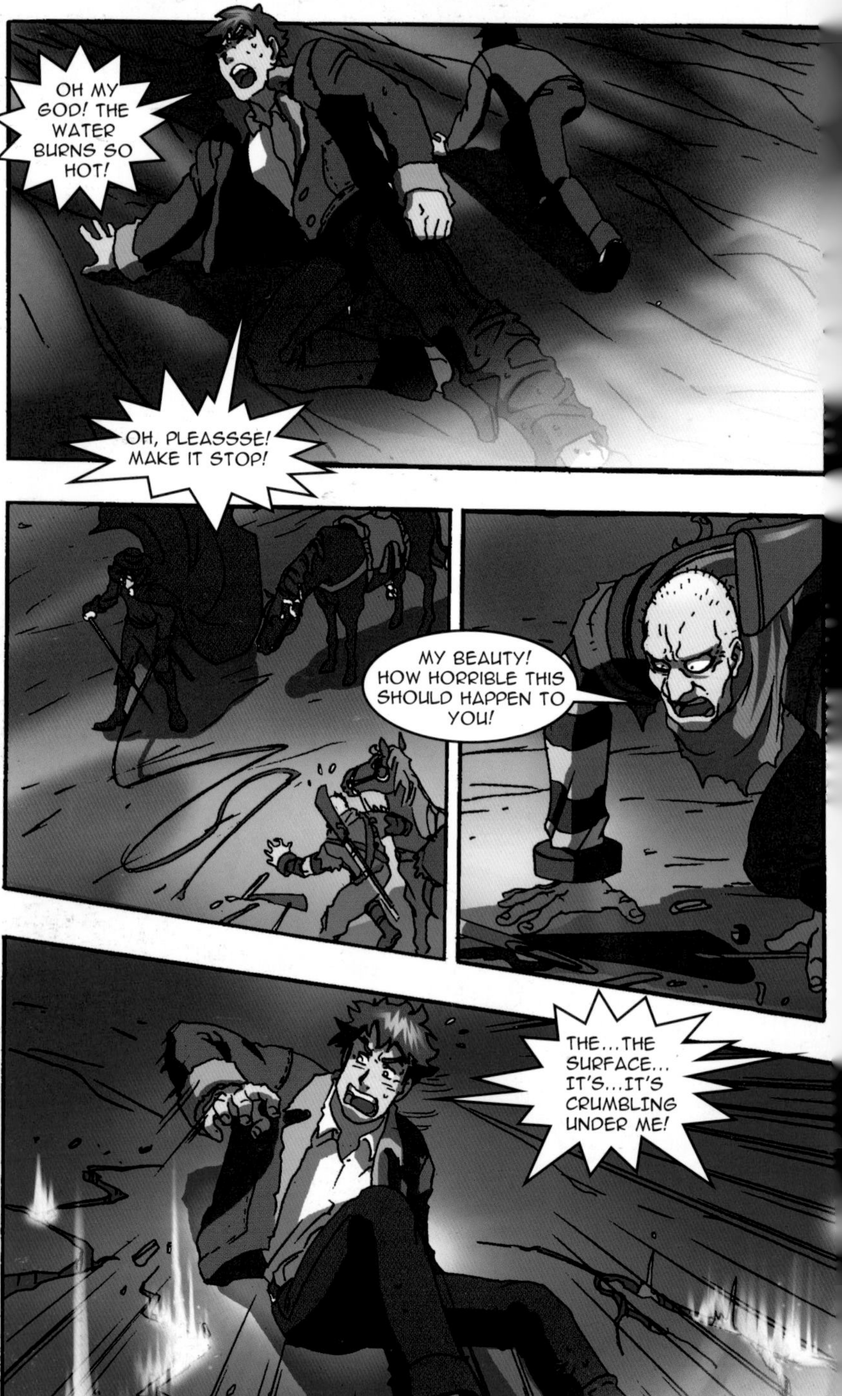
OH MY GOD! THE WATER BURNS SO HOT!
OH, PLEASSSE! MAKE IT STOP!
MY BEAUTY! HOW HORRIBLE THIS SHOULD HAPPEN TO YOU!
THE...THE SURFACE... IT'S...IT'S CRUMBLING UNDER ME!

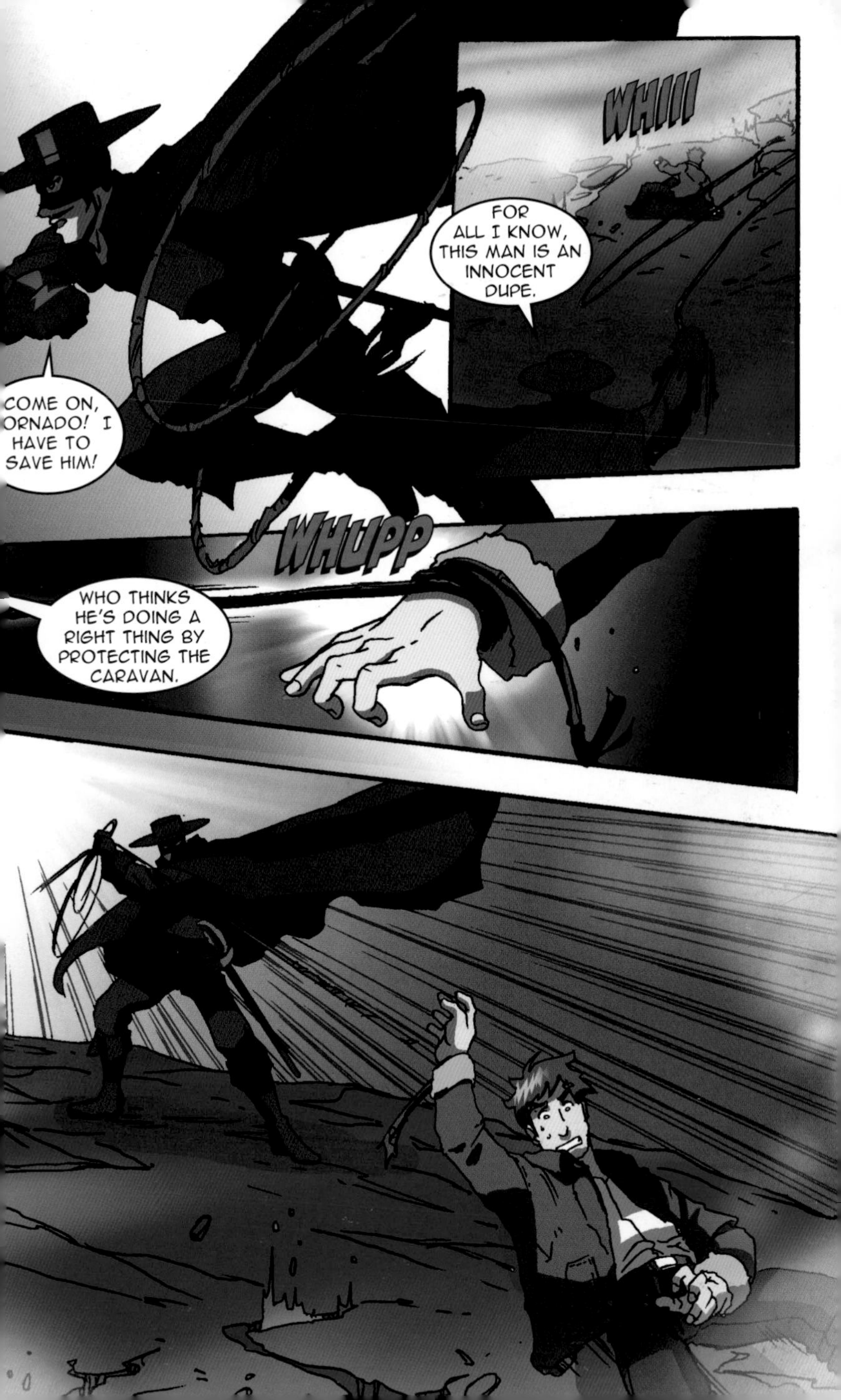
WHIII
FOR ALL I KNOW, THIS MAN IS AN INNOCENT DUPE.
COME ON, ORNADO! I HAVE TO SAVE HIM!
WHUPP
WHO THINKS HE'S DOING A RIGHT THING BY PROTECTING THE CARAVAN.

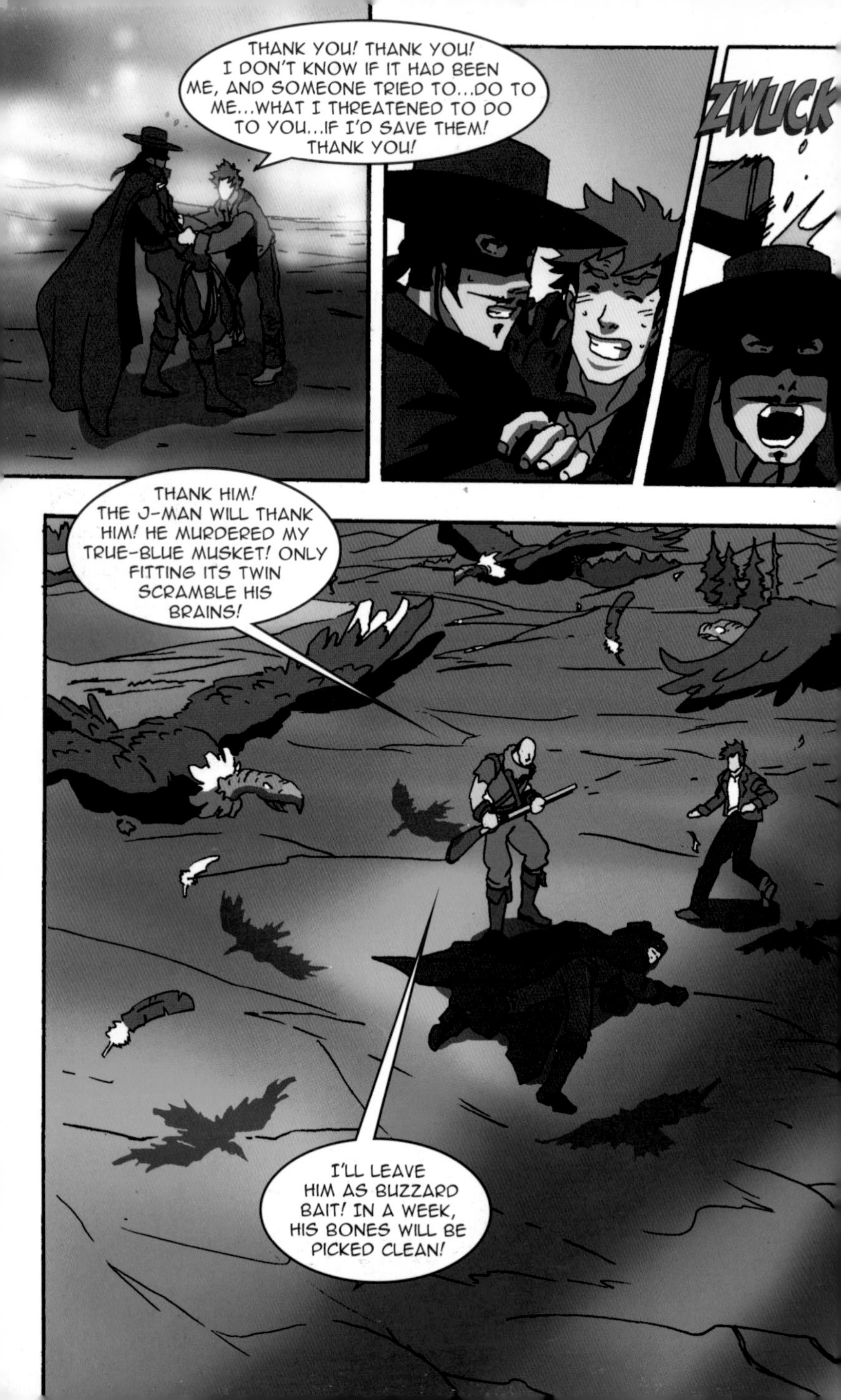

THANK YOU! THANK YOU! I DON'T KNOW IF IT HAD BEEN ME, AND SOMEONE TRIED TO...DO TO ME...WHAT I THREATENED TO DO TO YOU...IF I'D SAVE THEM! THANK YOU!
ZWUCK
THANK HIM! THE J-MAN WILL THANK HIM! HE MURDERED MY TRUE-BLUE MUSKET! ONLY FITTING ITS TWIN SCRAMBLE HIS BRAINS!
I'LL LEAVE HIM AS BUZZARD BAIT! IN A WEEK, HIS BONES WILL BE PICKED CLEAN!

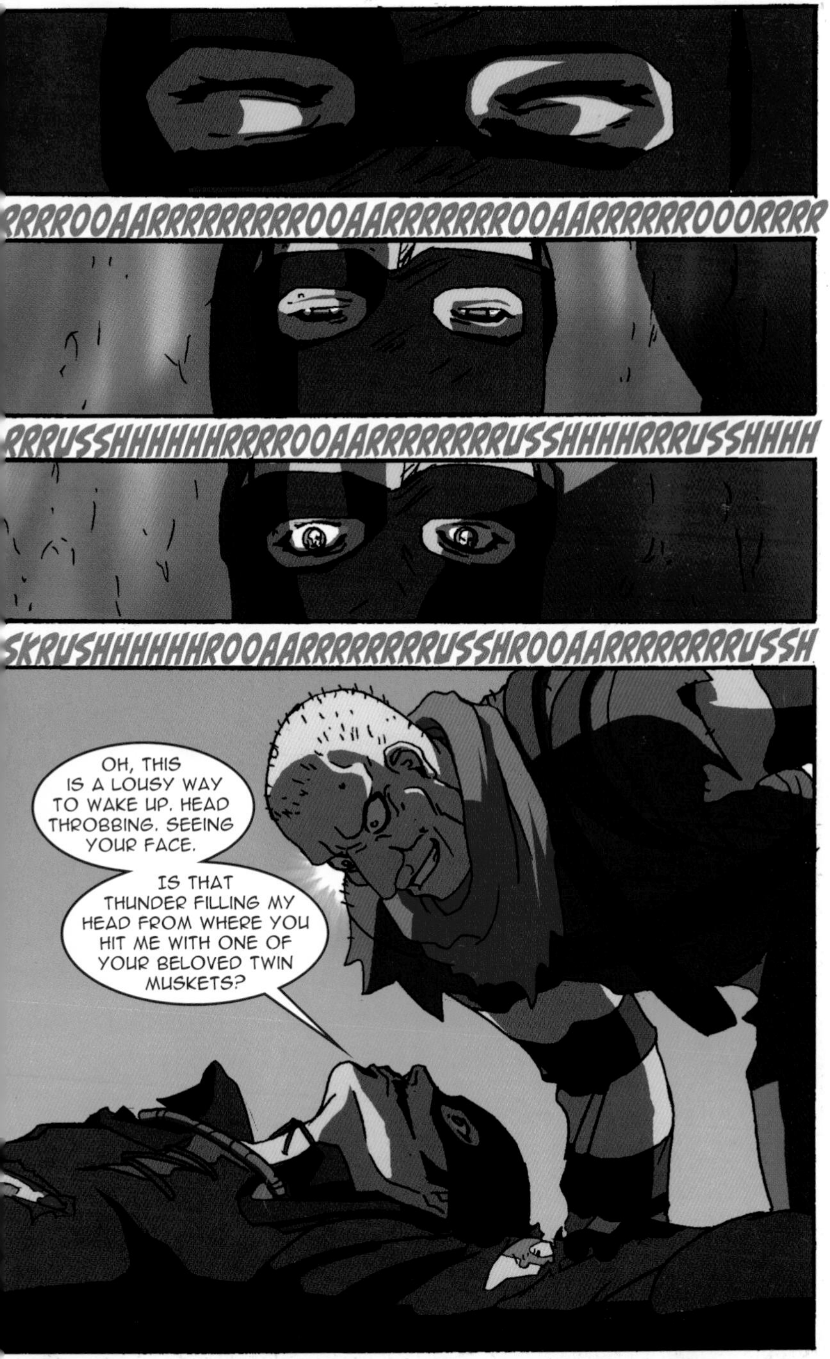
RRRROOAARRRRRRRRROOAARRRRRRROOAARRRRRROOORRRR
RRRUSSHHHHHHRRRROOAARRRRRRRUSSHHHHRRRUSSHHHH
SKRUSHHHHHHROOAARRRRRRRRRUSSHROOAARRRRRRRRUSSH
OH, THIS IS A LOUSY WAY TO WAKE UP. HEAD THROBBING. SEEING YOUR FACE.
IS THAT THUNDER FILLING MY HEAD FROM WHERE YOU HIT ME WITH ONE OF YOUR BELOVED TWIN MUSKETS?

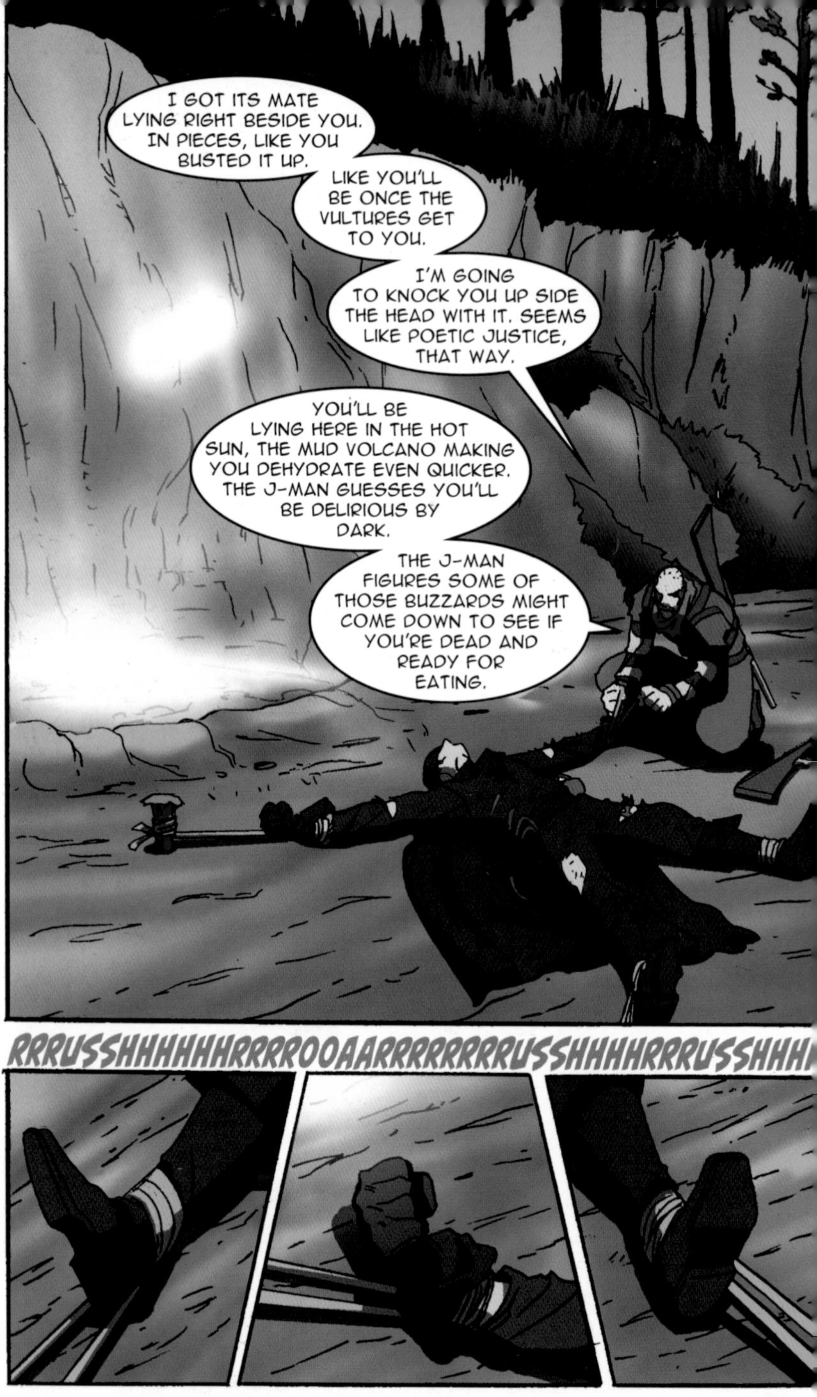

I GOT ITS MATE LYING RIGHT BESIDE YOU. IN PIECES, LIKE YOU BUSTED IT UP.
LIKE YOU'LL BE ONCE THE VULTURES GET TO YOU.
I'M GOING TO KNOCK YOU UP SIDE THE HEAD WITH IT. SEEMS LIKE POETIC JUSTICE, THAT WAY.
YOU'LL BE LYING HERE IN THE HOT SUN, THE MUD VOLCANO MAKING YOU DEHYDRATE EVEN QUICKER. THE J-MAN GUESSES YOU'LL BE DELIRIOUS BY DARK.
THE J-MAN FIGURES SOME OF THOSE BUZZARDS MIGHT COME DOWN TO SEE IF YOU'RE DEAD AND READY FOR EATING.
RRRUSSHHHHHHRRRROOAARRRRRRRRUSSHHHHRRRUSSHHH

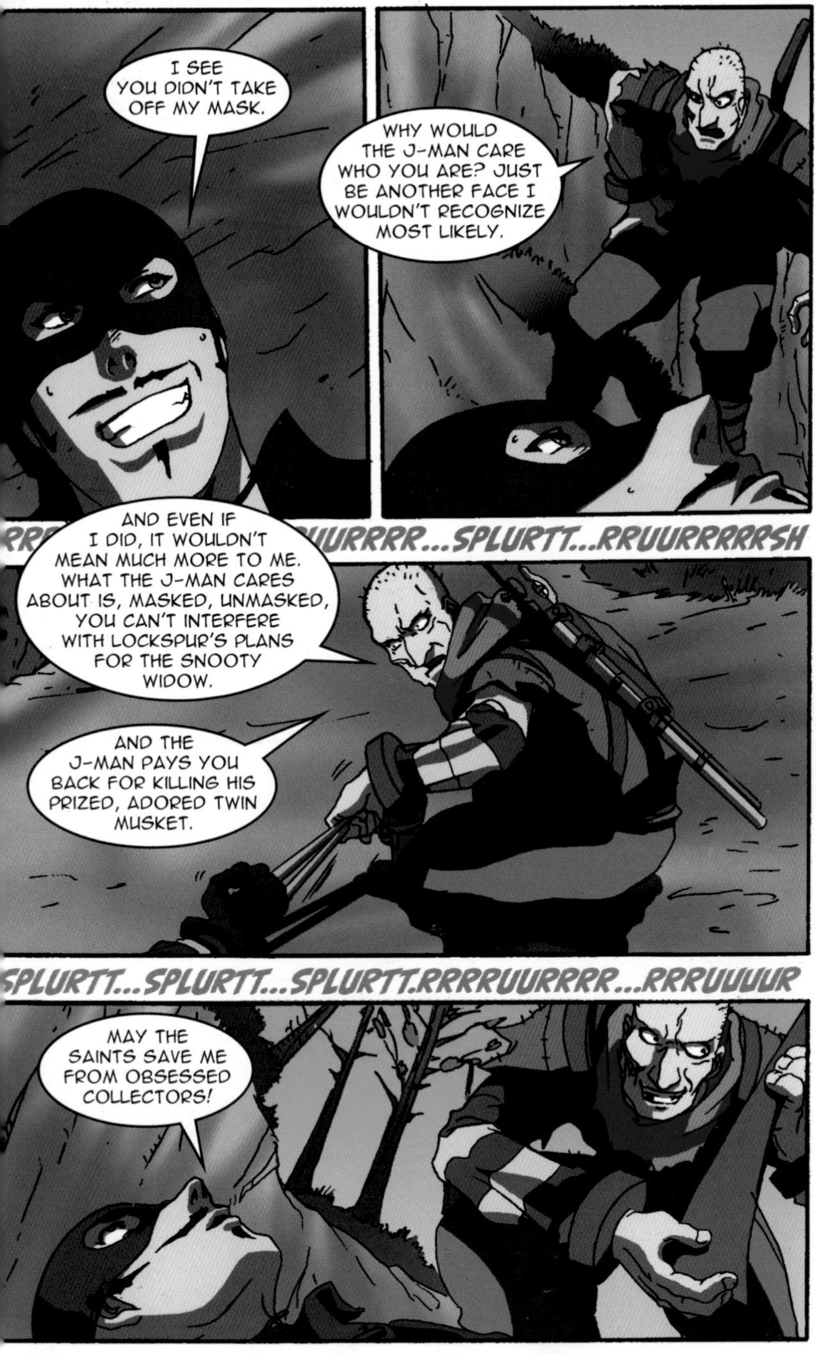
I SEE YOU DIDN'T TAKE OFF MY MASK.
WHY WOULD THE J-MAN CARE WHO YOU ARE? JUST BE ANOTHER FACE I WOULDN'T RECOGNIZE MOST LIKELY.
UURRRR...SPLURTT...RRUURRRRRSH
AND EVEN IF I DID, IT WOULDN'T MEAN MUCH MORE TO ME. WHAT THE J-MAN CARES ABOUT IS, MASKED, UNMASKED, YOU CAN'T INTERFERE WITH LOCKSPUR'S PLANS FOR THE SNOOTY WIDOW.
AND THE J-MAN PAYS YOU BACK FOR KILLING HIS PRIZED, ADORED TWIN MUSKET.
SPLURTT...SPLURTT...SPLURTT.RRRRUURRRR...RRRUUUUR
MAY THE SAINTS SAVE ME FROM OBSESSED COLLECTORS!

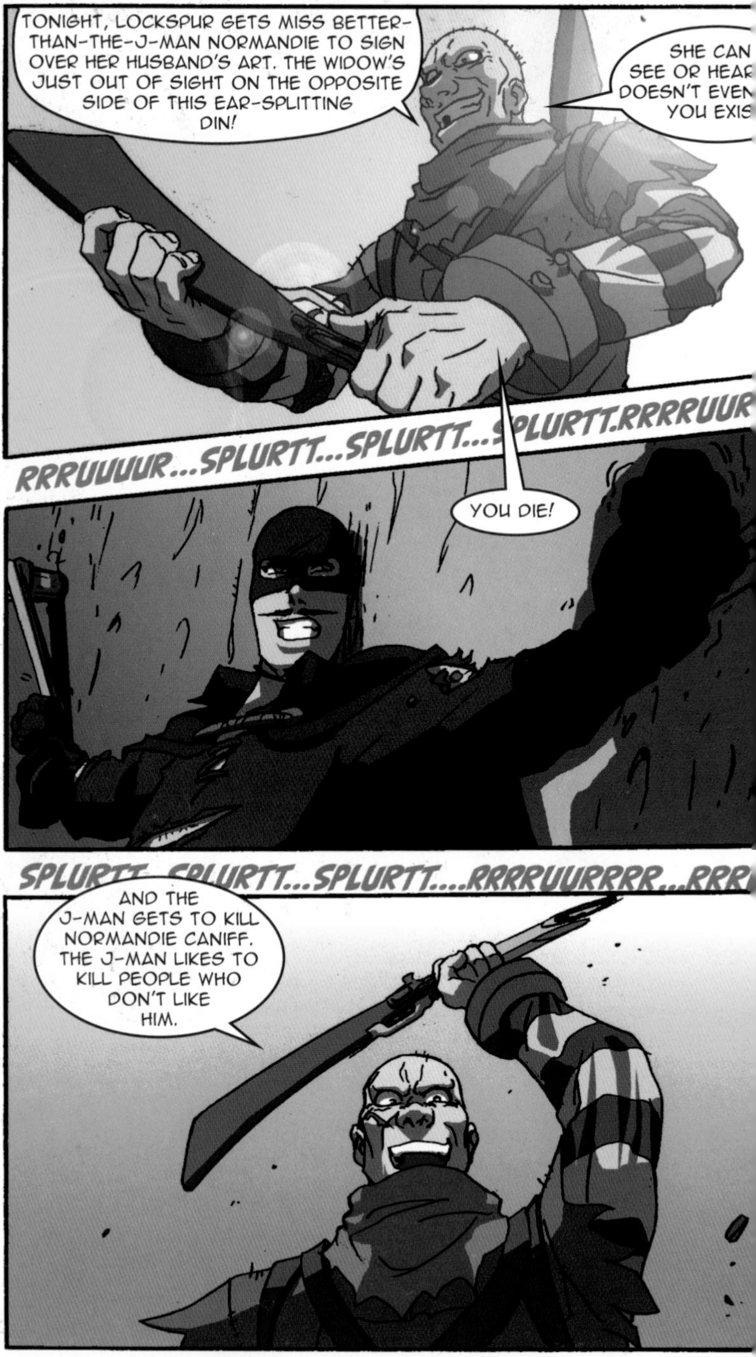
TONIGHT, LOCKSPUR GETS MISS BETTER-THAN-THE-J-MAN NORMANDIE TO SIGN OVER HER HUSBAND'S ART. THE WIDOW'S JUST OUT OF SIGHT ON THE OPPOSITE SIDE OF THIS EAR-SPLITTING DIN!
SHE CAN SEE OR HEAR DOESN'T EVEN YOU EXIS
RRRUUUUR...SPLURTT...SPLURTT...SPLURTT.RRRRUUR
YOU DIE!
SPLURTT...SPLURTT...SPLURTT....RRRRUURRRR...RRR
AND THE J-MAN GETS TO KILL NORMANDIE CANIFF. THE J-MAN LIKES TO KILL PEOPLE WHO DON'T LIKE HIM.

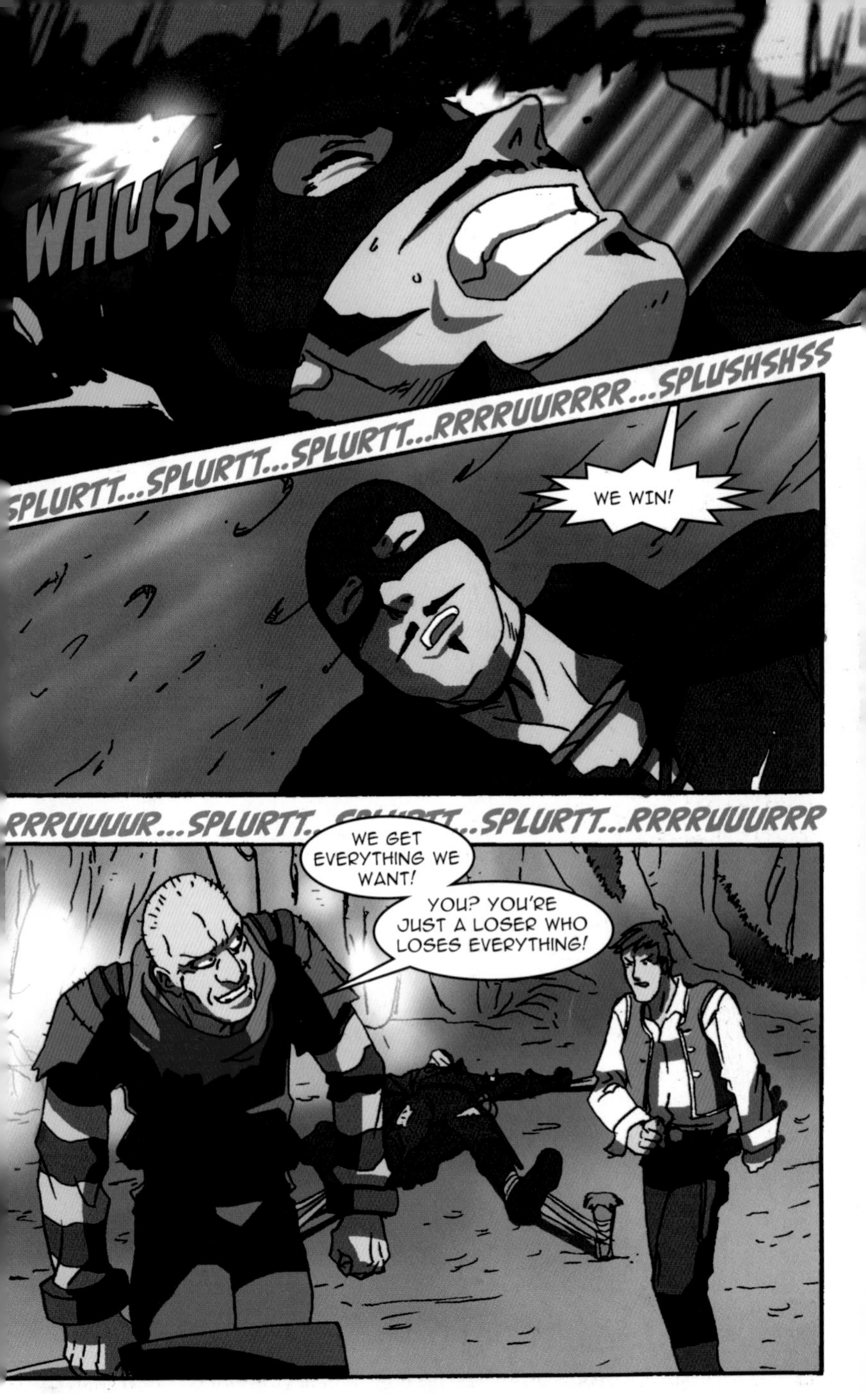
WHUSK
SPLURTT...SPLURTT...SPLURTT...RRRRUURRRR...SPLUSHSHSS
WE WIN!
RRRUUUUR...SPLURTT...SPLURTT...SPLURTT...RRRRUUURRR
WE GET EVERYTHING WE WANT!
YOU? YOU'RE JUST A LOSER WHO LOSES EVERYTHING!

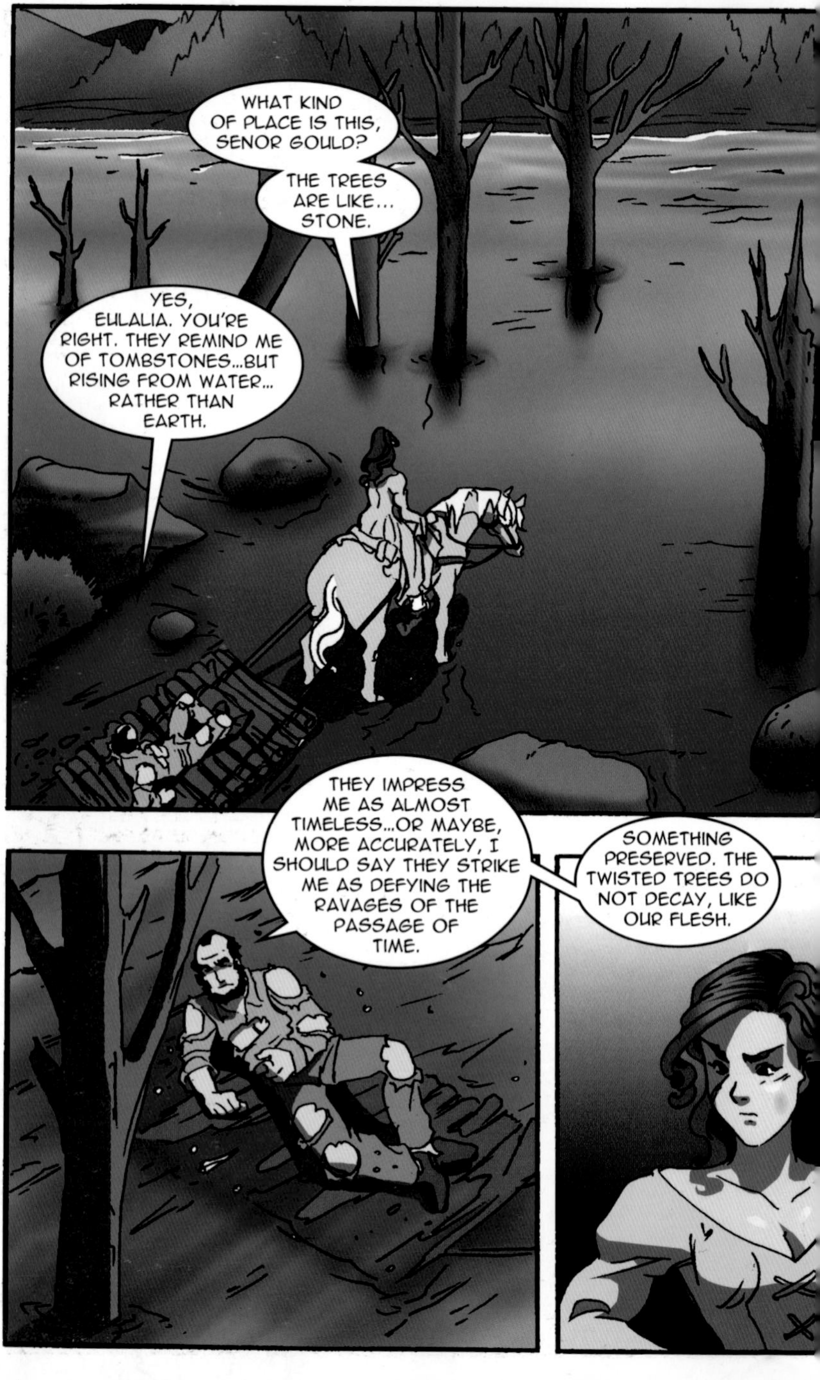
WHAT KIND OF PLACE IS THIS, SENOR GOULD?
THE TREES ARE LIKE... STONE.
YES, EULALIA. YOU'RE RIGHT. THEY REMIND ME OF TOMBSTONES...BUT RISING FROM WATER... RATHER THAN EARTH.
THEY IMPRESS ME AS ALMOST TIMELESS...OR MAYBE, MORE ACCURATELY, I SHOULD SAY THEY STRIKE ME AS DEFYING THE RAVAGES OF THE PASSAGE OF TIME.
SOMETHING PRESERVED. THE TWISTED TREES DO NOT DECAY, LIKE OUR FLESH.

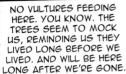

NO VULTURES FEEDING HERE. YOU KNOW. THE TREES SEEM TO MOCK US, REMINDING US THEY LIVED LONG BEFORE WE LIVED. AND WILL BE HERE LONG AFTER WE'RE GONE.

LOCKSPUR DID NOT LIE ABOUT THE UNIQUE QUALITIES OF THIS PLACE WHEN HE DESCRIBED IT TO NORMANDIE, AND CONVINCED HER TO TRAVEL OUT HERE.

WHICH DOESN'T MEAN LOCKSPUR, OR HIS CRAZED PARTNER, THAT J-MAN, WON'T KILL.

I'D LIKE THE FOX NOT TO GET HIMSELF DEAD.

AND KEEP HIS PROMISE TO FIND ME A NEW LIFE.

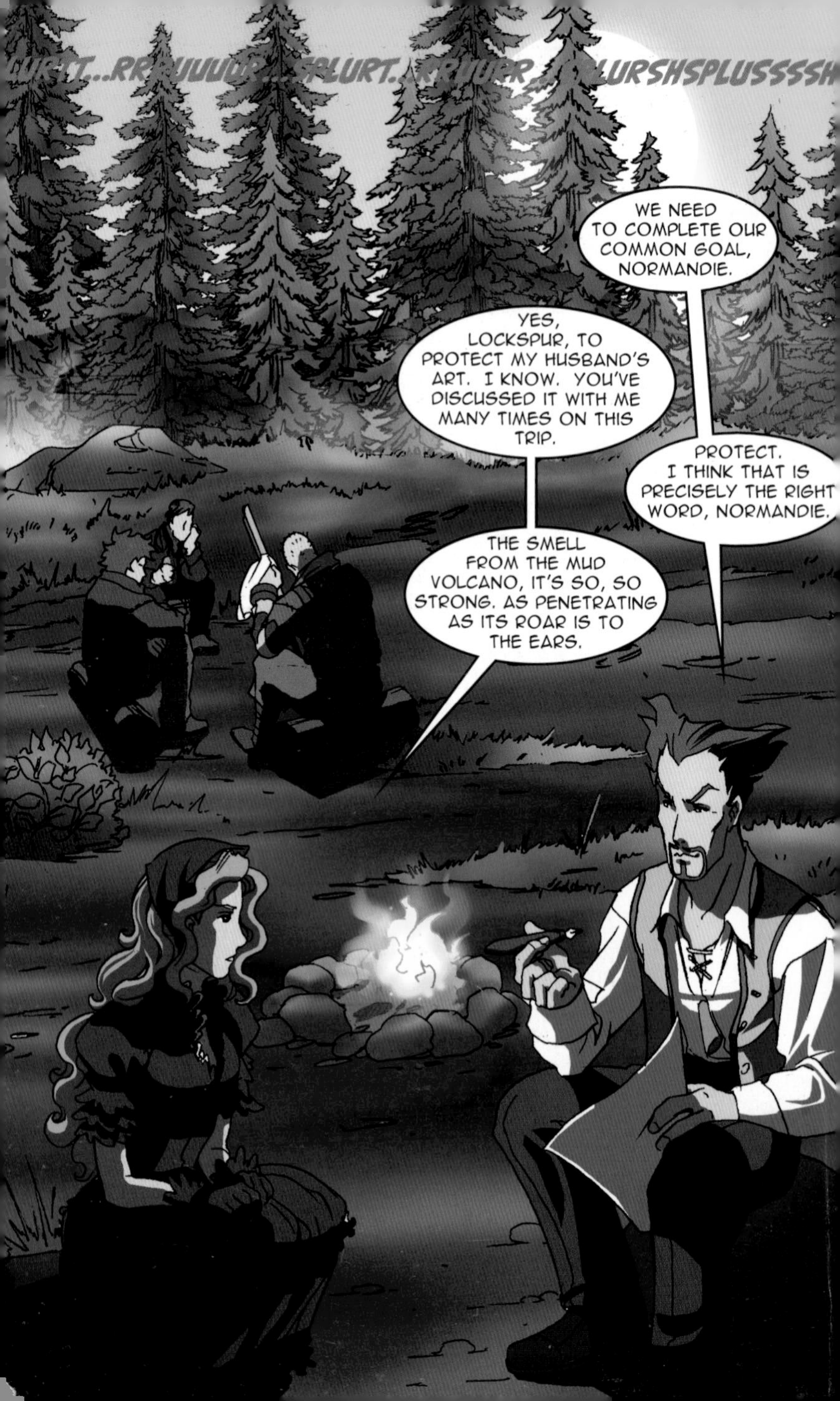
SPLURT...
URSHSPLUSSSSH
WE NEED TO COMPLETE OUR COMMON GOAL, NORMANDIE.
YES, LOCKSPUR, TO PROTECT MY HUSBAND'S ART. I KNOW. YOU'VE DISCUSSED IT WITH ME MANY TIMES ON THIS TRIP.
PROTECT. I THINK THAT IS PRECISELY THE RIGHT WORD, NORMANDIE.
THE SMELL FROM THE MUD VOLCANO, IT'S SO, SO STRONG. AS PENETRATING AS ITS ROAR IS TO THE EARS.

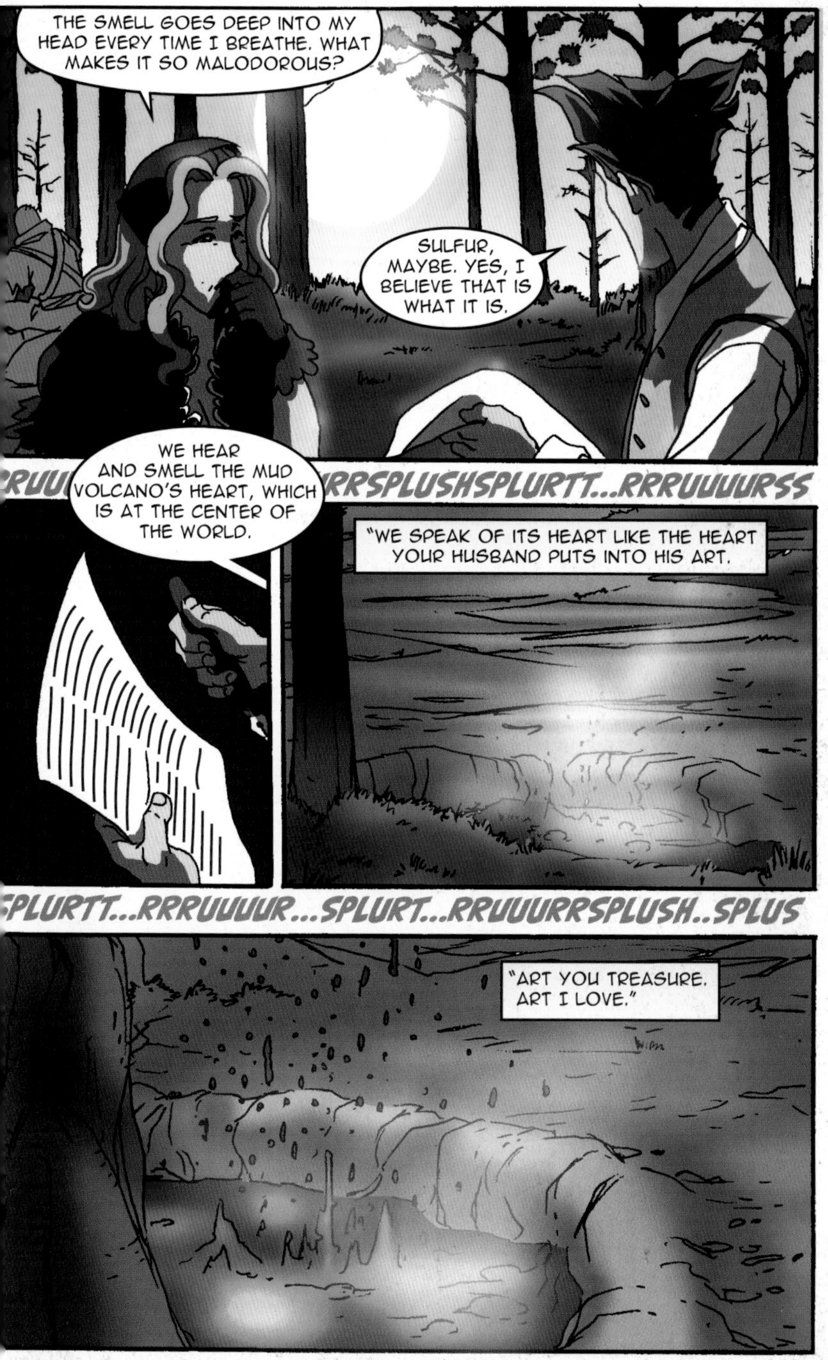
THE SMELL GOES DEEP INTO MY HEAD EVERY TIME I BREATHE. WHAT MAKES IT SO MALODOROUS?
SULFUR, MAYBE. YES, I BELIEVE THAT IS WHAT IT IS.
WE HEAR AND SMELL THE MUD VOLCANO'S HEART, WHICH IS AT THE CENTER OF THE WORLD.
RRSPLUSHSPLURTT...RRRUUUURSS
"WE SPEAK OF ITS HEART LIKE THE HEART YOUR HUSBAND PUTS INTO HIS ART.
SPLURTT...RRRUUUUR...SPLURT...RRUUURRSPLUSH..SPLUS
"ART YOU TREASURE. ART I LOVE."

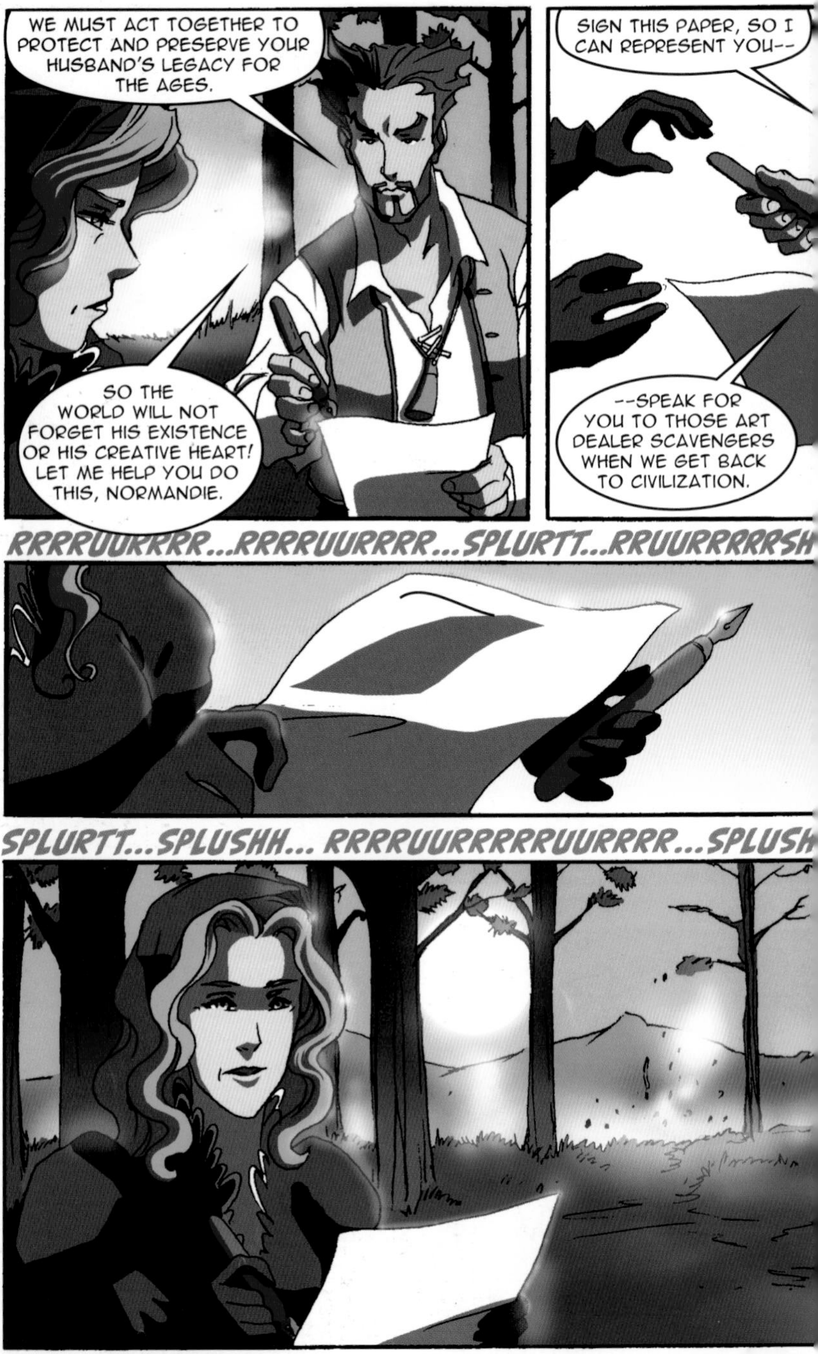
WE MUST ACT TOGETHER TO PROTECT AND PRESERVE YOUR HUSBAND'S LEGACY FOR THE AGES.
SO THE WORLD WILL NOT FORGET HIS EXISTENCE OR HIS CREATIVE HEART! LET ME HELP YOU DO THIS, NORMANDIE.
SIGN THIS PAPER, SO I CAN REPRESENT YOU--
--SPEAK FOR YOU TO THOSE ART DEALER SCAVENGERS WHEN WE GET BACK TO CIVILIZATION.
RRRRUURRRR...RRRRUURRRR...SPLURTT...RRUURRRRRSH
SPLURTT...SPLUSHH... RRRRUURRRRRUURRRR...SPLUSH

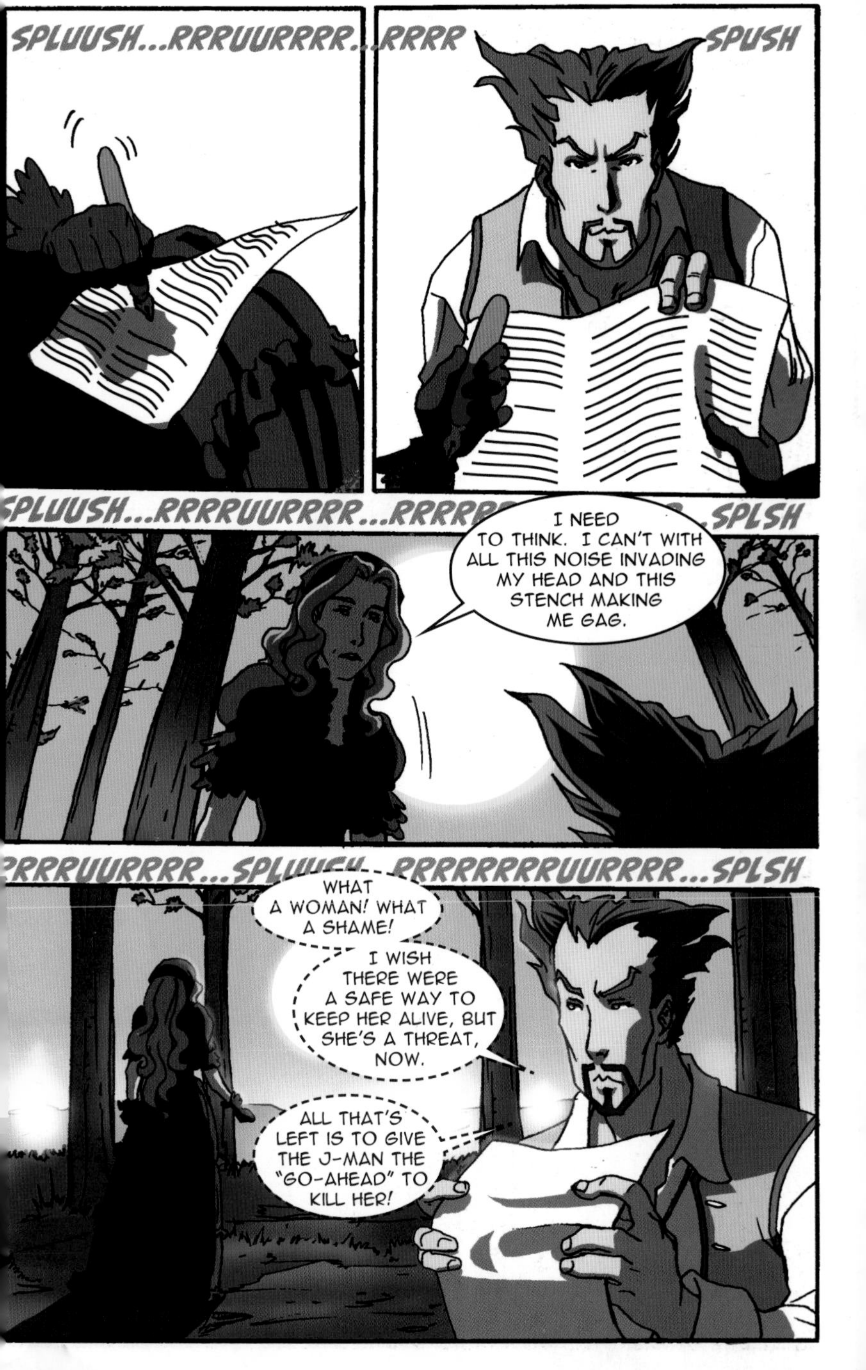

SPLUUSH...RRRUURRRR...RRRR
SPUSH
SPLUUSH...RRRRUURRRR...RRRR
..SPLSH
I NEED TO THINK. I CAN'T WITH ALL THIS NOISE INVADING MY HEAD AND THIS STENCH MAKING ME GAG.
RRRRUURRRR...SPL
RRRRRRRRUURRRR...SPLSH
WHAT A WOMAN! WHAT A SHAME!
I WISH THERE WERE A SAFE WAY TO KEEP HER ALIVE, BUT SHE'S A THREAT, NOW.
ALL THAT'S LEFT IS TO GIVE THE J-MAN THE "GO-AHEAD" TO KILL HER!

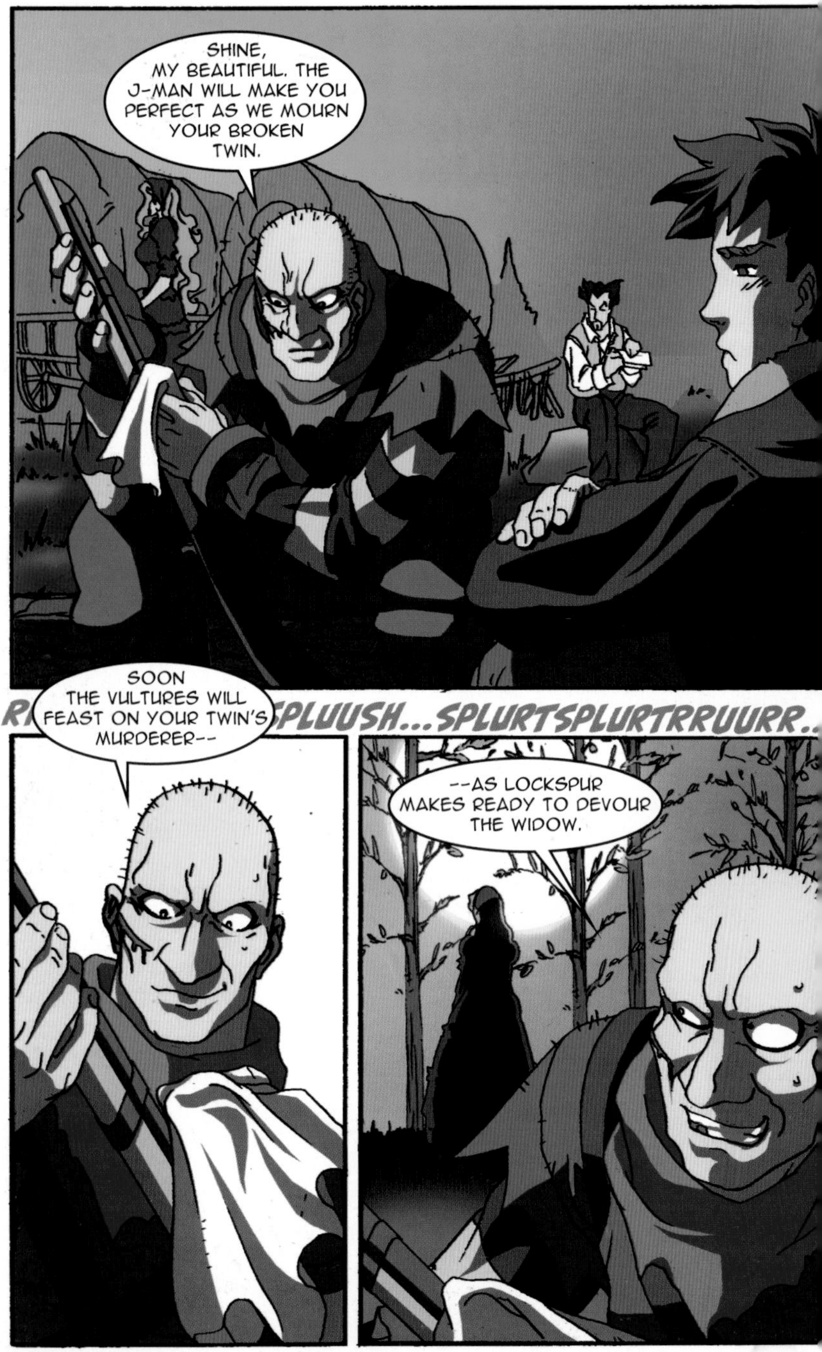
SHINE, MY BEAUTIFUL. THE J-MAN WILL MAKE YOU PERFECT AS WE MOURN YOUR BROKEN TWIN.
SOON THE VULTURES WILL FEAST ON YOUR TWIN'S MURDERER--
SPLUUSH...SPLURTSPLURTRRUURR..
--AS LOCKSPUR MAKES READY TO DEVOUR THE WIDOW.

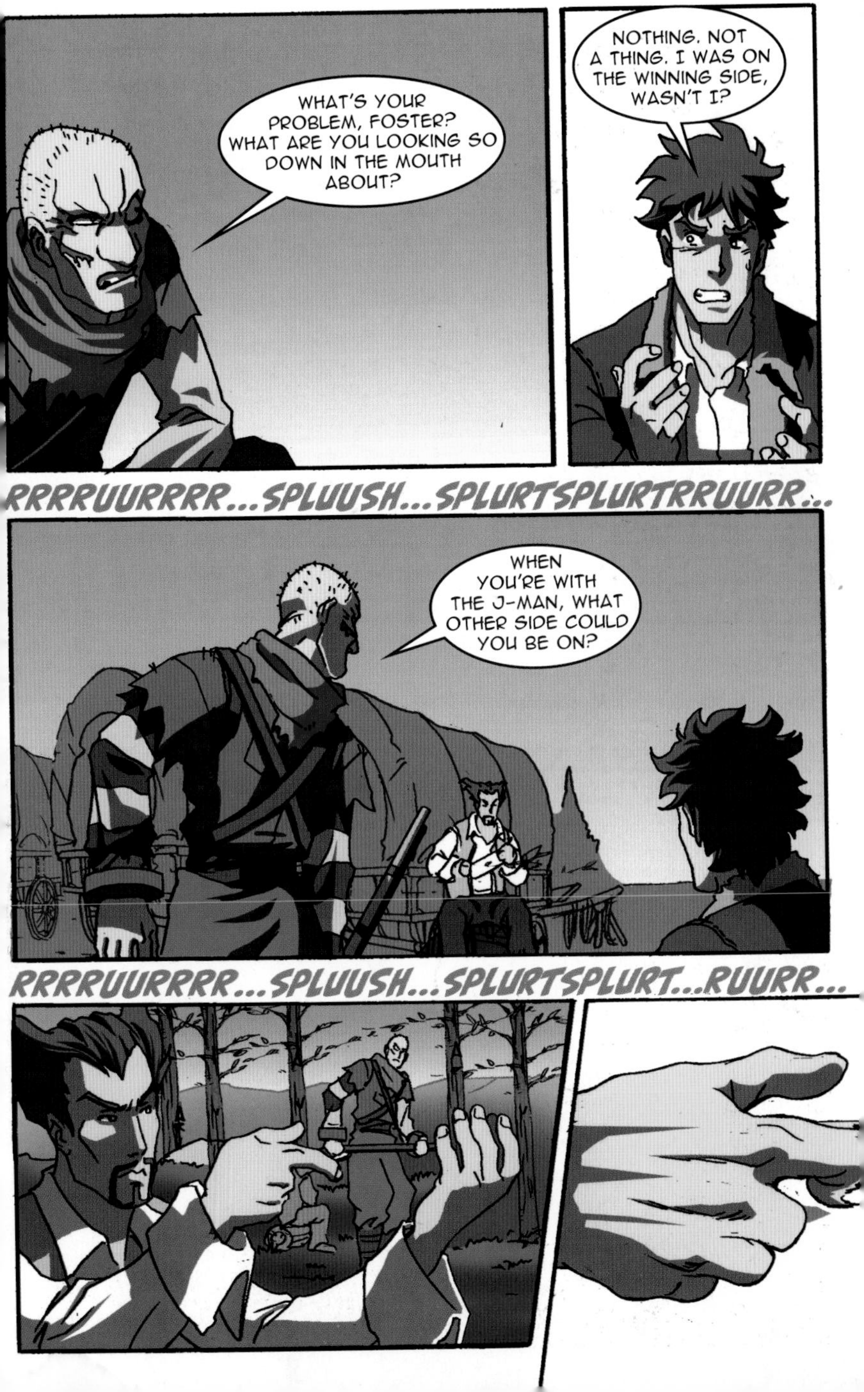
WHAT'S YOUR PROBLEM, FOSTER? WHAT ARE YOU LOOKING SO DOWN IN THE MOUTH ABOUT?
NOTHING. NOT A THING. I WAS ON THE WINNING SIDE, WASN'T I?
RRRRUURRRR...SPLUUSH...SPLURTSPLURTRRUURR...
WHEN YOU'RE WITH THE J-MAN, WHAT OTHER SIDE COULD YOU BE ON?
RRRRUURRRR...SPLUUSH...SPLURTSPLURT...RUURR...

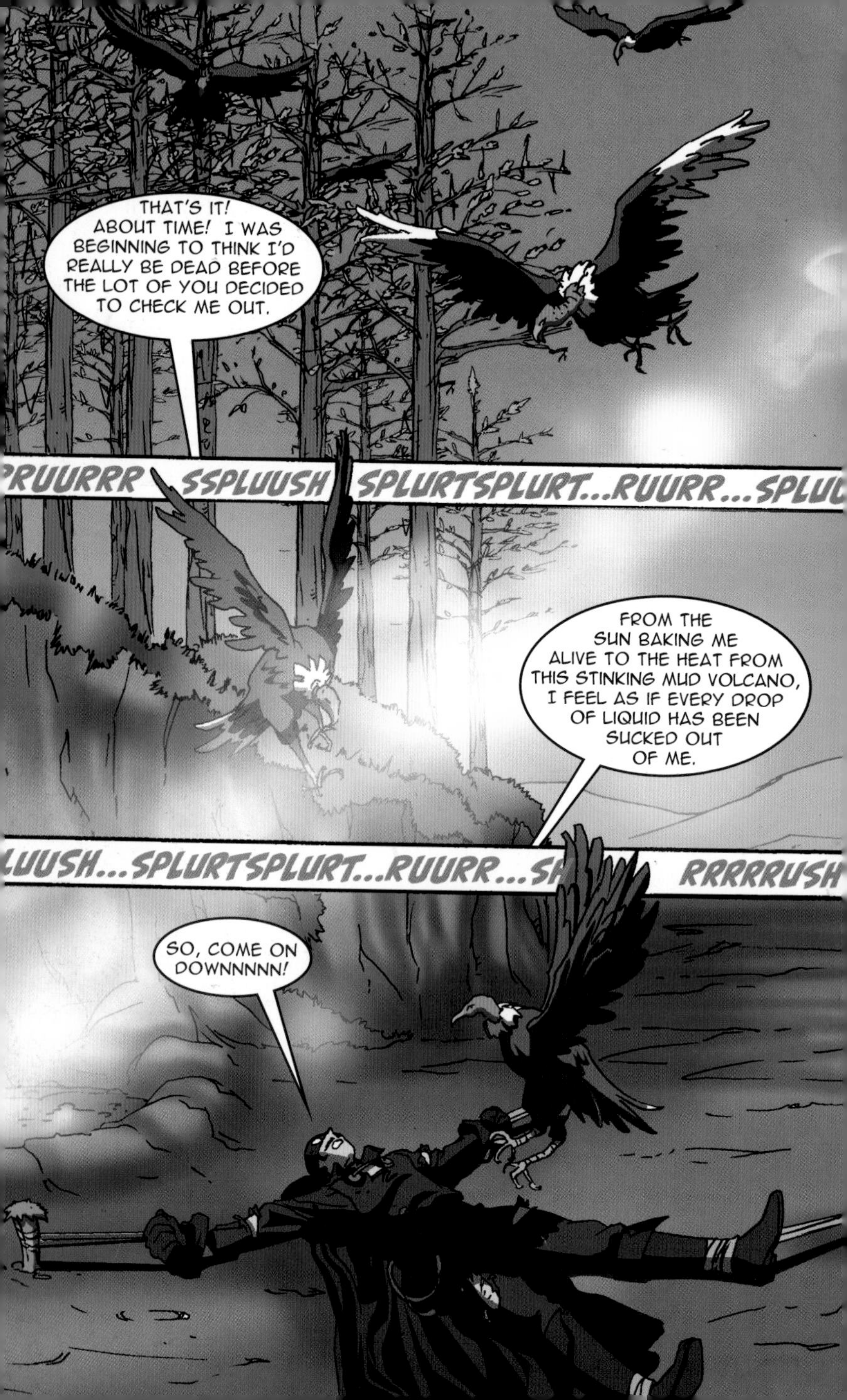
THAT'S IT! ABOUT TIME! I WAS BEGINNING TO THINK I'D REALLY BE DEAD BEFORE THE LOT OF YOU DECIDED TO CHECK ME OUT.
RUURRR SSPLUUSH SPLURTSPLURT...RUURR...SPLU
FROM THE SUN BAKING ME ALIVE TO THE HEAT FROM THIS STINKING MUD VOLCANO, I FEEL AS IF EVERY DROP OF LIQUID HAS BEEN SUCKED OUT OF ME.
LUUSH...SPLURTSPLURT...RUURR...SP RRRRRUSH
SO, COME ON DOWNNNNN!

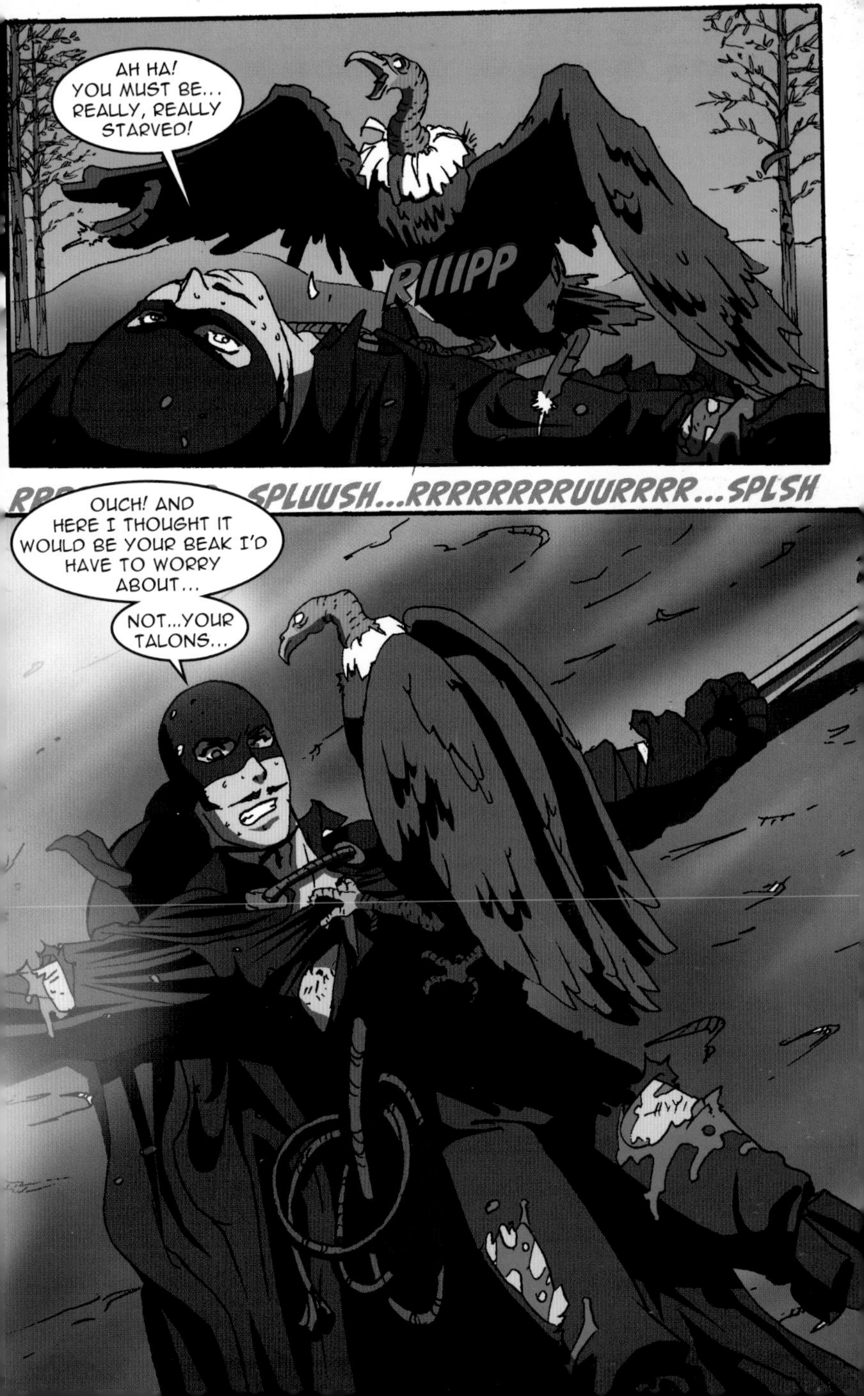
AH HA! YOU MUST BE... REALLY, REALLY STARVED!
RIIIPP
SPLUUSH...RRRRRRRRUURRRR...SPLSH
OUCH! AND HERE I THOUGHT IT WOULD BE YOUR BEAK I'D HAVE TO WORRY ABOUT...
NOT...YOUR TALONS...

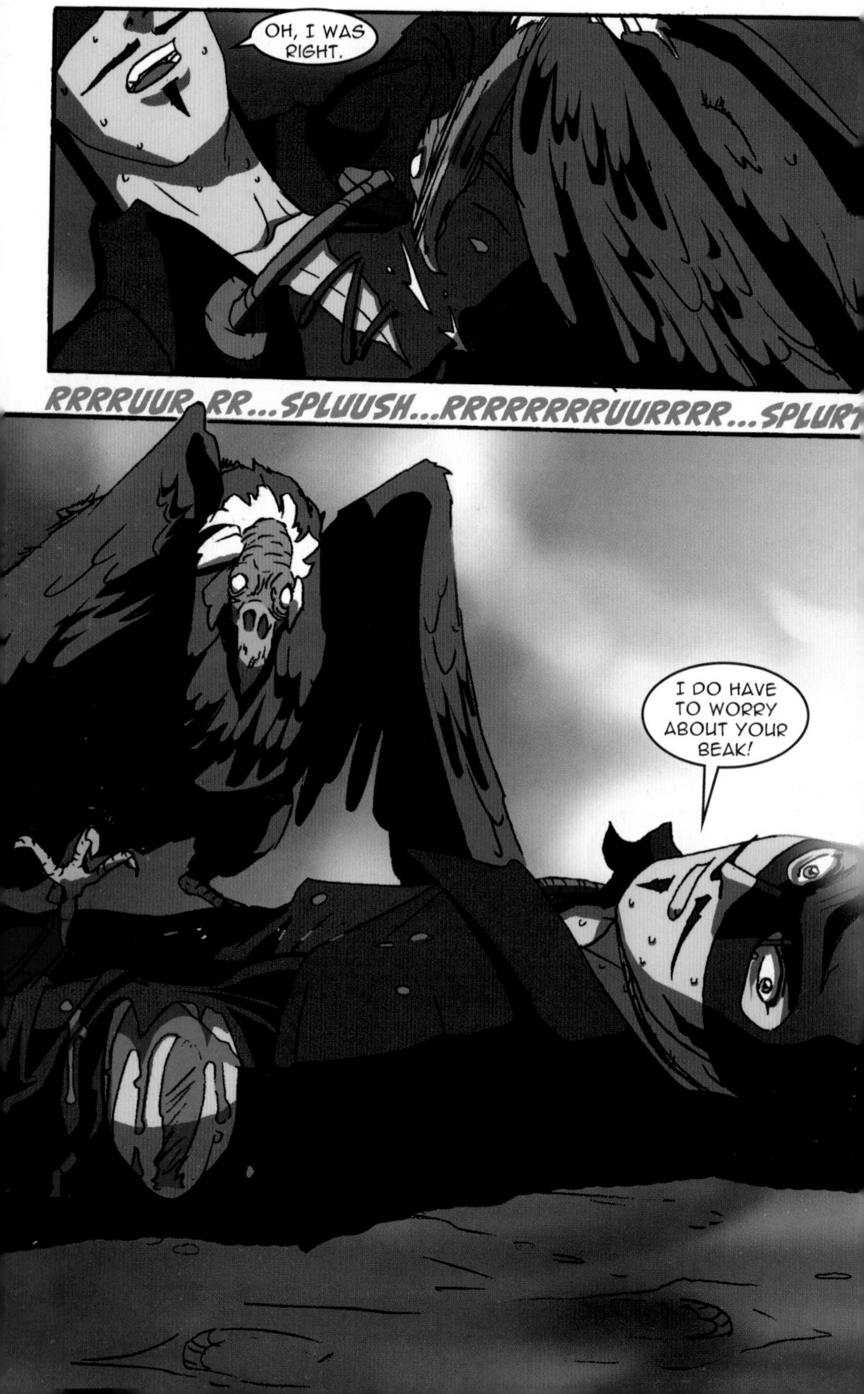
OH, I WAS RIGHT.
RRRRUUR RR...SPLUUSH...RRRRRRRRUURRRR...SPLURT
I DO HAVE TO WORRY ABOUT YOUR BEAK!

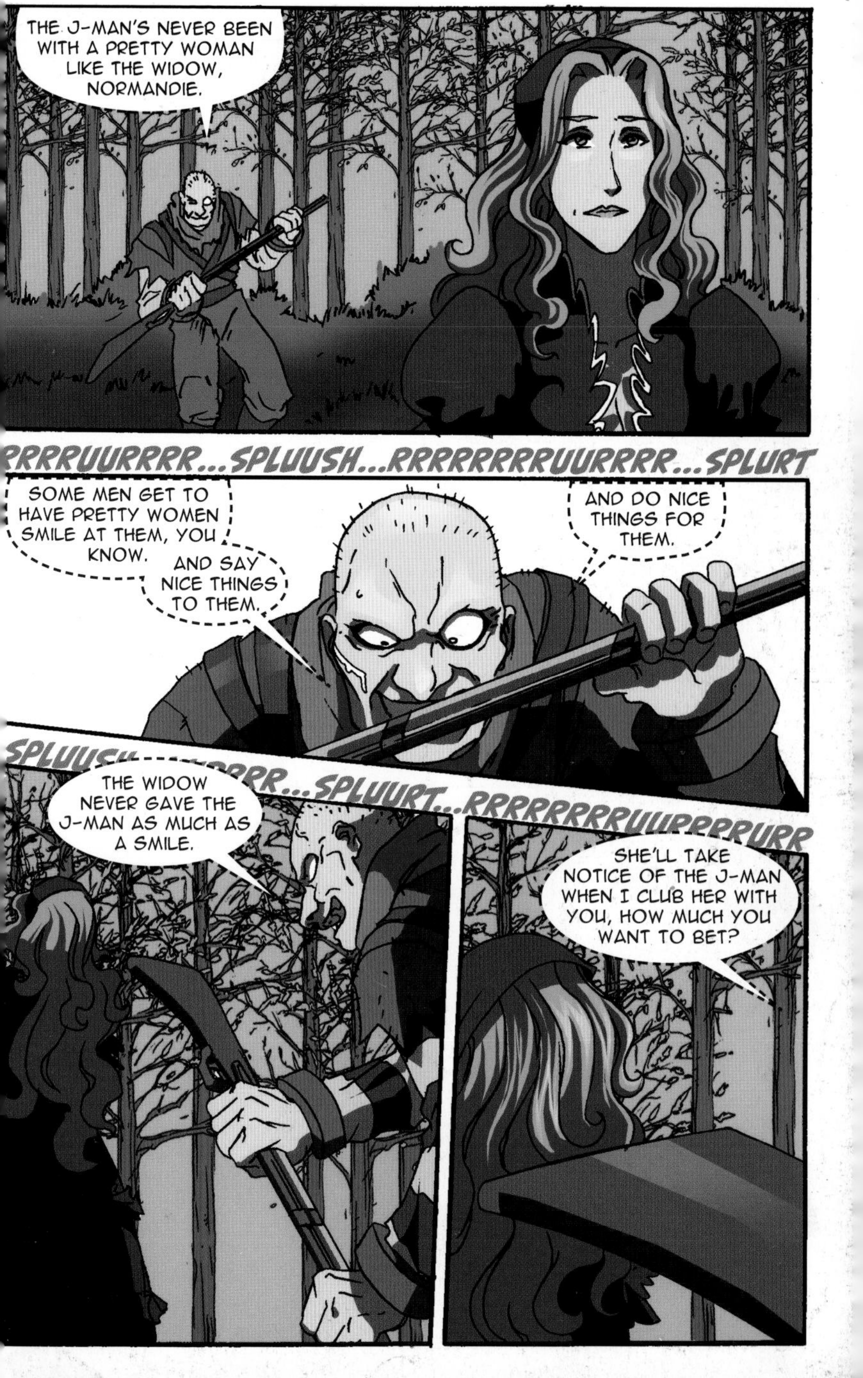
THE J-MAN'S NEVER BEEN WITH A PRETTY WOMAN LIKE THE WIDOW, NORMANDIE.
RRRRUURRRR...SPLUUSH...RRRRRRRRUURRRR...SPLURT
SOME MEN GET TO HAVE PRETTY WOMEN SMILE AT THEM, YOU KNOW.
AND SAY NICE THINGS TO THEM.
AND DO NICE THINGS FOR THEM.
THE WIDOW NEVER GAVE THE J-MAN AS MUCH AS A SMILE.
SHE'LL TAKE NOTICE OF THE J-MAN WHEN I CLUB HER WITH YOU, HOW MUCH YOU WANT TO BET?

RRRRUURRRR...SPLUUSH...RRRRRRRUURRRR...SPLURT

SPLURT...RRRRUURRRR...SLURRRRP..RUURRRRRR..RUURP

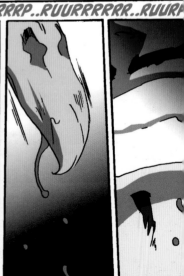

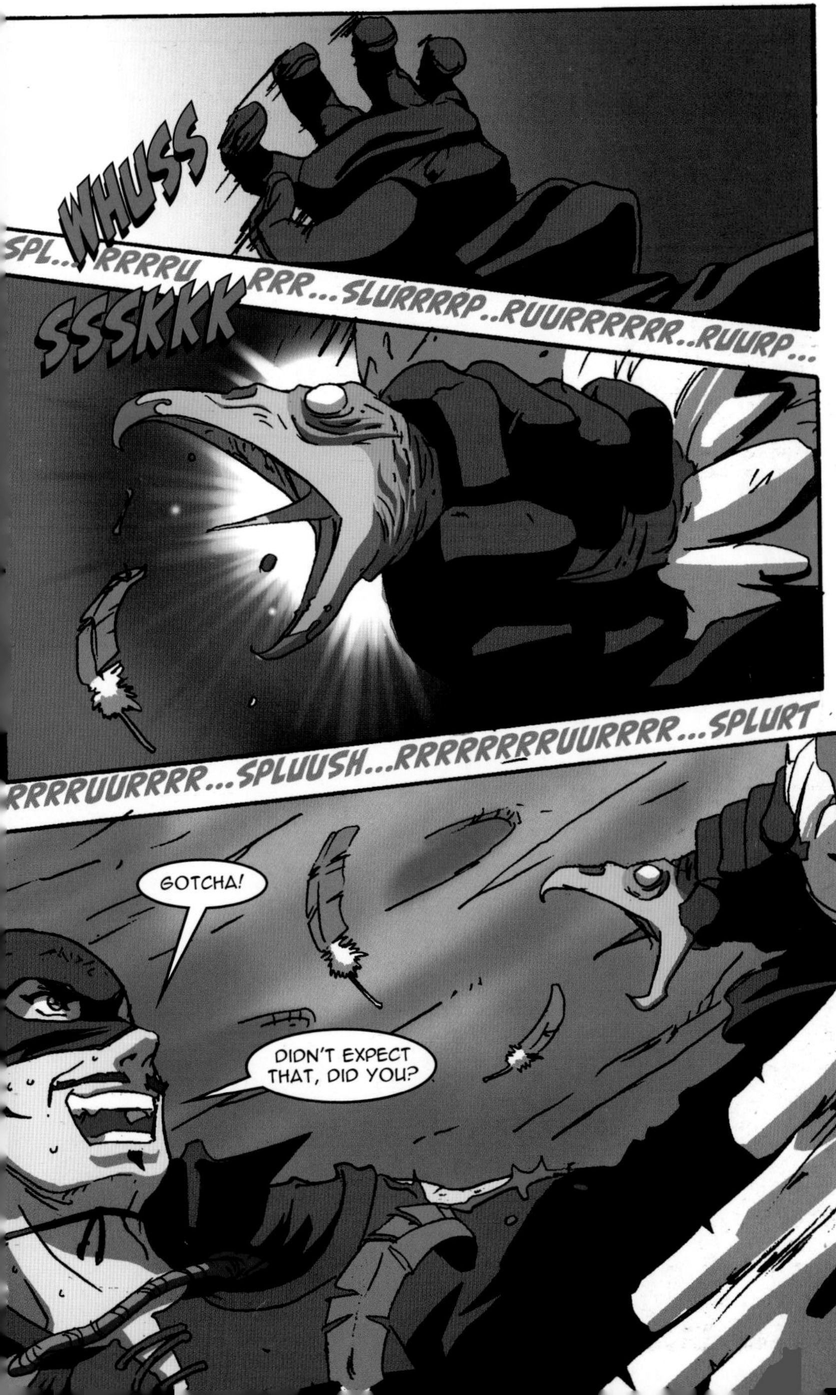
WHUSS
SPL... RRRRU
SSSKKK
RRR...SLURRRRP..RUURRRRRR..RUURP...
RRRRRRRRUURRRR...SPLURT
RRRRUURRRR...SPLUUSH...
GOTCHA!
DIDN'T EXPECT THAT, DID YOU?

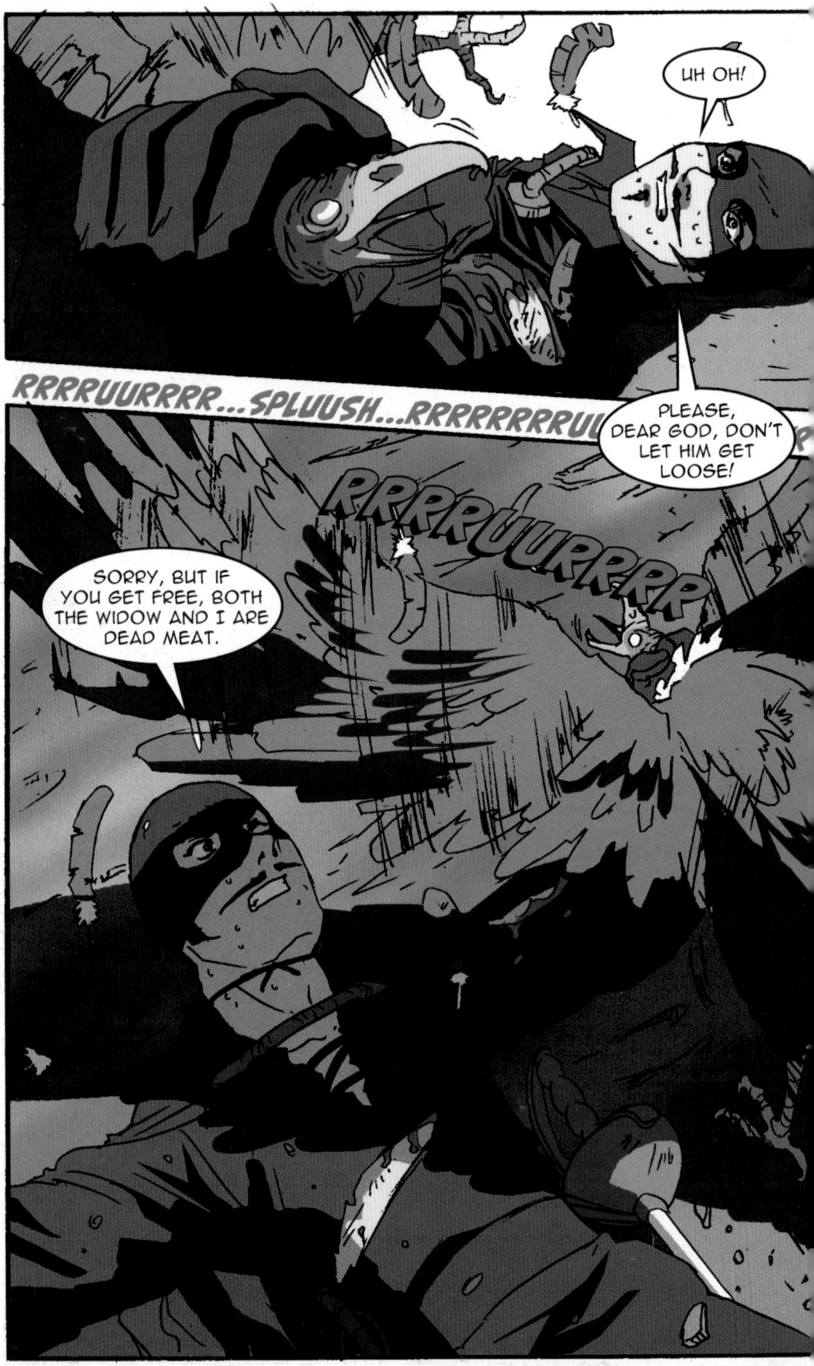

UH OH!
RRRRUURRRR...SPLUUSH...RRRRRRRRUU
PLEASE, DEAR GOD, DON'T LET HIM GET LOOSE!
RRRRUURRRRR
SORRY, BUT IF YOU GET FREE, BOTH THE WIDOW AND I ARE DEAD MEAT.

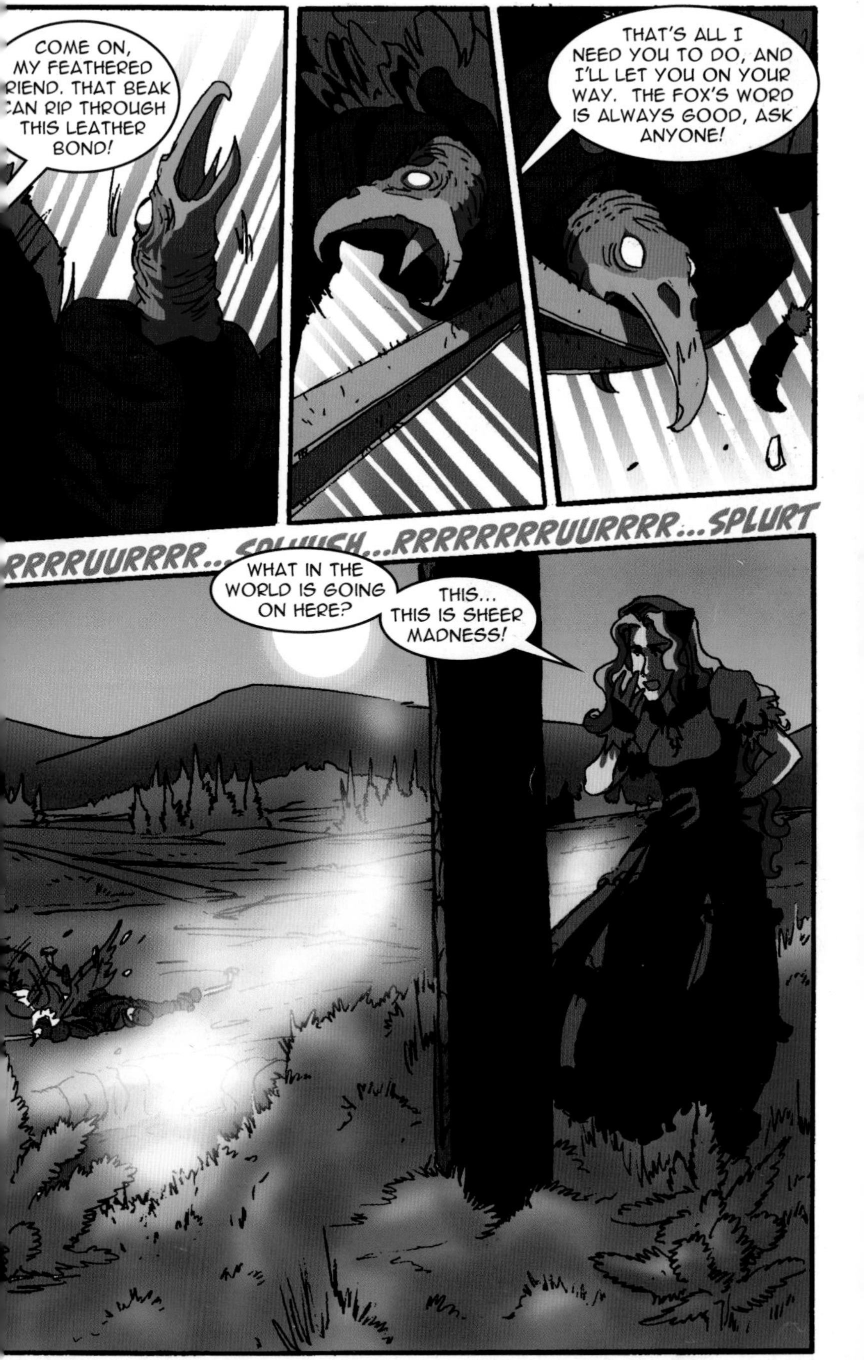
COME ON, MY FEATHERED FRIEND. THAT BEAK CAN RIP THROUGH THIS LEATHER BOND!
THAT'S ALL I NEED YOU TO DO, AND I'LL LET YOU ON YOUR WAY. THE FOX'S WORD IS ALWAYS GOOD, ASK ANYONE!
RRRRRRRRUURRRR...SPLURT
WHAT IN THE WORLD IS GOING ON HERE?
THIS... THIS IS SHEER MADNESS!

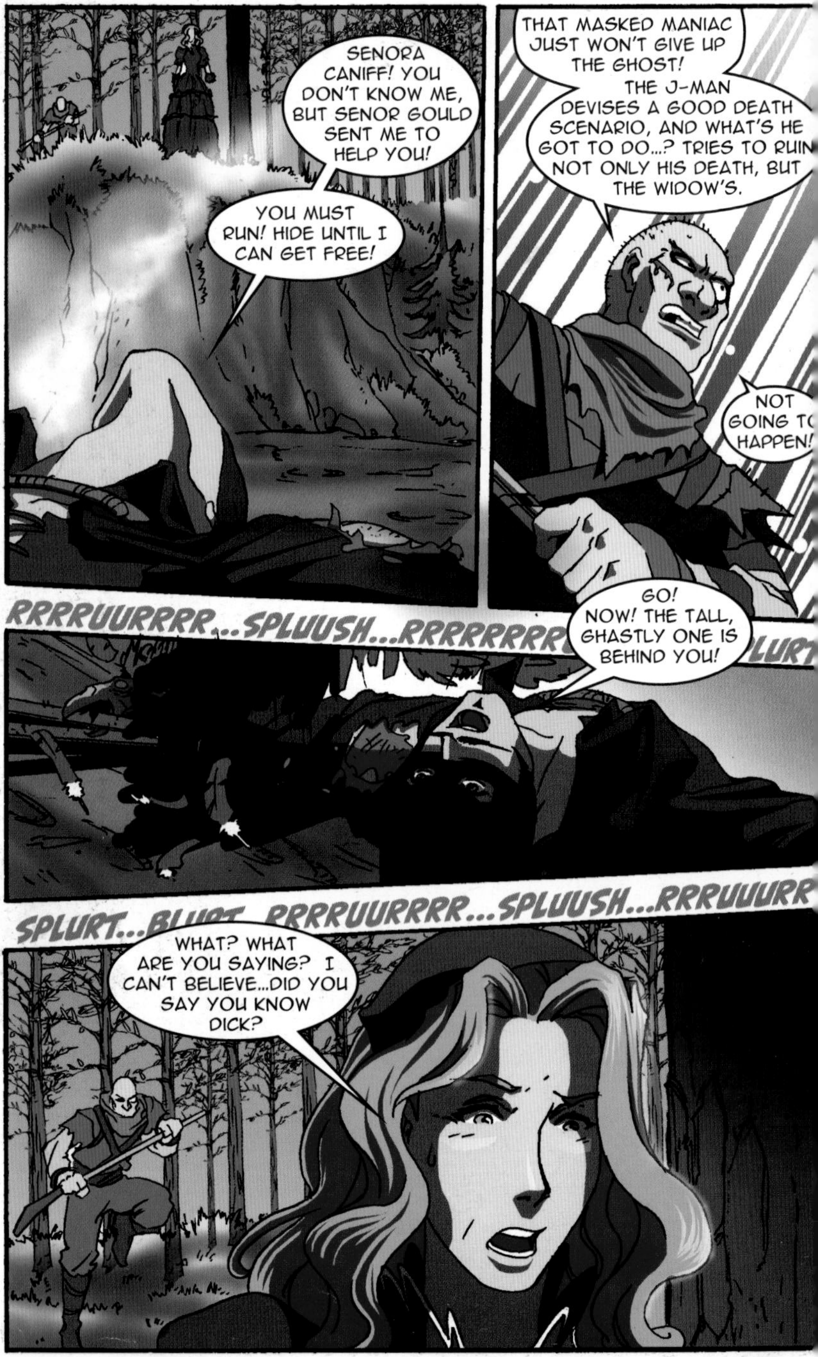
SENORA CANIFF! YOU DON'T KNOW ME, BUT SENOR GOULD SENT ME TO HELP YOU!
YOU MUST RUN! HIDE UNTIL I CAN GET FREE!
THAT MASKED MANIAC JUST WON'T GIVE UP THE GHOST!
THE J-MAN DEVISES A GOOD DEATH SCENARIO, AND WHAT'S HE GOT TO DO...? TRIES TO RUIN NOT ONLY HIS DEATH, BUT THE WIDOW'S.
NOT GOING TO HAPPEN!
RRRRUURRRR...SPLUUSH...RRRRRRRR
GO! NOW! THE TALL, GHASTLY ONE IS BEHIND YOU!
SPLURT...
RRRRUURRRR...SPLUUSH...RRRUUURR
WHAT? WHAT ARE YOU SAYING? I CAN'T BELIEVE...DID YOU SAY YOU KNOW DICK?

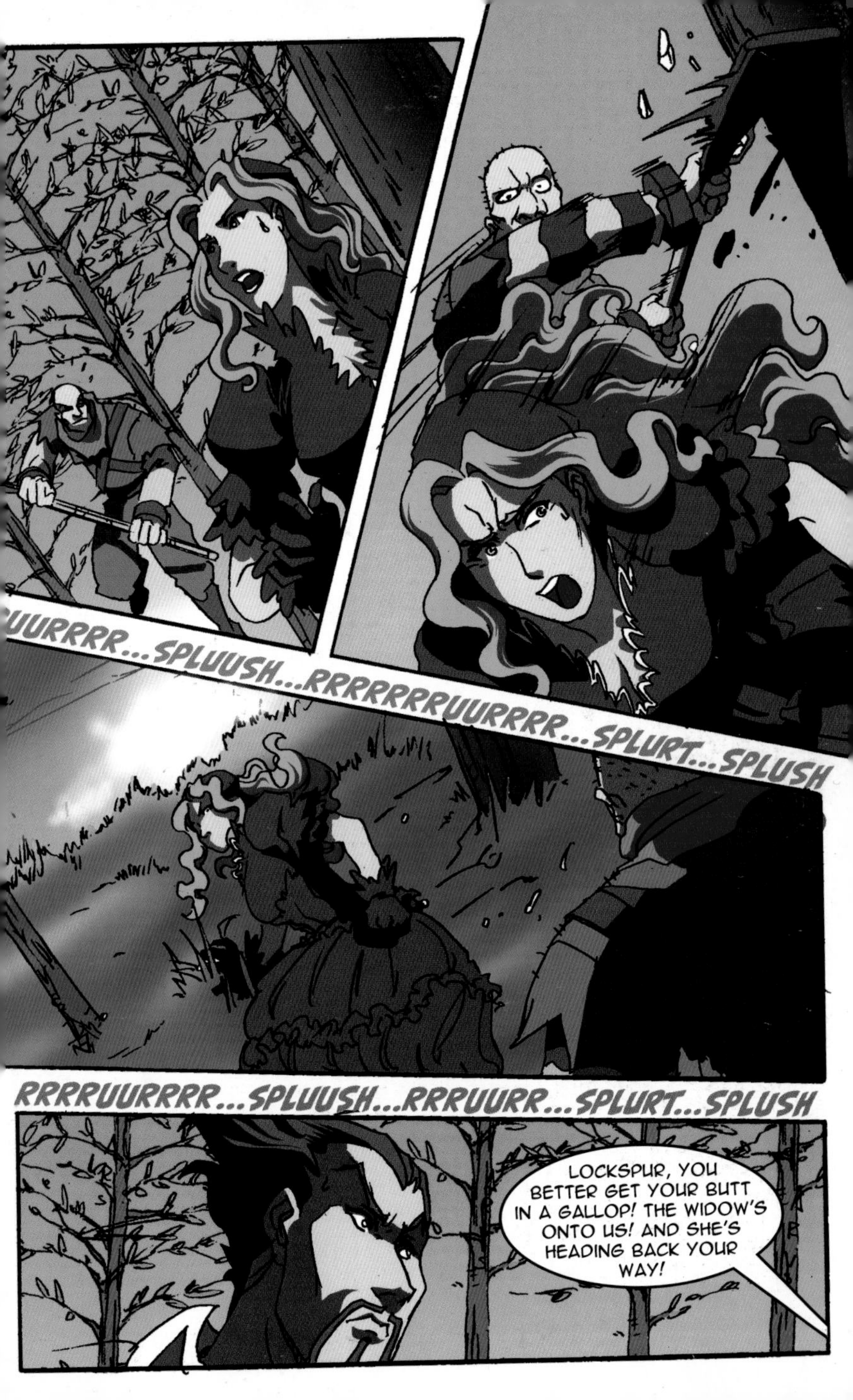
UURRRR...SPLUUSH...RRRRRRRUURRRR...SPLURT...SPLUSH
RRRRUURRRR...SPLUUSH...RRRUURR...SPLURT...SPLUSH
LOCKSPUR, YOU BETTER GET YOUR BUTT IN A GALLOP! THE WIDOW'S ONTO US! AND SHE'S HEADING BACK YOUR WAY!

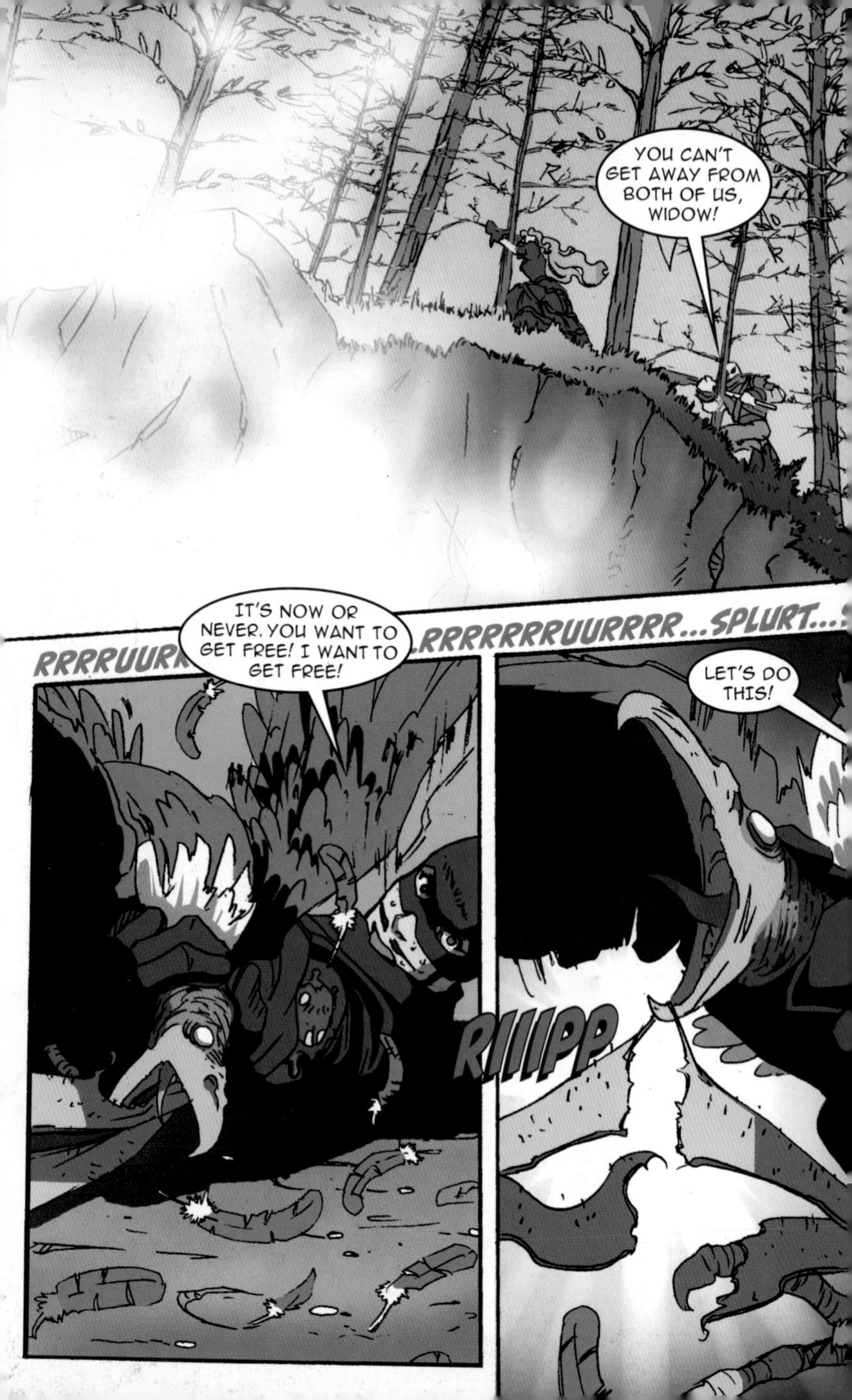
YOU CAN'T GET AWAY FROM BOTH OF US, WIDOW!
RRRRUURR
IT'S NOW OR NEVER. YOU WANT TO GET FREE! I WANT TO GET FREE!
...RRRRRRRUURRRR... SPLURT...
LET'S DO THIS!
RIIIPP

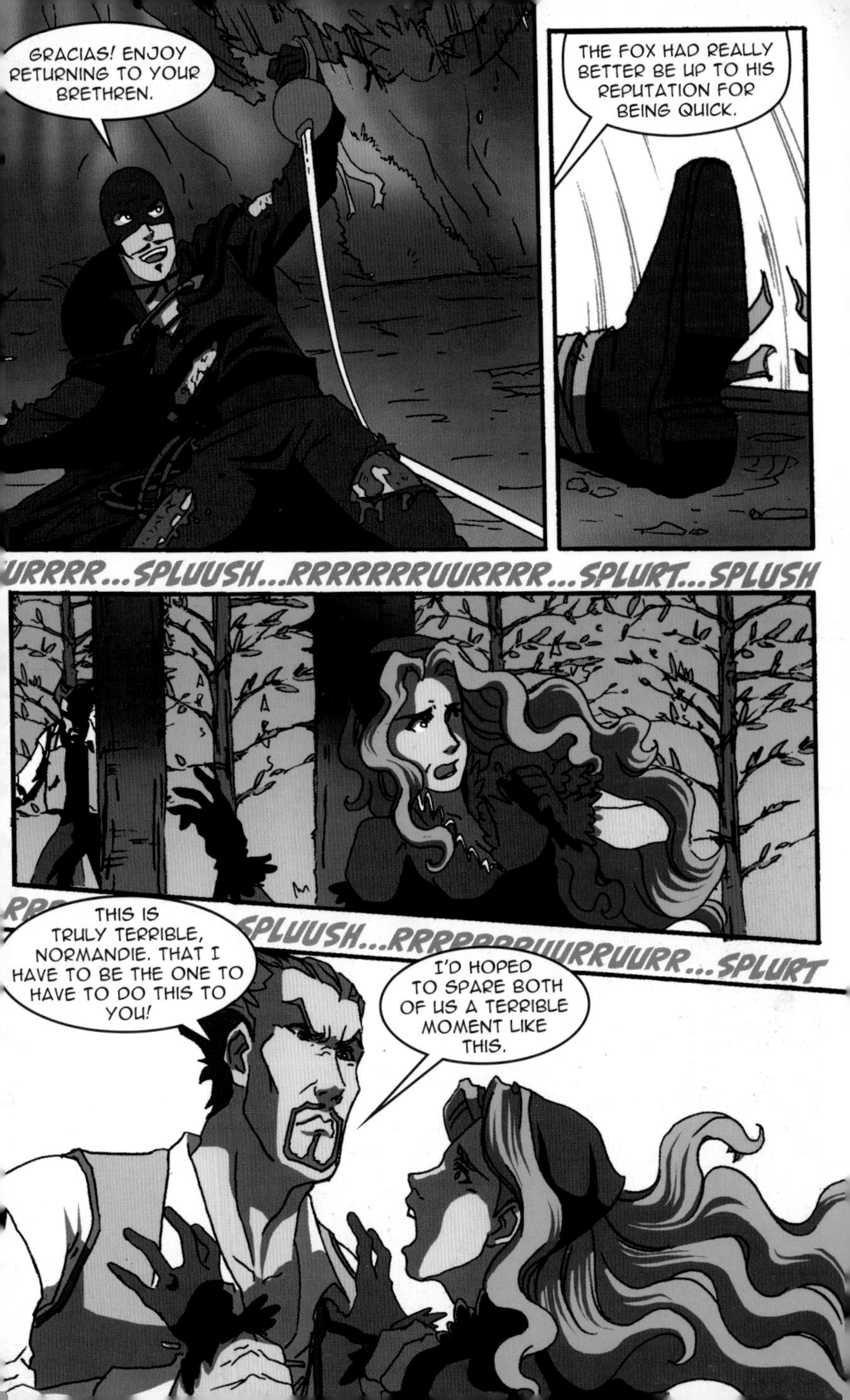
GRACIAS! ENJOY RETURNING TO YOUR BRETHREN.
THE FOX HAD REALLY BETTER BE UP TO HIS REPUTATION FOR BEING QUICK.
URRRR...SPLUUSH...RRRRRRRUURRRR...SPLURT...SPLUSH
SPLUUSH...
THIS IS TRULY TERRIBLE, NORMANDIE. THAT I HAVE TO BE THE ONE TO HAVE TO DO THIS TO YOU!
URRRUURR...SPLURT
I'D HOPED TO SPARE BOTH OF US A TERRIBLE MOMENT LIKE THIS.

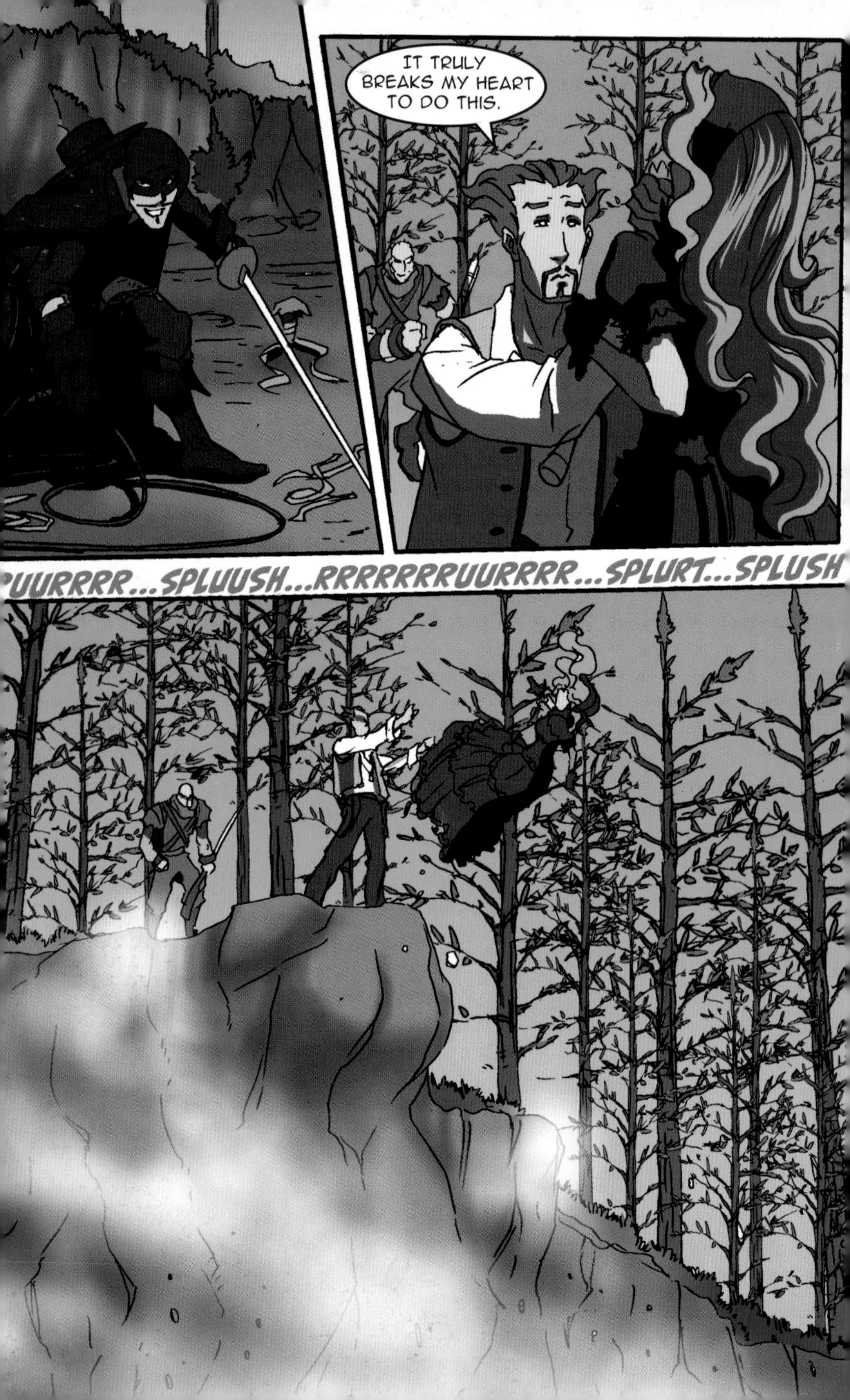
IT TRULY BREAKS MY HEART TO DO THIS.
RUURRRR...SPLUUSH...RRRRRRRUURRRR...SPLURT...SPLUSH

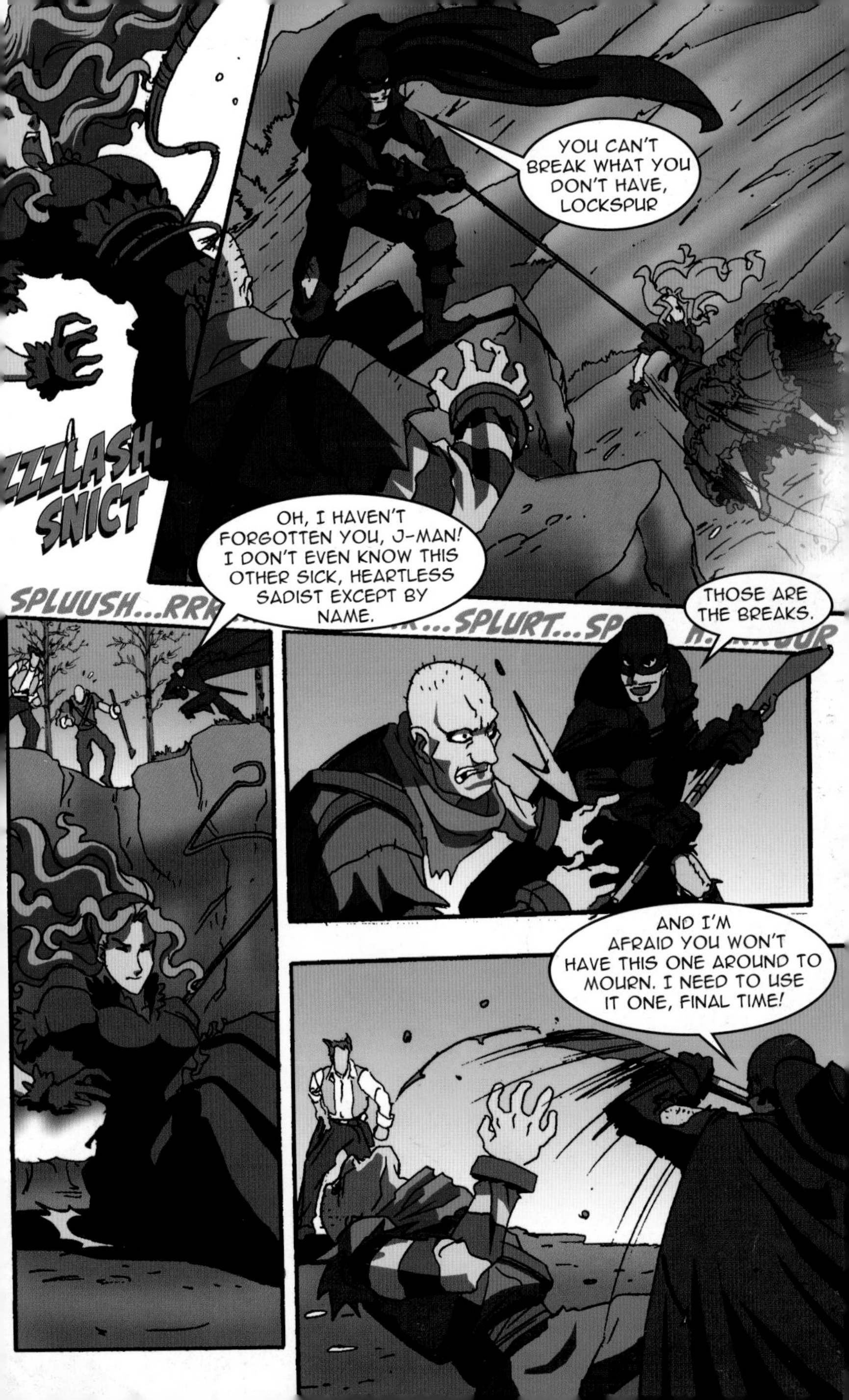
YOU CAN'T BREAK WHAT YOU DON'T HAVE, LOCKSPUR
ZZZLASH-
SNICT
OH, I HAVEN'T FORGOTTEN YOU, J-MAN! I DON'T EVEN KNOW THIS OTHER SICK, HEARTLESS SADIST EXCEPT BY NAME.
SPLUUSH...RRK
...SPLURT...SP
THOSE ARE THE BREAKS.
AND I'M AFRAID YOU WON'T HAVE THIS ONE AROUND TO MOURN. I NEED TO USE IT ONE, FINAL TIME!

SKRASH

SMU[

RRUURRRR...SPLUUSH...RRRUUPPPP...SPLURT...SPLUSH

WELL, WHATEVER'S GOING ON, I SEE IT'S ALL OVER. NOW WE CAN GET BACK TO WHAT WE'RE GOING TO DO ABOUT ME.

ONCE, I THOUGHT WHATEVER SOLUTION I CAME UP WITH, TO FIND YOU A SAFE PLACE, WOULD BE A SIMPLE AFFAIR.

I'M OLDER AND WISER NOW. I SEE I DIDN'T KNOW AS MUCH AS I THOUGHT I DID.

YOU'LL FIGURE SOMETHING OUT. YOU ALWAYS DO. THAT'S WHY YOU'RE THE FOX. AND IT LOOKS LIKE HERE, YOU HAD A HAPPY ENDING. YOU CAN'T ASK FOR MUCH MORE THAN THAT.

BURRRP

SPLUSK

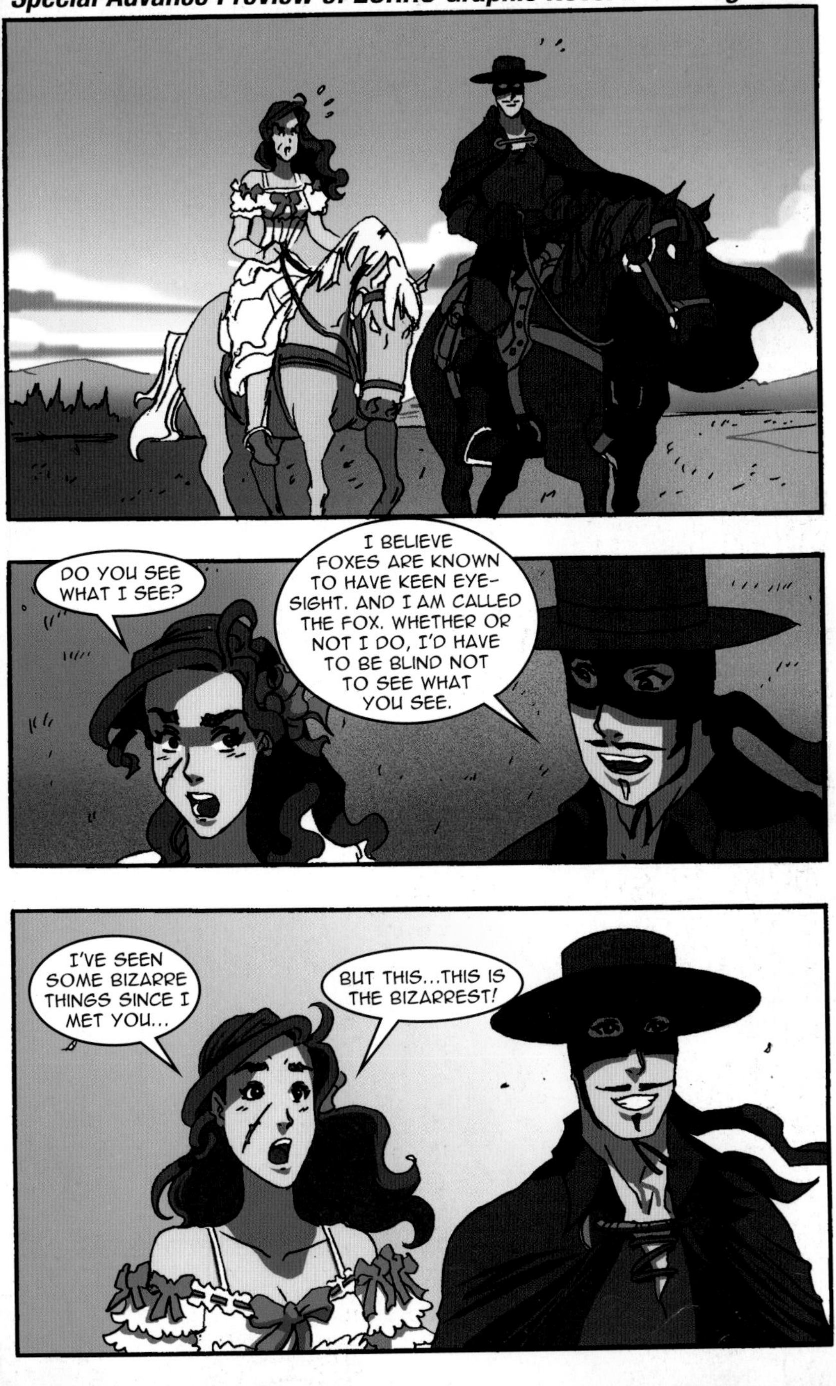
DO YOU SEE WHAT I SEE?
I BELIEVE FOXES ARE KNOWN TO HAVE KEEN EYE-SIGHT. AND I AM CALLED THE FOX. WHETHER OR NOT I DO, I'D HAVE TO BE BLIND NOT TO SEE WHAT YOU SEE.
I'VE SEEN SOME BIZARRE THINGS SINCE I MET YOU...
BUT THIS...THIS IS THE BIZARREST!

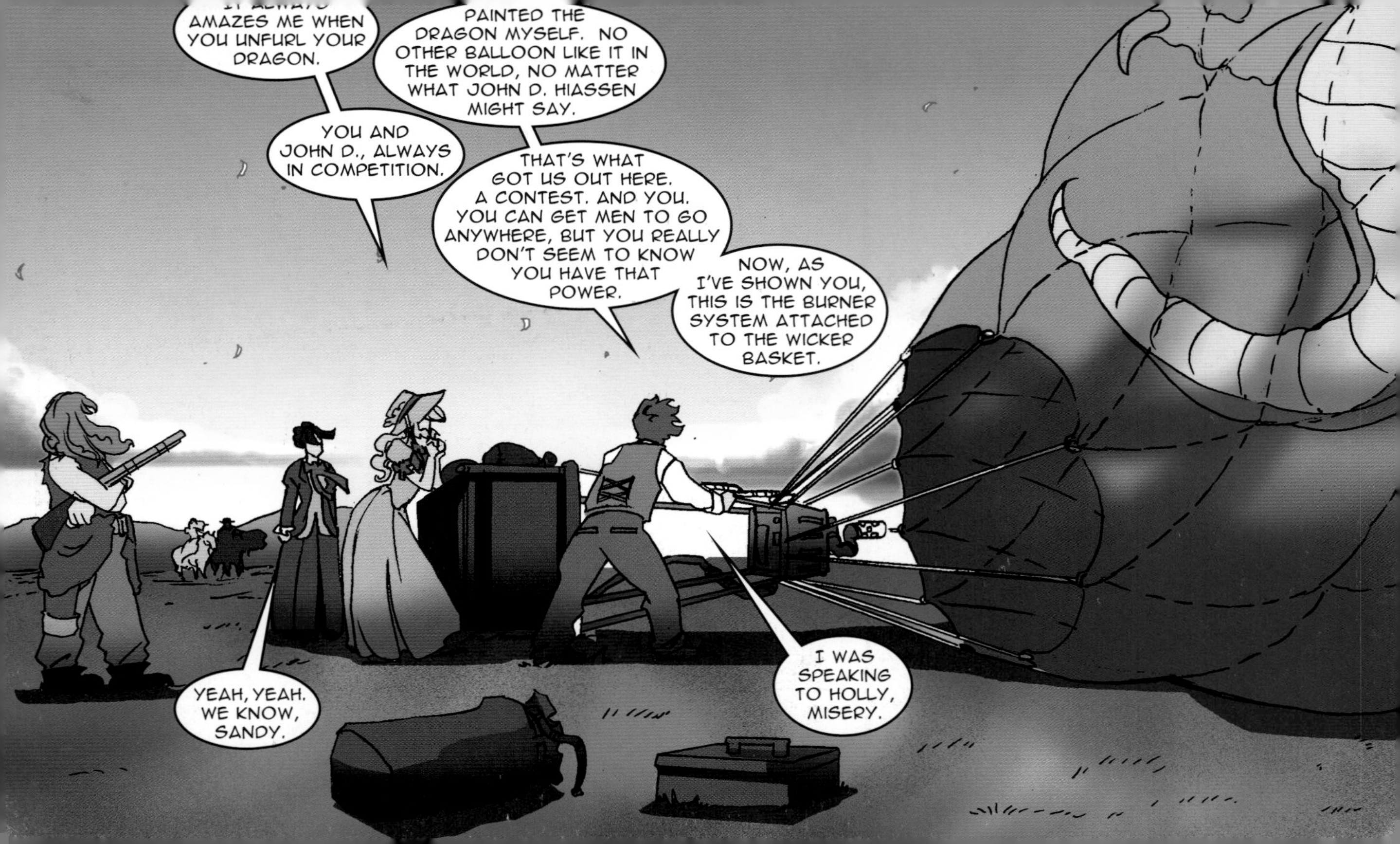
AMAZES ME WHEN YOU UNFURL YOUR DRAGON.
YOU AND JOHN D., ALWAYS IN COMPETITION.
PAINTED THE DRAGON MYSELF. NO OTHER BALLOON LIKE IT IN THE WORLD, NO MATTER WHAT JOHN D. HIASSEN MIGHT SAY.
THAT'S WHAT GOT US OUT HERE. A CONTEST. AND YOU. YOU CAN GET MEN TO GO ANYWHERE, BUT YOU REALLY DON'T SEEM TO KNOW YOU HAVE THAT POWER.
NOW, AS I'VE SHOWN YOU, THIS IS THE BURNER SYSTEM ATTACHED TO THE WICKER BASKET.
YEAH, YEAH. WE KNOW, SANDY.
I WAS SPEAKING TO HOLLY, MISERY.

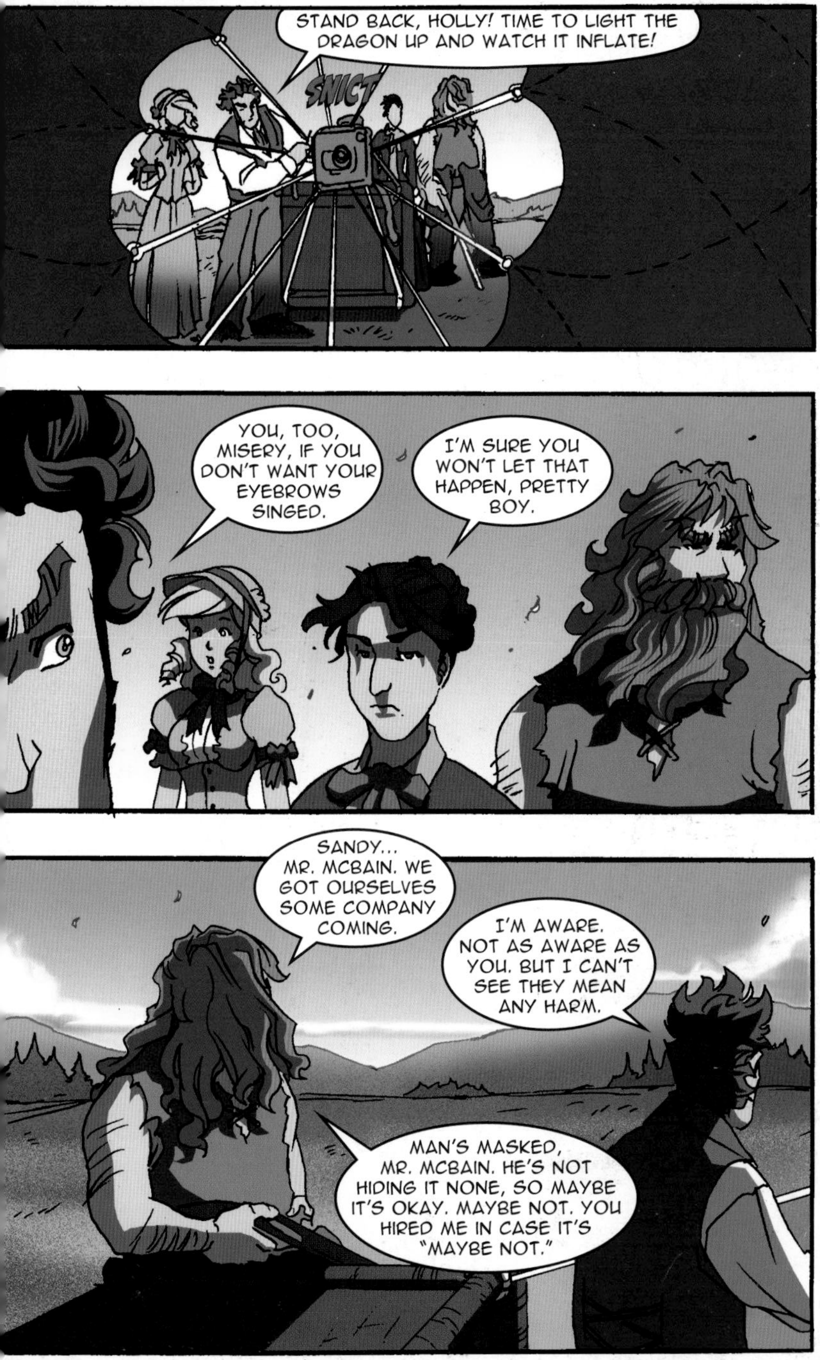
STAND BACK, HOLLY! TIME TO LIGHT THE DRAGON UP AND WATCH IT INFLATE!
SNICT
YOU, TOO, MISERY, IF YOU DON'T WANT YOUR EYEBROWS SINGED.
I'M SURE YOU WON'T LET THAT HAPPEN, PRETTY BOY.
SANDY... MR. MCBAIN. WE GOT OURSELVES SOME COMPANY COMING.
I'M AWARE. NOT AS AWARE AS YOU. BUT I CAN'T SEE THEY MEAN ANY HARM.
MAN'S MASKED, MR. MCBAIN. HE'S NOT HIDING IT NONE, SO MAYBE IT'S OKAY. MAYBE NOT. YOU HIRED ME IN CASE IT'S "MAYBE NOT."

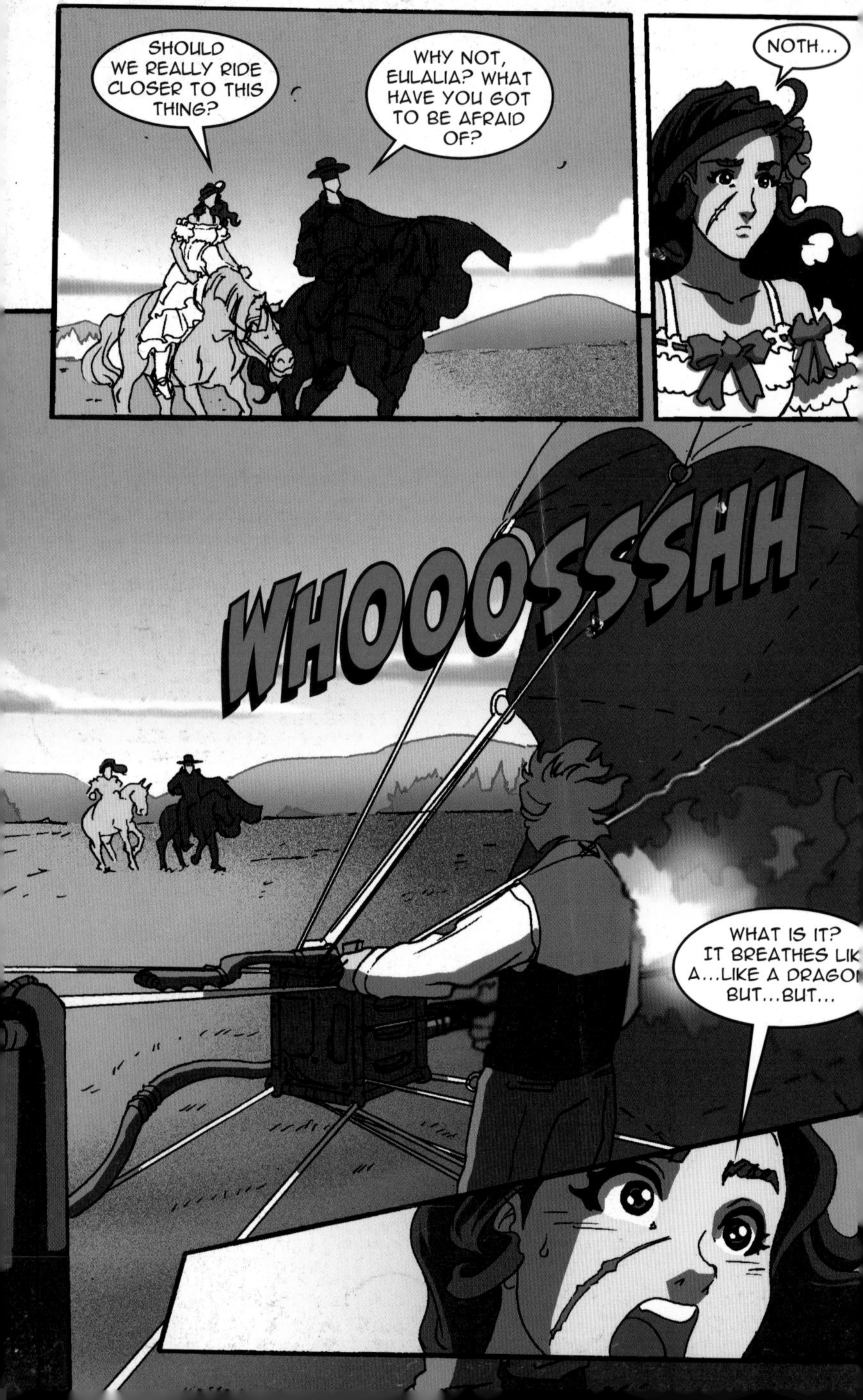
SHOULD WE REALLY RIDE CLOSER TO THIS THING?
WHY NOT, EULALIA? WHAT HAVE YOU GOT TO BE AFRAID OF?
NOTH...
WHOOOSSSHH
WHAT IS IT? IT BREATHES LIK A...LIKE A DRAGO BUT...BUT...

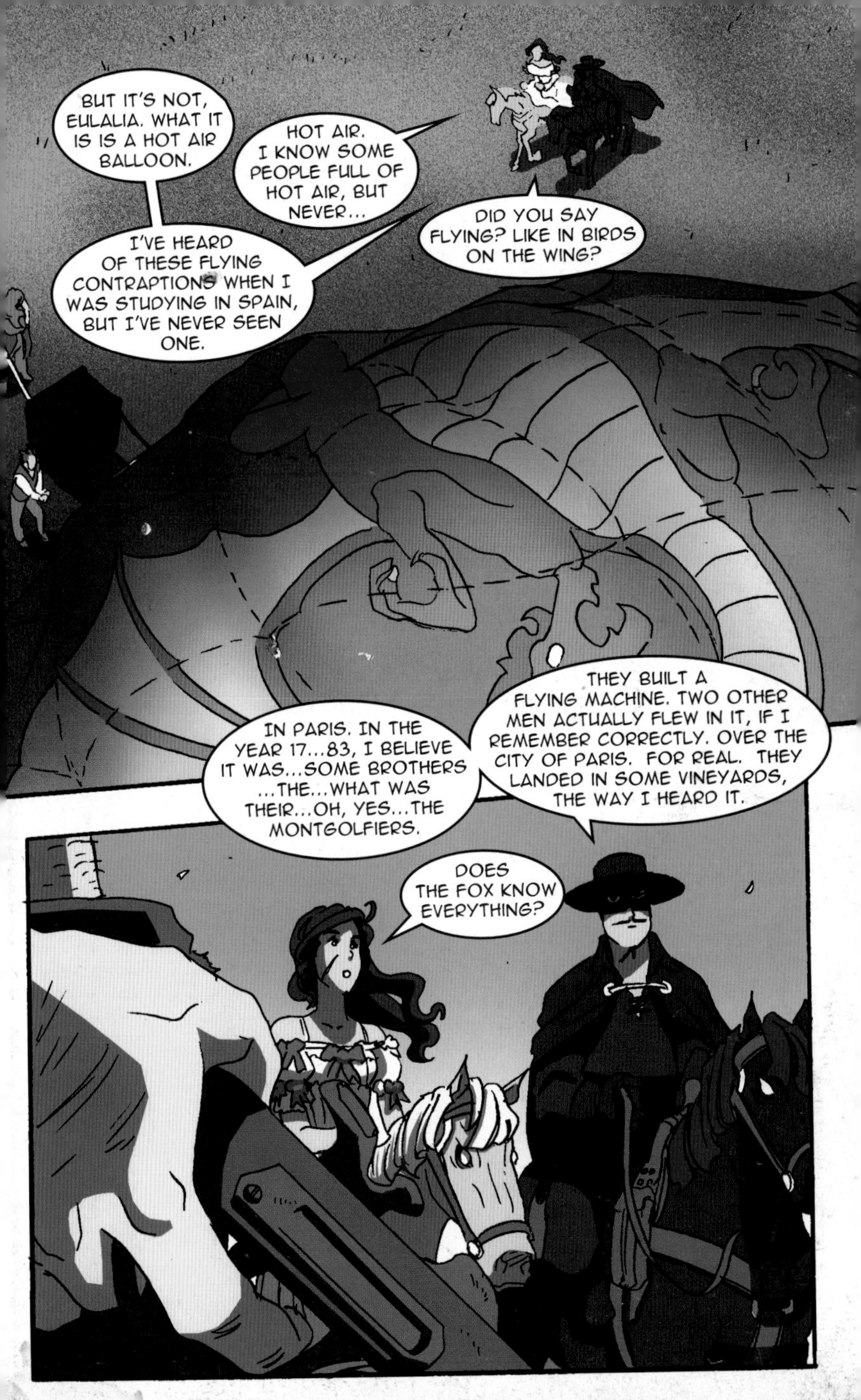
BUT IT'S NOT, EULALIA. WHAT IT IS IS A HOT AIR BALLOON.
HOT AIR. I KNOW SOME PEOPLE FULL OF HOT AIR, BUT NEVER...
I'VE HEARD OF THESE FLYING CONTRAPTIONS WHEN I WAS STUDYING IN SPAIN, BUT I'VE NEVER SEEN ONE.
DID YOU SAY FLYING? LIKE IN BIRDS ON THE WING?
IN PARIS. IN THE YEAR 17...83, I BELIEVE IT WAS...SOME BROTHERS ...THE...WHAT WAS THEIR...OH, YES...THE MONTGOLFIERS.
THEY BUILT A FLYING MACHINE. TWO OTHER MEN ACTUALLY FLEW IN IT, IF I REMEMBER CORRECTLY. OVER THE CITY OF PARIS. FOR REAL. THEY LANDED IN SOME VINEYARDS, THE WAY I HEARD IT.
DOES THE FOX KNOW EVERYTHING?

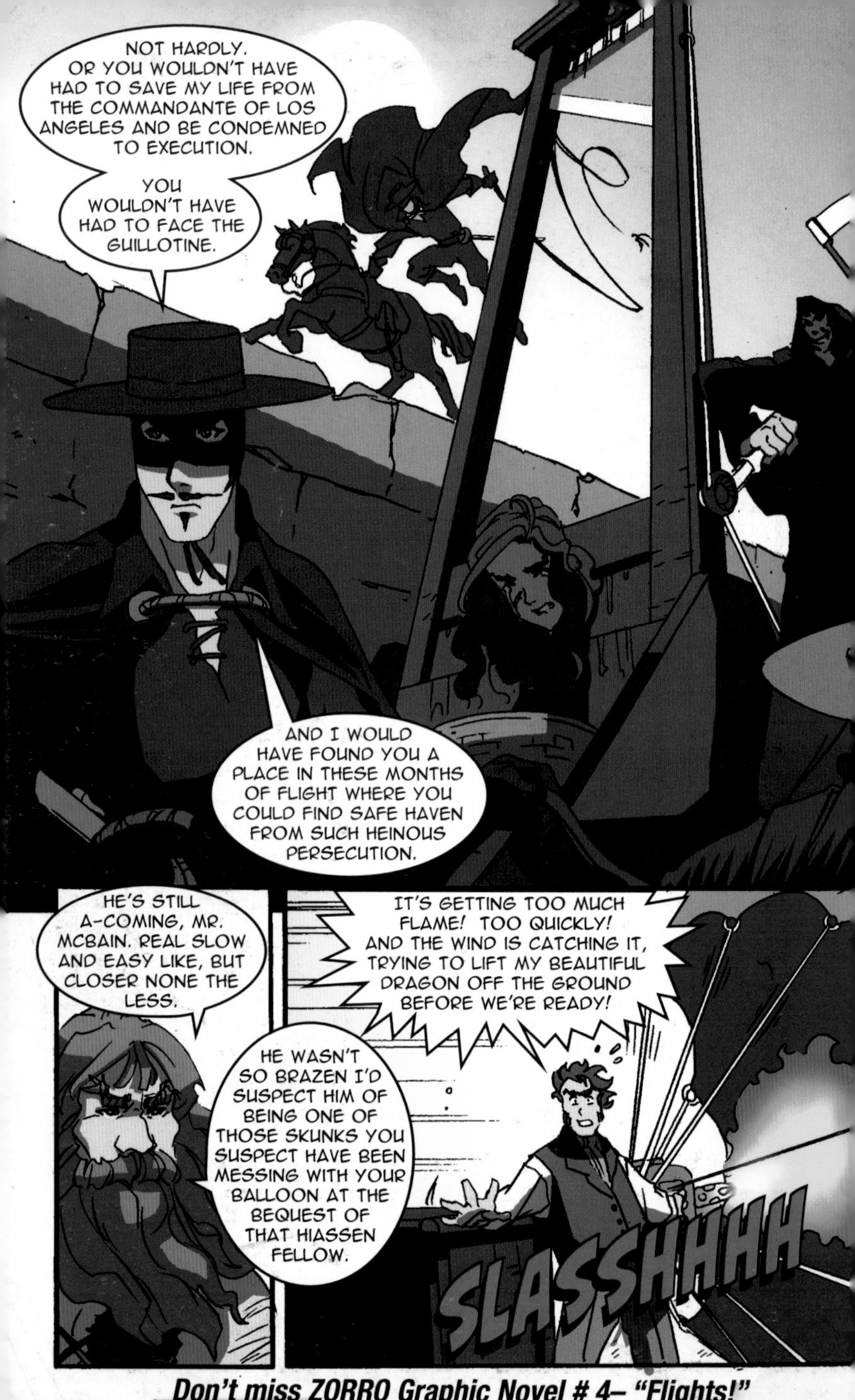
NOT HARDLY. OR YOU WOULDN'T HAVE HAD TO SAVE MY LIFE FROM THE COMMANDANTE OF LOS ANGELES AND BE CONDEMNED TO EXECUTION.
YOU WOULDN'T HAVE HAD TO FACE THE GUILLOTINE.
AND I WOULD HAVE FOUND YOU A PLACE IN THESE MONTHS OF FLIGHT WHERE YOU COULD FIND SAFE HAVEN FROM SUCH HEINOUS PERSECUTION.
HE'S STILL A-COMING, MR. MCBAIN. REAL SLOW AND EASY LIKE, BUT CLOSER NONE THE LESS.
HE WASN'T SO BRAZEN I'D SUSPECT HIM OF BEING ONE OF THOSE SKUNKS YOU SUSPECT HAVE BEEN MESSING WITH YOUR BALLOON AT THE BEQUEST OF THAT HIASSEN FELLOW.
IT'S GETTING TOO MUCH FLAME! TOO QUICKLY! AND THE WIND IS CATCHING IT, TRYING TO LIFT MY BEAUTIFUL DRAGON OFF THE GROUND BEFORE WE'RE READY!
SLASSHHHH

Don't miss ZORRO Graphic Novel # 4– "Flights!"